Why couldn't he just say what he meant?

Lissa felt there was something lurking beneath Jared's words, but she couldn't tell what it was. As he continued to stare at her, she sensed he had never been more serious about anything in his life. She shivered again, not from the brisk ocean wind but from the smoldering darkness of his eyes; they seemed to dig into her, to cut through her skin and grip her, hold her fast, tug her toward him.

Jared's lips moved against hers, and Lissa felt herself tumbling over the edge, tumbling down into a place far deeper than her intellect could grasp. This was not a kiss of lust or even of friendship — it was a kiss of need, of raw, brutal necessity. When they parted, Lissa was afraid to open her eyes, afraid of what she might see. She forced herself to look, and she found Jared watching her with the same trembling wonder that she was feeling. Neither of them was able to speak. The only sound was the rhythm of the ocean breaking against the sand....

ABOUT THE AUTHOR

Judith Arnold says she can't remember ever not being a writer. She wrote her first story at age six and pursued a successful playwrighting career after getting her master's degree from Brown University. Judith devotes herself to writing full-time, except for a rather large diversion — her year-old son. She and her family live in rural Connecticut.

Come Home to Love

JUDITH ARNOLD

Harlequin Books

TORONTO • NEW YORK • LONDON
AMSTERDAM • PARIS • SYDNEY • HAMBURG
STOCKHOLM • ATHENS • TOKYO • MILAN

Published May 1985
First printing March 1985

ISBN 0-373-16104-2

Chapter One

"The man is impossible!" Lissa wailed as she sank wearily into her high-back swivel chair. "Four hours, Candy, and all I could get from him was 'ishes.'"

"'Ishes'?" Lissa's secretary cast her a confused look before applying herself to the chore of gathering up the flotsam and jetsam her boss had scattered about the office: the sample books into their slots on the built-in bookcases; the purse onto the coffee table by the sofa; the portfolio atop the Formica workbench along the windowed wall; the brown leather pumps, which Lissa had kicked off at the doorway, paired and placed neatly beneath Lissa's ultramodern sculpture of a desk, a flattened arch of highly polished teak.

Lissa gratefully watched the slender young secretary move with deft precision through the office. "Bless you, Candy," she said with a sigh. "I promise to remember you in my will."

Candy smiled and smoothed her bangs across her high forehead. "I'd just as soon you remember me at Christmas, when it comes to bonuses," she hinted. "What do you mean about 'ishes'?"

Lissa groaned and shook her head. "Everything Max Michaels wants for his restaurant, he wants 'ish.' The carpet is not to be maroon, it's to be 'maroon-ish.' The walls he wants not beige but 'beige-ish.' Not a big main dining room but a 'big-ish' one. I swear, Candy, once this restaurant opens, I am going to march in and order me a 'rare-ish' steak and a 'dry-ish' martini." Candy laughed appreciatively. "So, did anything exciting happen here while my back was turned?"

Candy fetched her notepad, which she had deposited on the coffee table before straightening up after her boss, and riffled through the pages. "Someone phoned from the advertising department of *Architectural Digest*—Paul talked to him." She turned a page. "The accountant called, claimed he never received the Talbot invoices. I photocopied our copies and got them out in the afternoon mail. McReed Custom Finishing said Mrs. Shelby's étagère was ready for delivery tomorrow."

"I'll have to call Mrs. Shelby," Lissa said and nodded for Candy to continue.

"I already did," said Candy, flipping the page. "A Jared Stone called and asked for you."

"Jared Stone?" Lissa frowned, accepting the sheet of paper Candy tore from her pad and handed to her. It contained only the name and a telephone number. "Never heard of him. Is he with a company, or is it a private job?"

"He didn't say," Candy replied. "He asked for you by name, and said it was personal."

Lissa shrugged and tossed the note onto her blotter. Leaning back in her chair, she asked, "Anything else?"

Candy checked her wristwatch. "It's currently four

forty-five, and you have to teach tonight. I suggest that you go home, take a hot bath and unwind."

Lissa's full pink lips spread into a grin. "That does it, Candy. You've just earned yourself first place on my Christmas list."

Candy refused to smile, though her eyes sparkled gaily as she pivoted on her heel and departed from Lissa's office, shutting the door quietly as she left.

Now that she was alone, Lissa's grin faded as her memory replayed her tiresome afternoon with the vacillating restaurateur. She untied the bow collar of her brown crepe de chine blouse, unfastened the top button and reached around to her nape to massage the tired muscles. Her fingers detected several loose strands of her honey-blond hair that had leaked out of her chignon, but she decided her coiffure wasn't worth repairing. She would be home soon enough, obeying Candy's order to collapse into a tub full of bath salts and steamy water.

But first she had to call this Jared Stone. Annoyed, she punched out his phone number on her push-button telephone. He was probably one of those smug, pompous businessmen who refuse to discuss anything with a secretary. If he only knew that in her two years as an employee of Cavender & Morris, Candy had learned as much about the business as Paul and Lissa could teach her.

The phone rang twice, and then Lissa heard the click as it was answered. "Jared Stone here."

Something about the man's crisp baritone voice jolted Lissa, and she snapped upright at the sound of it. It was as smooth and hard as forged steel, and after having spent several long hours debating with the wishy-washy Max Michaels, Lissa was utterly unprepared to hear a voice so clear, so sure, so forceful. She swallowed, regained her composure and said, "This is Lissa Cavender of Cavender & Morris returning your call—"

"Lissa Cavender, yes. Thank you. I'd like to talk to you about Curtis Wade."

Curtis? Lissa fell back into her chair. Not after all this time. Would it never end? Would the badgering never cease? She exhaled, and when she spoke again her voice was drenched in the sensuous mountain drawl that always dominated her pronunciation when she was emotionally aroused. "Mr. Stone," she said in soft, velvety tones, "I'm afraid that as far as Curtis Wade is concerned, this well has run dry."

"What do you mean?" he asked.

"I mean, Mr. Stone, that I am no longer in the practice of covering Curtis's bad debts. If he owes you money. I'm terribly sorry, but even my generosity has its limits."

An edgy silence rippled along the wire before the man on the other end spoke. "He doesn't owe me any money. I've recently come into ownership of a painting he did, and I like it, and I'm curious to learn whatever I can about the artist."

A painting? One of Curtis's creations? Lissa's eyebrows arched in puzzlement. Obviously, since he knew nothing about Curtis, Mr. Stone hadn't purchased the painting directly from him; therefore, he must have obtained it from someone else. Yet Curtis had never sold a thing in his life—or if he had, he had never bothered to let Lissa know about it. Perplexed, uncertain of what Mr. Stone was after, she said nothing.

"Do you know where I might find him?"

"I've heard he's in Montana, and I've heard he's in France. I confess I've done nothing to verify these rumors. Curtis Wade's whereabouts are not my concern."

"Could you tell me anything about him?"

What was with this man? What in the world did he want? Lissa entertained the bizarre thought that Jared Stone was an FBI investigator, or perhaps an organized-crime figure hunting Curtis for nefarious reasons. Well, whatever he wanted Curtis for, Lissa was not going to help him. Bad blood may have passed between her and Curtis, but all she wanted was to forget, not revive old wounds and heartaches. And she wasn't a vindictive person. She had no interest in seeking revenge for her former husband's bad treatment of her.

"Mr. Stone," she said coolly, "I've had a long, exhausting day, and it's not nearly over yet. I'm sorry I can't assist you. Good day."

"Good-bye, Ms. Cavender. I'm sure we'll talk again."

Lissa was too stunned to hang up. She listened to the line go dead, then shook her head, bewildered and resentful. What audacity! How dared he assume they would talk again. Who the hell was he, anyway?

Her irritation invigorated her, and she forgot how tired she was as she slipped her feet into her pumps, snatched her purse from the coffee table and stalked from the office. She issued Candy a curt farewell before swinging out of the reception area and into the hallway by the elevator bank. Waiting for the elevator, she paced restlessly, then dived into the elevator car when it finally arrived. She was so full of nervous energy that she would gladly have hiked the rugged two miles to her apartment on Providence's cliff-hugging

East Side, but her automobile was waiting in the parking lot across the street from her office. The rush-hour traffic was beginning to build, and she felt her tension and anger increase as her economy car wheezed up the steep incline of College Street. Now that both Brown University and the Rhode Island School of Design were in session for the fall term, the narrow tree-lined streets of the East Side were clogged with parked cars, jaywalking students and careless cyclists. Lissa drummed her manicured fingers impatiently against the steering wheel as she maneuvered her way to the sunny floor-through apartment she rented in a pleasant Victorian-style house north of the campuses.

She parked in the small tenant lot behind the house, stalked to the front door, gathered her mail out of her box and climbed the stairs to her apartment on the second floor. Although Lissa was fully capable of decorating a house or apartment in any style, her own home reflected her Appalachian roots. Despite the high ceilings with their ornate moldings, and the black marble fireplace, the apartment had an aura of rustic simplicity. The matching cane rockers by the bay window, the plain pine dining table with its ladder-back chairs, the loomed rugs scattered across the waxed plank floor and the sofa and two armchairs set about the hearth gave the living-dining room an earthy warmth. A hall, one wall of which contained a gallery of photographs of Lissa's hometown and her family, led past the kitchen to her bedroom, a tiny study and a bathroom. She entered the bedroom, tossed her clothing across the handmade quilt on her brass bed, then crossed to the bathroom and turned on the faucets above the tub. Plucking the pins from what remained of her chignon, she shook out her thick golden tresses and tucked them into a shower cap. After adding scented salts to the bath, she returned to her bedroom to hang up her clothing, and then finally eased herself into the nearly scalding water.

She shut her eyes as the heat worked its way into her, melting her tension and relaxing her muscles. *I mustn't let Curtis get to me this way,* she thought. It was three years since the divorce was final and her memory now was as if she had finally awakened from a bad dream. Yet being his wife hadn't been a total loss, she learned she was strong enough to survive a divorce.

"Ridiculous!" she blurted aloud. "That's like saying the good thing about surviving a car wreck is that you learn you can survive a car wreck!" She laughed at her own frazzled logic.

Opening her eyes, she studied her body, which seemed to undulate beneath the water's milky surface. Her skin was still clearly marked with the outlines of her bikini, thanks to the few weekends she had spent this past summer at Narragansett and Newport beaches. Her figure was lean and tight, compact curves on a small frame. Lord, she had been scrawny as a child, she remembered with a smile. It wasn't until she had arrived at the Rhode Island School of Design as a student and, desperate to supplement her scholarship, had taken a job modeling for the life-drawing classes that she had finally come to accept her shape. She had been so frightened the first time although her roommate had assured her that there was nothing to it. "Remember Lissa, they're not staring at *you* they're studying musculature and skeleton. If you really get tense, just remind yourself of how much you're getting paid to sit still for an hour."

As it turned out, one student *did* stare at her: Curtis Wade. And he drew some marvelous sketches. In retrospect, Lissa realized that the one thing she truly loved about Curtis was his talent. He had hungry good looks, and the sort of boyish personality only a fool would consider charming, but what talent! Enough to dazzle Lissa for a while, at least; enough to entice her into believing the myth that if one was brilliant enough, one didn't have to be kind or responsible or considerate.

So now, supposedly, somebody was in possession of one of Curtis Wade's masterpieces, and he wanted to know about the artist. "I could tell him a thing or two," Lissa said out loud, bitterness in her sarcasm. She could tell this Jared Stone about how the money she had given Curtis to pay his bills at the art supplies store instead vanished during his poker games, about how Curtis had a theory that a painter needs to "know" his model intimately before he can really paint her—and about how, even after they were married, Lissa was not his only model, though she didn't learn that until the end. She could tell the inquisitive Mr. Stone about the squandering of talent, about the fiery arrogance that can incinerate an artist's soul until he's nothing but a shell, a hollow posture. She could tell Jared Stone lots of things, if he really wanted to know.

Lissa realized that her skin was beginning to prune; she unstopped the drain, stood up in the tub and toweled herself off. For some reason, she was no longer able to think of Curtis. All she could think of was the potent, supremely confident voice of the stranger whose call she had returned this afternoon, the stranger who was sure they would talk again.

She forced him from her mind as she dressed in wool slacks and a cream-colored cowl-neck sweater. Being invited to teach a course at R.I.S.D., her alma mater, was one of the most thrilling events in Lissa's life. Her class in interior design met one evening a week, so it didn't drain her energies excessively, and she enjoyed the mild schizophrenia of being a sleek, chic business-woman by day and a philosophical professor by night. In fact, the change from her linen skirt and silk blouse to her collegiate outfit was motivated by more than comfort—it helped to remind Lissa of which person she was. She brushed her thick hair and let it hang loose down her back, dried the bathroom steam from the long, spidery lashes that fringed her round gray eyes and hastened to the kitchen to prepare herself a light supper.

Once she had finished her meal and cleaned the dishes, she tied on her suede boots, pulled her Harris tweed blazer from the closet and gathered her lecture notes from her desk in the study. The bath, the food, the bracing autumn air, and her half-mile stroll south to the R.I.S.D. campus refreshed and rejuvenated her.

The classroom was nearly full when Lissa entered and strode to the lectern. As usual, the first few rows of seats were filled with the most eager and energetic students. Behind them sat the sullen and sluggish ones, and the back row held auditors. In the three weeks Lissa had been teaching, the back row had been populated by a wide variety of onlookers: curious students from adjacent Brown University, R.I.S.D. professors

checking up on their former pupil and visiting friends
of the enrolled students. Lissa never minded the auditors. She was terribly flattered that people who didn't
have to take her class wanted to observe just for the fun
of it.

As the noise in the room gradually died down, Lissa
ticked off the attendance, then opened her lecture notes.
"This evening," she began, "I'd like to talk about the
case of the pink prison cell." Several students chuckled
as they scribbled notes. Before Lissa could continue, the
door to the room swung open and a straggler entered.

Lissa had never seen him before. He was tall and
muscular, substantially older than the predominantly
adolescent students, with slightly mussed black hair
splayed out from his face in dense waves. His eyes were
a piercing dark color, his nose long and even, his jaw
thick and square. He apparently spent a great deal of
time in the sun, because his face and hands, visible
where they shot out from the sleeves of a brown corduroy blazer, were a rich coppery color. As he eased
toward the back of the room, he gave Lissa a small
apologetic smile for his tardiness, and his teeth glinted
straight and white behind his thin lips.

Lissa waited for him to find a seat, but even after he
had wrestled his long limbs into a semblance of comfort within one of the desk-chairs, she was afraid to
resume her lecture. Something about the man's dark,
unrelenting eyes, which stared at her like two glowing
coals, seemed to tie her tongue and scramble her
thoughts. She cleared her throat and turned to one of
the girls in the front row, "What was I saying?"

"The pink prison cell," the student replied.

Lissa nodded, focusing her attention on her lecture

notes. "Yes, the pink prison cell. In a recent experiment, several prisons and detention centers painted one of their rooms a specific shade of pink. Not just any pink, mind you—a carefully developed and mixed pink. What they discovered was that if they had a particularly rowdy or violent prisoner and they shut him into this pink cell, after a short while—say thirty minutes or so—the prisoner would emerge subdued and totally manageable. More research has to be done on this, naturally, but law-enforcement officials are intrigued, and so are psychologists. And you should be, too, because what this experiment tells us is that the colors of our environment work on us in ways we are only beginning to comprehend. If a pink cell can subdue a violent prisoner, then isn't it possible that some other color can rile a lethargic person? Can wall colors affect the hospital patient's ability to heal? How about the colors in a nursery? By choosing one color paint over another, can you help to create a docile child or a hyperactive child? Can a shopkeeper choose colors to make his customers want to buy more? Can a restaurateur choose colors to make diners hungrier?" Or "hungry-ish," Lisa added silently as she recalled her tedious afternoon.

To maintain her students' interest, she avoided burying herself in her notes, but whenever she glanced up, seeking eye contact with her audience, she saw the unfamiliar man in the back row staring at her with a disconcerting intensity. Every time their eyes met she flinched and had to turn away. Yet even looking elsewhere, Lissa sensed his gaze fixed on her, his attention wrapping itself so tightly about her she was afraid he would strangle her.

Lord, is he handsome, she thought, her mind wandering off in its own direction even though her mouth continued to discuss psychological theories of color. *Maybe not feature for feature, but the impression he creates is remarkably bold and virile.* Lissa found herself remembering the frequently told tales of professors having affairs with their students. She wondered if the unfamiliar visitor was a student at R.I.S.D. She wondered if he modeled for the life-drawing classes—and if he did, if part-time lecturers were allowed to spy....

She paused when the three-hour class was half over so the students could take a short break. This was the time for cigarette and coffee addicts to race from the room and satisfy their habits, for other students to stand and stretch, and for auditors who had failed to introduce themselves to the teacher before class to explain their attendance. Lissa dared to glance up at the rangy, dark-eyed man at the back of the room, and indeed, he had unwedged himself from his chair and was shaking his snug jeans back down his long legs as he approached her. But before he could reach her, she was surrounded by a gaggle of frantic students anxious to discuss their first major homework project, which was due the following week. By the time Lissa had listened to each of their plaintive tales about the difficulties they were having with the assignment, fifteen minutes had elapsed and the rest of the class had returned, taken their seats and brought their attention back to her. Her gaze fell upon the visitor as he was resuming his seat; he offered her a light shrug and another stunning smile.

Lissa wasn't entirely sure how she made it through the remainder of the class. The man at the back of the room distracted her more and more, and she found herself rushing through the lecture, eager to finish. At the end of the class, she knew, one of two things would happen: he would leave, in which case she would no longer have to deal with his disturbing presence, or he would introduce himself to her, in which case...in which case she would just have to see.

She ended the class at nine-thirty, and before she had a chance to shut her folder of notes, she was once again surrounded by panicked students chattering about the upcoming homework project. From the corner of her eye Lissa saw the stranger loitering patiently near the door, waiting for the people swarming around her to depart. When she had finished conferring with the last of the students, he approached, arm outstretched, and said, "Ms. Cavender? I'm Jared Stone."

He didn't have to identify himself. Lissa recognized the cool, self-assured voice immediately. She reflexively shrank from him, but not before he had grasped her hand in his, offering such a firm handshake that she teetered on the balls of her feet. As soon as he released her, she busied herself with her lecture notes, waiting for her agitation to dissipate enough for her to speak calmly to him.

If he was aware of her uneasiness, he did nothing to show it. Leaning casually against one of the front-row desks, he watched her fumble with her papers. "I'm sorry I barged in after you had begun," he offered. "I had some trouble finding the right classroom." He waited for Lissa to respond, and when she didn't, he continued. "It was a fascinating lecture. I always thought interior decorating had to do with matching the slipcovers to the drapes."

"Interior decorating does." Lissa spoke in a quiet, testy voice. "This is interior design. It encompasses a whole lot more. How did you find me here?"

"The same way I found you this afternoon," he explained. Noticing her clumsiness with her blazer, he pushed away from the desk, took the jacket from her and held it by its shoulders for her to ease her arms through the sleeves. The glance she gave him was one of gratitude laced heavily with distrust, and his grin expanded. "What does one do when he comes into possession of a painting by an unfamiliar artist? If he happens to be in the same city as one of the nation's finest art schools, he calls the school. I tried the R.I.S.D. museum first, and they suggested I talk to a professor of painting on the faculty. He told me Mr. Wade was an alumnus of R.I.S.D., and while his whereabouts were unknown, a certain Lissa Cavender might be able to help me out."

"I'm so glad to hear they protect their lecturers' privacy," she muttered.

"Consider your privacy protected. All he told me was that you had a firm downtown and you taught a class here one night a week."

Buttoning her blazer, Lissa felt her discomfort about the man transform itself into resentment at his complacency. Oh, he was proud of himself, all right. He had found Lissa without any difficulty, and then, once he had decided this afternoon that they should speak again, he had arranged to do just that. "What precisely do you want with me, Mr. Stone?"

"I'd like to talk. Can we go someplace for a drink?"

Lissa scowled and glimpsed at the large electric clock

on the wall behind the lectern. It read a quarter to ten. "I go to work in the morning," she said.

"Is there anyplace close by?" In spite of her scowl, he persisted. "A cup of coffee, maybe?"

Lissa conceded with a reluctant smile. As imposing as the man was, she didn't think having a cup of coffee with him would be all that dreadful. He certainly didn't seem like a federal agent or a loan shark out for Curtis's hide. She had to admit she was curious about how he had gotten Curtis's painting. Besides, she allowed sheepishly, he was mighty appealing to look at. "There's a campus coffeehouse just across on Waterman Street," she informed him.

Pleased, Jared Stone followed Lissa from the classroom, down the hall and out of the building. His hands in his pockets, he ambled beside her with an easy gait, his long strides forcing Lissa to increase her pace. At the corner, he watched to see where she would lead, and when she stepped into the street he chivalrously took her elbow, releasing it as soon as they reached the opposite corner. The gesture seemed so unexpectedly gallant to Lissa that she had to suppress a laugh.

"It's in here," she said nodding toward a stodgy fieldstone building, and Jared acompanied her up the front steps and through the heavy door. Toward the end of the hall an open doorway led into the coffeehouse. As they entered she was relieved to see the place nearly empty. Sometimes it was jammed with boisterous students, but right now, as tired and perplexed as she was, Lissa felt the relative seclusion of the place, the soft lights and the classical guitar music

being piped through the ceiling speakers would help
her unwind after her long day.

At the counter, she filled a mug with hot water and
plucked a bag of herbal tea from a plate. Jared Stone
studied the meager offerings, finally selecting hot
chocolate and a large green apple from a bowl. He took
a plate and a paring knife, and as he paid for the snack,
Lissa scouted out a vacant small round table in a
corner. She removed her blazer before sitting, then arranged her things about the table. Jared watched with
fascination as she dipped her tea bag into the steaming
water. *What in the world is he staring at,* she wondered;
her uneasiness in his company returned slightly. *Hasn't
he ever seen anyone prepare a cup of tea before?* She
forced herself to glare at him, and was shocked to discover him smiling, as if to observe her dunking the tea
bag in and out of the mug was the most entertaining
thing he had ever done. "Mr. Stone." She kept her
voice steady. "Would you mind explaining what this is
all about?"

"I was right about you," he confessed, leaning back
in his chair, slowly polishing his apple on the sleeve of
his blazer. "I had a hunch that your face would match
your voice, and I was right."

Lissa felt her cheeks burn as they flooded with color.
"What's that supposed to mean?" she challenged him.
"I look like a backwoods hillbilly?"

His smile deepened. "It means you look soft and sul-
try."

Lissa's face grew hotter, and she concentrated on
squeezing the moisture from the tea bag so she could
avoid looking at Jared Stone. *If he's simply on the prowl to
pick up a woman,* she thought irately, *he shouldn't have*

*bothered to go to all this trouble. Given how handsome he is,
he probably doesn't have to go through any trouble at all.*
Surely he was here with her right now for a better reason
than merely to flirt. "Mr. Stone—" she began.

"Jared."

Casting him a flinty glance, she repeated, "*Mr.
Stone,* are you after Curtis Wade for some reason? Is
he in trouble?"

The man across the table regarded her quizzically,
then cut himself a wedge of apple. "I wouldn't know
about it if he was. Do you care?"

"I care to know what you're after."

Jared chewed his apple slice, then cut another. "I
told you this afternoon. I have a painting by him, and
I'm interested in finding out about the artist."

"Why didn't you ask whoever you got the painting
from?"

"He's dead." Jared said it with such bluntness that
Lissa cringed. She was suddenly overcome with regret
for her haughty tone.

"I'm sorry," she said.

He shrugged, his face clouded briefly by a shadow.
"The painting belonged to my father. I discovered it
yesterday in a closet off his bedroom, of all places. It's
really got me baffled."

"Your father?" Lissa's remorse swelled. "Oh, I'm
terribly—"

"Forget it," he said, extending a slice of apple to
Lissa. Hoping to make amends for her earlier tactlessness, she accepted the apple slice, and Jared smiled.
"He was seventy-nine years old, he had everything he
ever wanted and he died in his sleep. Not a bad way to
go, if you ask me."

"You seem awfully accepting of it," Lissa observed. Jared said nothing as he sliced another sliver of apple. "So he kept the painting in his closet? Was that sort of behavior unlike him?"

Jared chuckled. "Buying a painting was unlike him, unless he bought it as an investment. Ms. Cavender...you see..." He sighed deeply, considering his words. "My father and I weren't very close. We had a falling out about eighteen years ago, and it wasn't until, oh, maybe nine years ago that we finally started to communicate again. I'm his only child, and I guess it's a little late in the day for me to be trying to figure out the person my father became at the end of his life, but when I found the painting, I hoped it might be a clue of some sort. As I said, it's not the sort of thing I would have expected him to own."

All of Lissa's resentment and anger vanished as she listened to Jared. Her sympathy for him in his bereavement mingled with her own curiosity about how one of Curtis's paintings ended up in the closet of Jared Stone's father. "Could you describe the painting to me?" she asked.

He presented an enigmatic expression to Lissa. "It's...a naked woman."

Lissa laughed sardonically. Of course it would be. Curtis loved to seek out attractive girls to pose for him, to get to "know" them. "One of his nude floozies, I reckon," she snorted.

Jared arched an eyebrow. "Did he paint many nudes?"

"Did he ever. He used to say that only an artist could truly appreciate the female form," Lissa said as she sipped her tea. "Does it shock you to think that per-

haps your father took a—how should I put it?—a pruri-
ent interest in art?''

Jared guffawed. "That wouldn't shock me at all," he
said, chuckling. "What shocked me was that he had the
thing lying in the closet.''

"What was your father's name?" Lissa inquired, trying to figure out how he might have been connected
with Curtis.

"Joseph Isaiah Stone.''

"Joseph Isaiah Stone," she echoed, then shook her
head. "It doesn't ring a bell.''

Jared mulled this over, then shifted forward in his
chair. "Did you know Curtis Wade very well?''

Lissa blushed again, and her lips twitched. "No,''
she replied quietly, recognizing that despite the fact
that she had been married to Curtis for over two years,
she hadn't known him well at all.

Jared slouched back in his seat, studying Lissa, his
gaze remaining on her even as he sipped his hot chocolate. When he lowered his mug, he asked, "Where did
you get that drawl of yours?''

"Tennessee.''

"Nashville?''

Lissa rolled her eyes. "That seems to be the only
place anyone's ever heard of in Tennessee," she complained. "Believe it or not, there's a whole lot more to
the state than the Grand Ole Opry.''

"Memphis?" he guessed. "Knoxville? Chattanoo-
ga?''

"O'cha' Crick.''

"Where?''

"Orchard Creek," she enunciated, then smiled. "Up
in the hills, northeast corner of the state. It's what

people quaintly refer to as a 'holler.' A little mining town. Spend enough time there, you call it O'cha' Crick."

"How did you end up in Rhode Island?"

"School of Design," she told him. "And then when I was finished with school..." *I got married,* she almost said, but restrained herself. "I just decided to stay on."

"Do you miss the mountains?"

Lissa grinned. "Every place has something to recommend it. I never saw so much red brick, so much three-dimensional history, in my life till I came up here. Anyway, there isn't a big demand for interior designers and architects in Orchard Creek. And where do you make your home, Mr....Jared?"

His face brightened at her use of his first name. "Mostly Colorado Springs," he said. "I grew up here, though." His eyes drifted as he reflected for a moment. "It's strange coming back after eighteen years."

"Lots of changes, I reckon."

He nodded in amazement. "The whole downtown, just to begin with—that pedestrian mall. And Thayer Street, by Brown University... The last time I was here, there were a few bookstores and Ronnie's Rascal House and, right across from Ronnie's, their big competition: the Exit. Now every other building is a restaurant or a fast-food place. And the Exit is gone."

"The Exit must have exited before I arrived," Lissa quipped. "I don't recall it." She gazed mischievously at Jared. "So tell me, was Thomas Wolfe right? Can you never go home again?"

Jared returned her mild, twinkling gaze. "Yes and no. Home isn't a place. It's something in here." He tapped his chest lightly with his fingers. "If you're doing what you want, and you're with someone you want to be with, you're home."

His words and his smoldering dark eyes wove a spell in Lissa's mind. Beneath his arrogant exterior, Jared Stone seemed sensitive, thoughtful, deeper than she had originally guessed. Conversing with him over a cup of tea was developing into a much nicer experience than she ever imagined. "Colorado Springs," she murmured. "Is that in the mountains?"

"Right in the shadow of Pike's Peak," he replied. "Have you ever been out West?"

"Lord, no," she said, chuckling. "But I saw the Mississippi once."

He joined her laughter. "You'd love Colorado Springs," he told her. "It's a beautiful town."

"Perhaps someday I'll visit it." Finishing her tea, she glanced ruefully at her watch. "I'm afraid I must be getting home. I have a busy day tomorrow."

"How about dinner?" Jared asked.

"I beg your pardon?"

"Have dinner with me tomorrow."

"Well...I..."

"I don't know anyone in town anymore, and I'm tired of eating alone. How about it? Or do you have plans already?"

Lissa floundered. Jared Stone was a total stranger, but he seemed intelligent and civilized—and he was awfully handsome. Why shouldn't she go out with him? It was a gamble, she knew, and after having been married to a gambler she was loath ever to take risks, but if he took her to a restaurant, what all that terrible could go wrong? "All right." She smiled shyly. "Dinner tomorrow."

Satisfied, Jared rose and once again helped Lissa on with her blazer. "Can I see you home?"

"It is rather late to walk alone," she realized. "Thank you, I'd appreciate that."

Stepping outside, they paused to adjust to the cool darkness of the late evening. "I've got my car parked up this way," said Jared with a nod toward the hill. Casually, almost without thinking it seemed, he slipped Lissa's hand through the crook of his elbow as they followed the curving slope of the road. Lissa didn't even consider pulling her hand away, not only because she had already agreed to have dinner with him, but because through the soft corduroy of his blazer and the cotton of his shirt his arm felt so solid and warm and strong. He probably expected her to keep her hand there, she thought wryly, just as he had expected, that afternoon, that they would talk again. He was obviously the sort of person who got what he wanted. Lissa inhaled the spicy autumn aroma in the air and pondered the man at her side. She would have to keep her guard up, at least until she knew him better. But walking arm in arm with him felt too agreeable to guard against.

Jared drew to a halt beside an enormous black Cadillac of a vintage Lissa could only guess at. Clearly, from its size, it was built when gasoline cost less than thirty cents a gallon. She was startled; Jared Stone didn't seem the type to drive such an enormous, staid vehicle. Someone with his steady eyes and cool manner ought to be cruising about in something sportier. "This is your car?" she verbalized her surprise.

Jared unlocked the door for her and chuckled. "Now that I've inherited it, it is. It was my father's, but since my car is in Colorado, this is all I've got." He shut the door behind Lissa, walked to the driver's side and slipped in beside her. "It's quite a monster, isn't it."

Lissa scanned the vast interior, the leather seats, the polished and paneled dashboard. "I reckon it must have cost a pretty penny when it was new."

"Maybe in a few years it'll be a collector's item," Jared said with a touch of sarcasm. Twisting the key in the ignition, he glanced out the side window and let his right hand grope toward Lissa, coming to rest on her knee. They both flinched simultaneously. "Excuse me," he said, laughing. "I'm used to four-on-the-floor."

Lissa joined in his laughter, congratulating herself on her assessment of him as totally unsuited to a car like this. He fumbled with the automatic shift on the steering column and eased out into the street. Lissa told him where to turn, and the car glided along the road. It had been so long since Lissa had been in a car this heavy that she sat dumbfounded at the smooth silence of the engine. Jared correctly read her wonder. "If you think it feels strange to ride in a tank this big, you should try driving it. I feel as if I'm taking up two and a half lanes—and parking is the challenge of a lifetime."

Lissa directed him to the yellow Victorian-style house where she lived, and he pulled up at the curb. "Is this still predominantly a student neighborhood?" he asked.

"There are some students in the area," Lissa replied, "but not in my building, thank heavens. My landlady and her sister live on the first floor, and a married couple, both junior faculty at Brown, live above me on the third floor. It's very quiet."

Jared escorted her up the front walk to the wooden

porch by the door. Noting the brass digits affixed to the shingles, he recited the number several times to memorize it, then turned to Lissa. "So you're on the second floor?" She nodded. "Fine. I'll pick you up around six-thirty."

"All right."

For an awkward moment neither of them moved or spoke, and then Jared bowed his head and touched his lips to Lissa's. It was a soft kiss, almost questioning, and when he separated from her his eyes scrutinized her face, seeking permission to continue. Apparently he saw what he was looking for, because he let his hand drift to the back of Lissa's head and drew her mouth to his for another kiss.

If there had been anything forced, anything demanding, in his kiss she would have pulled away. But as his lips gently caressed hers, Lissa felt only a warm pleasure spreading through her, relaxing her body into his tentative embrace. His skin smelled tangy, his cheek was smooth beneath her fingers as she reached up to trace his jaw, and when his tongue tenderly essayed her lips, they willingly parted for him. He explored her mouth with quiet assurance, and as his arms tightened around her, drawing her closer, Lissa succumbed without any resistance. What she felt within his arms, what she felt as her tongue reveled in his clean, tart flavor, was a tranquillity so total that she could not conceive of anything more soothing, more comfortable, more utterly right than to be kissing Jared Stone.

Her body seemed to melt into his, and she gloried in the strength of his hand against the small of her back. She believed they were dancing, their hips swaying as their fingers wove through each other's hair, Jared's thick and dark with waves and curls, Lissa's long and slippery as silk. She felt her cells drink him up as if she were blotting paper, and the sweet delight he imparted to her through his mouth and his hands and his hard thighs against hers gradually grew from warm to warmer to hot.

Lissa abruptly became aware that the rhythm their hips were following belonged to a dance more sensual than she at first had realized. Breathless, she broke the kiss, her vision struggling to focus on the ruggedly chiseled face of the man holding her. His eyes were half closed, glowing with a desire Lissa had no difficulty comprehending, a desire that throbbed imploringly in her own body. "God, you feel wonderful," Jared said with a groan, his fingers trailing through her hair.

Lissa knew she ought to extricate herself from him, but her body continued to nestle against him, refusing to shatter the delectable enclosure of his arms. "Jared," she whispered, her voice quivering. "We can't stand out here necking like this, my landlady will see us."

His eyes seethed with a dark fire. "You could invite me in," he murmured.

Longing to savor more fully what she had just tasted, her body entreated her to say yes, but her mind sternly refused. "I...I hardly know you."

He studied her. His eyes were still ablaze but his hands released their grasp. "I intend to change that," he said, the hint of a smile hovering on his lips. "Tomorrow at six-thirty, Lissa. May I call you Lissa?"

"Of course," she said, half laughing, half sighing, her chest heaving with relief and dismay as he backed off the porch and down the walk, refusing to turn his face from her until he had reached his car. She leaned against the porch support, watching him ease the bulky Cadillac away from the curb and out of sight. Lingering in the chilly autumn night air until her pulse had slowed to normal, Lissa hugged her arms about herself, shivering and giggling and feeling less like a jaded divorcée than like a giddy, infatuated schoolgirl.

JARED HAD A HUNCH about Lissa, and when he had a hunch, he was never wrong.

He had always had hunches, strange premonitions about things, like an inner radar receiving what seemed to him obvious messages about the world around him. Even as a child he had been that way. He had known his mother was dying although no one would tell him the truth; when he had asked his father if she were dying, his father had snapped, "If you talk that way, maybe she will." And she did. He was a small boy, and such a coincidence had filled him with dread about his own intuition.

But later he had grown to trust it. He had had a hunch about leaving home, and it had been the right thing to do. He had had a hunch about the factory when his newspaper had sent him there to do a story on its closing down; he had had a hunch that the plant could be saved, run profitably. And he had been right about that, too.

And he had had a hunch about Lissa Cavender. The moment he heard her voice, he had known, deep inside himself, that he would have to meet her.

Part of it was her accent. He had never heard one like it before, definitely Southern but not that slow, thick drawl one associated with the Deep South. No, it was somehow sharper, more tangy, oddly exotic.

And the things she had said about Curtis Wade: "This well has run dry," "His whereabouts are not my concern." Her comments were understated; implying a dark pain that Jared could only guess at, and it piqued his curiosity.

Her words, yes, but her accent, the soft, rich purr of her voice... he had known, by the time he hung up the telephone, that he had to meet her.

And when he saw her, he wasn't at all surprised. Maybe he should have been, but he wasn't. That was the way it was with his hunches.

He steered the huge black Cadillac east toward his father's house, his dark eyes instinctively absorbing the light traffic while his mind followed its own meandering course. She was beautiful, no question about that. He had known she would be. Her honey-blond hair was stunning, so lush and luxurious when it whispered through his fingers; and her full, soft lips; and her eyes, pale in color but haunted by shadows, the cool, life-filled shadows one finds in a dense forest. Holding her had felt marvelous. Kissing her... kissing her had staggered him. He was a grown man, experienced. He wasn't used to reacting to a woman's kiss so strongly.

Jared reached the driveway, shifted into neutral and left the car to open the gate. Then he cruised up to the looming house at the end of the driveway, his thoughts far from the mechanics of parking and figuring out which of his father's keys was to be inserted into which lock. He would kiss her again tomorrow, he realized, and the thought made him smile. He would kiss her, maybe even make love to her. She had bought his line about not having anyone to eat dinner with, thank God, and he would be spending the night with her. He was supposed to visit Nina, but that had been tentative—he had told her that if he were free he'd give her a call. And now, much to his delight, he wasn't free. Nina would understand.

He had a hunch that tomorrow night would be special, that Lissa Cavender was about to become very important to him. The thought pleased him so much that he didn't mind the overpowering gloom of his father's house as he shut and locked the door and headed for the stairs.

Chapter Two

"Anyway," Paul was saying, "I know it's a status thing to advertise in *Architectural Digest*, but I don't see millions of dollars in business coming out of it. I hope you don't mind my nixing it without asking you first." He waited for Lissa to respond, but she was staring dreamily into her coffee cup. Every morning, in the cramped conference room that separated their offices, Paul and Lissa met to discuss business and exchange ideas over coffee. Today, Lissa tried to pay attention to Paul, but her mind kept drifting, drifting back to last night. "You haven't heard a word I've said," Paul chided her, too amused by the glazed expression on her face to be annoyed by her inattentiveness.

She tore herself from the mist rising out of her mug—and the mist that filled her brain—and sheepishly bit her lip as she eyed her colleague. More than a colleague, Paul Morris was, with the possible exception of his wife, Peggy, Lissa's closest friend. An owlish, intense man two years her senior, he had invited Lissa to help him found his own design firm and had insisted on creating an equal partnership with her, even after she found herself deeply in debt from Curtis. Paul had negotiated generous terms so she could meet her obligations to their corporation while she paid off Curtis's accounts, and he and Peggy had offered Lissa the moral support she had needed to get through the misery of her divorce. As a business partner, Paul complemented Lissa perfectly; they rarely disagreed, and when they did they knew how to disagree constructively. In response to his accusation this morning, she smiled guiltily at him and said, "Don't scold me. I've heard a word or two. 'Status.' 'Nixon.'"

"Nix*ing*. As in vetoing. Turning down. Saying no. You look tired, kid. Didn't you sleep last night?"

"Not much," she admitted truthfully. She had spent most of the night tossing and turning, mashing her pillows and reshaping them, tasting Jared Stone on her lips and feeling his hand roaming through her hair, and then fuming and trying futilely to order herself to sleep.

"Why don't you come home with me for dinner tonight?" Paul suggested. "You haven't been over for a while. We've done a lot of work since you were last by. I'll give Peggy a call. What do you say?" Paul and his wife had purchased a ramshackle farmhouse the previous spring, and the remarkable improvements they had made on the house were a source of great pride to them. "Come on. I'll tell Peg to throw another cup of water into the soup."

Lissa laughed. "Can't," she told Paul. "I've got a date tonight." Simply saying this caused her cheeks to swell into a grin, and she felt them grow warm.

"Oh, yeah?" Paul regarded her curiously. "Who's the lucky guy?"

"You don't know him," she said.

"Try me," Paul challenged her. He had grown up in Providence, and the city was small enough for him to know an uncommon number of its citizens.

"His name is Jared Stone," said Lissa. "He lives in Colorado."

"Colorado?" Paul's eyebrows shot up. "Boy. I used to complain when I had to travel more than ten minutes to pick up a date."

"Fool!" Lissa laughed, not at all minding Paul's teasing. "He's in Providence now. He's here to settle his father's estate or some such thing."

"Oh, so you met him while you were hanging out at the Probate Court. Why can't you go to a singles' bar like normal people?"

Lissa laughed again and sipped her coffee. As the caffeine entered her veins, she felt her brain sharpening, coming fully awake. "Paul," she asked as she lowered her cup. "Did you ever know Curtis to sell a painting?"

Surprised by the question, Paul crossed to the counter on which the coffee maker sat, lifted the glass pot, and refilled his cup. "I never knew him to sell anything," he replied. "He thought every painting he did was either so bad he wouldn't humiliate himself by selling it, or so good he couldn't bear to part with it. Why do you ask?"

"Did Curtis ever mention to you that he knew someone named Joseph Isaiah Stone?"

Paul dropped the decanter onto the hot plate, his eyes bulging. "Joseph Isaiah Stone? Are we talking about J. I. Stone, as in *the* Stones of Rhode Island?"

Lissa watched Paul recover from his astonishment enough to reseat himself. "I reckon we are," she said with a shrug. "Does this signify something I don't know about?"

"Lissa, in Rhode Island, the Stone family is like royalty. You've never heard of J. I. Stone? That's right, he died a few weeks ago. Didn't you read about it?"

"I don't make a habit of reading the obituary pages," Lissa said, her flippant tone failing to conceal her fascination with what Paul was telling her.

"It wasn't on the obituary page. It was on the *front* page. J. I. Stone: financier, megabuck mogul, king-maker, wheeler-dealer and friend of presidents.... And you've got a date with his son?"

"I..." Lissa shook her head in amazement. "Jared seemed nothing like that at all, Paul. He was wearing an old pair of dungarees when I met him, and...well, he didn't seem..." She shook her head again. "He said he didn't get on well with his father. I guess being a wheeler-dealer didn't rub off on him."

"If he's a Stone—hell, Lissa, it's royalty. You can't disown your blood. Wow," he said, exhaling. "So you're having dinner with a Stone. I hope you won't forget about the little folks you left behind."

"Oh, come now," Lissa said, chuckling.

"What does J. I. Stone have to do with your erstwhile husband?"

"That's a good question," she said. "It seems one of Curtis's paintings is a part of J. I. Stone's estate. Lord, doesn't that sound absurd? Now what would a man you say is royalty—what would such a man be doing with a painting of Curtis's?"

"Beats me," Paul said, shrugging his shoulders. "But I'm intrigued."

"So am I." Lissa shared Paul's smile.

Paul leaned forward intently. "What's Stone Junior like?"

"Not like his father, I would guess," Lissa commented. "He certainly didn't seem—I mean, he didn't wave around a wad of hundred-dollar bills or anything. He's dark-eyed, kind of intense...intelligent. He sat in on my lecture last night."

"And then he asked you out."

"I think he likes my drawl," Lissa said, snickering.

"Well, keep pumping that Mason-Dixon charm, honey," Paul said. "The son and heir of J. I. Stone is well worth pouring on the ol' Southern Comfort for."

Lissa knew Paul was ribbing her, but she didn't mind. It seemed appropriate that she should be teased by her brotherly friend. Anyone who could lie awake all night replaying the conversation she had had with a man, anyone who could stand necking on the front porch in full view of the neighbors, anyone who could act so dewy-eyed and ingenuous deserved to be treated with a healthy dose of good-natured mocking. But there was work to get through today, and after a long draught of her coffee, Lissa turned the conversation to Max's, the restaurant she had been commissioned to design, and unrolled her blueprints in order to discuss with Paul the various placements of walls and partitions.

She spent most of the day at Max's restaurant. Fortunately, she had a construction contractor with her to help dampen the effect of the wavering Max Michaels. "Well, I think I'd like a wall here," he would begin. "A screen kind of wall, I guess. Maybe a little more to the left, with a row of yellow-ish lights above it...."
Lissa and the contractor exchanged glances of exas-

peration as the owner prattled uselessly; trying to get a straight answer from him took so much of Lissa's energy that she had little time or strength to let herself think about her impending date with Jared. Finally, by four-thirty, the contractor had wheedled enough information from Mr. Michaels to be able to formulate a bid on the job, and exhausted, Lissa telephoned her secretary. There was nothing worth returning to the office for, Candy reported. "Paul says you have a hot date tonight," she added mischievously. "Go home and shine your shoes."

Lissa groaned in protest, but as she steered over the Providence River and up the steep incline to the East Side, Candy's teasing gnawed at her and she began to fret over what to wear. She had assumed a date—even a dinner date—with Jared would be an informal thing. But now that she knew a little bit about his background, she couldn't help wondering whether the son of J. I. Stone would consider dinner a grand occasion, something more formal than what Lissa might expect.

Climbing the stairs to her apartment, Lissa realized that she hadn't been this excited about a date in a long, long time. Even before she had married Curtis, they had rarely gone out; there simply hadn't been the money. She had been a scholarship student, paying her own way through school, and although Curtis came from more comfortable circumstances, he was always squandering his money, always in over his head. She knew now it had been his stupid poker games, although back in school Curtis had sworn they were penny-ante. Then, after they were married and Lissa had begun to earn a good income with a company in Boston, her salary was eaten up by the rent on their house, which was much larger than they needed because Curtis insisted on renting a place with a south-facing detached garage that he could use as a studio. She had spent a small fortune on commuting costs, and all the money she had given Curtis, supposedly for his canvases and paints.... And then she had quit the Boston job to start up the firm with Paul, right in town, close to home — too close, as it turned out — and her marriage had fallen apart.

Even after the divorce, it was a long time before she felt able to socialize again. To Lissa, the shock of Curtis's behavior was surpassed only by the shock of her own stupidity and blindness, and for many months she shut herself up in her apartment, certain that she was too dumb, too sullied by what she had been through to be deserving of male companionship. "Stop punishing yourself!" Peggy would nag at her while Paul suggested various single friends of his as possible escorts. "You don't have to do penance for Curtis's sins." Gradually, Lissa emerged from her self-imposed exile, but none of the men she met were able to erase the scars with which Curtis had left her.

She frequently thought of her marriage as a night-mare from which she had awakened. Yet like a person arising from a troubled, fevered slumber, she found the world unfamiliar, untrustworthy, an alien territory she had to learn anew. Curtis had done more than be-tray her. He had wounded her. He had left her feeling sordid and stained. Only through great effort had she mastered the motions of dating, but she hadn't met a man who could make her want to transcend the motions, who could make her want to take a chance on him.

Not until last night.

As she stepped into the tub and adjusted the faucets for her shower, Lissa allowed herself to consider the possibility that Jared Stone was a man worth waking up for, worth losing sleep over. Maybe she had resented his overbearing confidence because she envied it, or because it awed her. From the moment she heard his cool, composed voice on the phone, she had known he was someone to be reckoned with. And then he had started grilling her about Curtis. No wonder her first impression of him hadn't been exactly positive!

But the first impression had dissolved into the second impression—that he was thoughtful, open, flattering...and magic with a kiss. As she shampooed her hair, Lissa tried to recall the last time she had enjoyed a kiss so much and came up blank. Not even Curtis had been able to warm her, to thaw her so completely with a single kiss. Giving her soapy head a shake, she marveled that she had the strength to refuse Jared's suggestion of retiring to her apartment. The strength, or maybe it was just downright stubborness. Jared Stone hadn't been the only person who had wanted to continue kissing, she admitted to herself.

And now she had to deal with the third impression: Jared Stone as scion of J. I. Stone, friend of presidents; Jared Stone as heir apparent, inheritor of the throne, blue blood and purebred.

"I shouldn't be so reverent about it," Lissa said aloud as she stepped out of the tub and wrapped a plush white towel about her hair. After all, she came from one of the finest families in O'cha' Crick herself. She stared at her reflection in the mirror above the sink. Her tawny skin glistened with moisture, her long lashes were matted together into spikes, and a large, undignified drop of water dangled from the tip of her nose. "Queen of the Hayseed Hicks," she said before walking into the bedroom to paw through her closet.

Slacks wouldn't do. What if J. I.'s princely successor arrived in a jacket and tie? She could wear a dress... but what if the Prodigal Son showed up in his faded jeans and corduroy blazer? Lissa opted for the obvious compromise: a skirt and blouse. After examining and then rejecting numerous outfits, she decided on a softly flared cashmere skirt of a rich burgundy and a delicate white sweater with a lacy knit, black shoes and her black velvet jacket. She spread the chosen ensemble across her bed and returned to the bathroom to dry her hair. By the time she had turned off the blow dryer, her mane of thick, silky waves shimmered with red and gold highlights. She twisted it into a knot atop her head, tried sweeping it dramatically back behind her ears, and finally decided to let it hang freely down her back. *Just in case he wants to set his fingers loose in it,* she thought, but then shook her head scornfully. "He's a man who gets what he wants," she reminded herself in a soft whisper. "Keep your guard up."

She dressed slowly, admiring the lovely clothing as she put each article on. It had all been purchased within the past year, when she was finally through paying off Curtis's debts and could at last splurge on a few elegant things for herself. When she was finally dressed she stood before the full-length mirror fastened to her bedroom door and critically appraised herself. Something was missing; then she remembered the dainty gold choker Paul and Peggy had given her for her birthday. "Of course," she said, crossing to her bureau and removing the slender chain from its box. As she fastened it about her neck, she heard a sharp, brisk knock on her door. She glanced at her wristwatch. "If it's Jared, he's early." She swallowed. "Now calm down, Lissa. Try not to act like a rube. This is a wealthy, sophisticated man."

Opening the door to the apartment, Lissa was so stunned by Jared Stone's strong, virile presence that she recoiled slightly. He looked neither like the inheritor of a kingdom nor like the denim-clad rebel; instead, he looked distinctively, serenely, utterly like himself. His hair was neatly combed, his cheeks freshly shaved, his eyes as dark and constant as a midnight sky. She was pleased to discover that he, too, had chosen a compromise between formal and informal attire by wearing dark gray trousers and a tan blazer of the softest suede Lissa had ever seen. His neck was unfettered by a tie, and the top two buttons of his white shirt were open, revealing an alluring hint of chest hair. "Hello," he said, his gaze wandering appreciatively over Lissa.

She swallowed again, willing herself to match his sauve confidence. "Come in, Jared. I'm sorry—I'm not quite ready—"

"No, *I'm* sorry," he interrupted as he stepped across the threshold. "I'm early. I finished my errands sooner than I expected, and decided I'd rather be with you than sitting alone waiting to be fashionably late. You go do what you have to do, and I'll be nosy."

Before Lissa could speak Jared had sauntered over to the cane rockers, their gracefully curving wood shining as the veneer caught the last of the sun's rays. He seemed to be ignoring her, so she moved back down the hall to her bedroom, closed her door and stuffed a small black purse with a comb, her wallet and her keys. She dashed a light cologne behind her ears, fluffed her hair out with her fingers, twisted anxiously in front of the mirror, and then exhaled with a small laugh. "This is not the senior prom," she told the nervous image in the glass, "and you're not a gawky teenager. You're a mature adult with a career, and you've been around the block once, and you've learned a few things along the way. So don't let the man daunt you."

Lifting her jacket from the bed and slipping her arms through the sleeves, she gathered up her purse and opened the bedroom door. Jared stood in the hallway, studying the photographs. He turned to her as soon as she appeared, his face radiating fascination. "I see you've found the gallery," she said, smiling. Hearing her voice emerge calm and poised reassured her.

"Introduce me," he said, nodding toward the pictures.

"If you insist," Lissa accommodated him. "Let's see, now this is Gramma Cavender, and Aunt Ida, my papa's sister.... They more or less raised me, once my parents were gone."

Jared touched her shoulder, his eyes shadowed. "Gone?"

"Mama died from complications of childbirth," Lissa steadily reported. "I lost Papa in a mine accident when I was three." She pointed to another photograph. "This one here, that's my parents. This is the house I grew up in," she said, indicating a photograph of a neat, modest cottage, its broad porch framed by gardenias and marigolds. "Papa designed and built it himself. I like to think I inherited his talent."

"It's very pretty," Jared concurred.

"As you can see," she gave him an impish grin, "we don't live in tarpaper shacks anymore. This here's Aunt Ida at her pharmacy. This is downtown O'cha' Crick. Our Main Street isn't exactly like Providence's, but it's got a smattering of markets and such."

"Your aunt's a pharmacist?"

Lissa nodded. "In fact, she used to be kind of an amateur doctor for the town. Around thirteen, fourteen years ago a regional clinic opened, but before that, the nearest doctor lived some dozen miles away, so if you weren't too sick, you'd go to Doc Ida at the pharmacy and she'd fix you up."

"Practicing without a license," Jared said with a chuckle. "Who's this?"

Lissa glanced at a portrait of a stern, heavyset elderly woman holding a small blond child on one knee. "This is Great Gramma Bodine, just a few months before she died. She was my mama's papa's mama. I don't remember her too well, only that she was kind of ornery."

"That's you on her lap?"

Lissa winced and nodded.

"You haven't changed a bit," Jared said, teasing. "Except for the platinum blond curls."

"Yes, well, time took care of that. By the time I was eight or so, my hair was about what it is now."

Jared studied her hair, a half-smile on his face. "I wouldn't complain if I were you. It's beautiful."

All of Lissa's self-assurance drained out of her. With one small compliment Jared had demolished her composure. She inhaled deeply, focusing on the floor, wishing her cheeks would cool off. Timidly raising her eyes, she forced a light tone. "Shall we go?"

The half-smile on Jared's lips widened into a full grin. His teeth sparkled and two dimples cut into his cheeks as he slipped his hand around Lissa's. "One more question." He pulled her down the hall into the living room and over to the fireplace. Pointing to a rustic implement comprised of wood and sticks woven together, he asked, "What is this?"

Lissa burst into laughter at his ignorance. "That's a besom."

"A what?"

"A besom. A round twig broom. This one's handcrafted. I use it to clean out the hearth. What did you think it was?"

"I thought," he said grimly, "that it was something a witch might use to fly across the moon."

Lissa continued to chuckle. "Come around at the end of October, I'll take you for a spin."

Jared's laughter mingled with Lissa's. "I'll mark it on my calendar," he said as he led her to the door and out to the stairway.

The oversized black car was parked by the curb, and Jared helped Lissa onto the seat. It was only when he let go of her hand that she realized he had been holding it all the way down the stairs and along the path from the porch to the street. The thick warmth of his fingers around hers seemed so natural to Lissa that she had hardly been aware of it, and now the absence of that warmth caused her palm to grow chilly. She folded her hands in her lap, unnerved by the ease with which the man beside her had insinuated himself into her consciousness. She was not used to a man's touch—barely used to men at all.

Yet with Jared...it was as if he hadn't even noticed

the crusty layers of disillusionment and distrust, as if
the layers had flaked away in his presence, revealing a
new woman willing, even eager, to try again with a
man. *He's in the right place at the right time,* Lissa
thought to herself to explain the phenomenon, although part of her argued that maybe it was simply a
matter of Jared's being the right man.

This was not a very good way of looking at things. He
was here only temporarily, to attend his father's estate.
He would be back in Colorado soon enough. Lissa was
only a diverson so he wouldn't have to eat alone. *Keep
your guard up,* she warned herself as he started the engine.

"Where are we going?" she asked.

"A new restaurant. Maybe it isn't so new, come to
think of it, but it wasn't here eighteen years ago. My
father's attorney recommended it." He steered around
the block, heading down the hill toward the center of
the city. "Of course, I may not have the same taste as
Bill Driscoll, but he said it was a nice place. I think
that's it over there." He pointed through the windshield.

"Capriccio's?" Lissa quietly exclaimed, drawing in
her breath. She had never been there before, but she
had heard that it was one of the classiest, most expensive restaurants in town.

Jared found a parking space a block away, and they
stepped outside into the mild evening. The sky was a
pearly pink color as the sun rode low on the horizon.
"Have you ever eaten here?" he asked, tucking Lissa's
hand through his elbow.

"No, but I've heard it's rather elegant." As if to
prove Lissa's assertion, a couple strolled ahead of them

into the restaurant, the woman clad in a modish designer dress with a fur boa draped exotically about her neck, and the man attired in a white silk suit. "I hope I'm not underdressed," Lissa apologized.

Jared grinned. "You look perfect," he said as he halted just outside the restaurant door. "And I came prepared." He reached into the pocket of his blazer and pulled out a gray-and-white striped tie. Releasing Lissa's hand, he fastened the top button of his shirt and slid the tie under his collar. Lissa laughed. "What's so funny?" He pretended indignation.

"Well...standing out here on the sidewalk and dressing yourself...."

"Find me a telephone booth," he joked, "and I'll change into my tights and cape. There." He slipped the end of the tie through the knot at his throat and measured the length. "How's that?"

Instinctively, Lissa reached up to straighten the knot and smooth the collar. When her eyes met his, she found him watching her with such a gentle, captivating smile that she dropped her hands, suddenly shy. What must he think of her, she thought, in panic—fussing with his tie as if she were his mother...or his lover.... Her discomfort seemed to delight him, however, because the smile lingered on his lips as he led her through the door into the dark ambiance of the restaurant.

A supercilious maître d' stopped them. "Jared Stone," Jared said, staring down the maître d'. "A reservation for two."

"Oh, Mr. Stone!" The host's manner instantly transformed into gushing obsequiousness. "Right this way, Mr. Stone."

Jared cast Lissa a wry glance as they followed the maître d' through the dining room to a secluded table. "I reckon," Lissa whispered, "when you're the son of J. I. Stone, it doesn't much matter whether you're wearing a tie."

As soon as the words slipped out she regretted them, and the swift look Jared gave her, full of fury and resentment and utter disappointment, froze Lissa's apology in her chest. She dropped weakly into the plush chair, afraid to lift her eyes, barely hearing the maître d's effusions about the fine meal he hoped they would have. When he departed, she shuddered as she waited for Jared to speak. He said nothing for an agonizing minute, during which Lissa felt him scorching her with his angry glare. Finally he muttered, "Last night you told me you'd never heard of him."

She steeled herself to meet his gaze. "Last night," she defended herself, "I *had* never heard of him."

"And this morning you decided to run me through the computer?"

"Of course not, I—" Her anger erupted, and she thrust her chin forward, too annoyed by his tone to be afraid of him. "I was trying to help you," she snapped. "You said you were interested in this painting of your father's, so I asked my business partner whether he knew if Curtis had ever been acquainted with someone named Joseph Isaiah Stone. He told me about your father's stature in Rhode Island. I'm sorry I brought it up." Turning to the cocktail waitress who had sidled up to their table, Lissa growled, "Bourbon neat. Jack Daniel's if you've got it in stock."

The waitress nodded and turned to Jared. Lissa turned to him as well, and was startled to see him wrestling with a laugh. "I'll have a Chivas, water on the side," he ordered. He waited until the waitress had disappeared before allowing a soft chuckle to emerge from his throat. "Bourbon neat. You are a hillbilly, aren't you?"

"Sure." She scowled. "But corn-mash whiskey is hard to come by in these parts, so I have to make do."

Jared chuckled again, then grew serious. "Well, Lissa, speaking of the painting, I did a little investigating myself. I found out that the artist is your husband."

"Not anymore he isn't!" she retorted through clenched teeth. "We've been divorced three years now."

"Excuse me—your ex-husband." He tapped his fingers quietly against the linen tablecloth. "Why did you tell me you didn't know him well?"

"Because I didn't," Lissa snarled. "Believe me, if I did I wouldn't have married him."

"Well, why didn't you tell me he had been your husband?"

She grimaced and was relieved to see the waitress bringing their drinks to the table. Once the waitress had vanished, Lissa exhaled, aware that Jared was still waiting for an answer to his question. "Because," she said softly, "I'm not the sort of person who likes to crow to strangers about my blunders and my follies. Having been Curtis Wade's wife is not something of which I'm terribly proud."

"He was awfully talented, though, wasn't he? The painting I've got is beautiful. He must have had some talent."

Lissa sipped her bourbon before speaking. "Oh, yes, he was talented. And I believed in that talent, more than I ought to have."

He regarded her thoughtfully for a long moment before speaking. "Did it ever occur to you that you might have been an inspiration to him?"

Lissa stared at Jared, her eyes round and bitter. "That's what he used to tell me—and I was fool enough to believe it. How did you find out I was married to him, anyway? Did your connection at R.I.S.D. spill the beans?"

"Marriages and divorces are a matter of public record, Lissa," Jared explained. "I had a hunch and I followed it through." He lifted his glass in a silent toast before drinking.

A toast to himself, Lissa thought caustically. "You do so well with your hunches," she said. "Why don't you get a hunch about how the painting ended up in your father's closet?"

Jared's eyes closed into mischievous slits. "I don't get hunches about everything," he confessed. "But I've been pretty accurate about you so far."

"Is that why you asked me out? So you could test your prognosticating abilities?"

His cheeks dimpled as he smiled. "I asked you out," he told her, "because you're attractive, intelligent, feisty and I like the way you talk...and I like the way you feel."

Lissa's face flushed a deep scarlet, and she was glad to see a waiter approaching their table with menus. She hid herself behind her menu, pretending to be engrossed in the listings, although in fact her only interest was in letting her complexion return to its normal shade. When her pulse had calmed somewhat she risked glimpsing over the top of her menu, only to find Jared watching her, seemingly charmed by her embarrassment. The waiter returned to take their orders, and without shifting his eyes from Lissa, Jared said, "I'll have the steak au poivre, rare, and a salad."

The waiter turned to Lissa, and she realized that she had no idea what was listed on the menu, so she coughed and mumbled, "I'll have the same."

The waiter removed the menus and Lissa reached for her bourbon. Before she could lift the glass, Jared had his hand clamped around hers. "That was an honest answer I gave you," he said with quiet intensity. "From here on in, let's be honest with each other, okay?"

Lissa swallowed, unprepared for such a request. She scarcely knew Jared; what kind of commitment was he demanding from her? Total honesty. Just the thing she had always demanded from Curtis, and never received. *Risk it,* her inner voice coaxed her. *Risk it,* Jared's dark eyes seemed to be urging her. "Okay," she relented.

He touched his glass to hers to seal the promise, and drank on it. Mustering her courage, Lissa drank, too. The bourbon spread its warmth along her tongue, down her throat, into her chest. *Honesty,* she thought, awed by the magnitude of what she had just toasted. "Tell me," she ventured, deciding to let Jared be honest first, "about Colorado."

"What do you want to know?"

"What do you do there?" she asked.

He relaxed in his seat. "I have a small factory that produces sophisticated sound equipment—parts for stereo components, that sort of thing. And I own three radio stations, one in Colorado Springs, one in Denver and one down in Phoenix. And I have a sound lab in

Los Angeles, sound processing for films and television shows."

"Good Lord," Lissa said with a gasp. "Sounds like you've built your own little dynasty in the West." *Stone blood,* she thought, recalling Paul's comments that morning. Maybe Jared had had a falling out with his father, but he was a wheeler-dealer just the same. "I take it you've had training as a sound engineer or something?"

He chuckled and shook his head. "Journalism."

"What?"

"I went to college out in Berkeley, became a rah-rah radical, majored in journalism and took a job with a newspaper in Colorado Springs. I was assigned to cover a plant closing—a sound components factory that the corporate owner had decided to shut down simply because he could make a bigger profit if he had the work done in Singapore. The plant was profitable, but the corporation wanted bigger profits than it could get by paying livable American wages." He grinned sheepishly. "I did something a journalist isn't supposed to do. I got involved. Next thing I knew, I had formed a new corporation, held half by me and half by the union local, and not only did we keep the plant open, but within five years we'd doubled profits."

"That's quite a success story. How did you do it?"

"Simple," he said with a shrug. "You give the workers a vested interest in improving productivity—like making them part owners—and they'll have the best incentive in the world to work harder. We're doing well now—we've expanded, improved our line.... Of course, I got fired from the newspaper."

"Obviously you've found other things to keep yourself occupied,'' Lissa noted. ''Are you still a 'rah-rah radical'?''

He smiled nostalgically. ''Well, the 1980s aren't the 1960s. I guess you could say I've learned to work within the system.''

''Or maybe you've redesigned the system to meet your needs,'' Lissa suggested.

''I guess I have.'' He sipped his Scotch. ''I had to rebel first, though. It was difficult to always be thought of as J. I.'s son; I still resent it, as you've seen for yourself. I had to break away. I didn't want to ride through life on his coattails, living off my trust funds and contributing nothing to society. I had to get away from him if I was ever going to be my own person.''

''And he didn't understand that?''

Jared paused as the waiter delivered their salads. ''My father,'' he said, jabbing his lettuce with his fork, ''thought it was the end of the world when I didn't want to go to Brown University. 'Stone boys go to Brown,' he claimed, as if it were holy writ. Only Stone *boys,* of course. When Brown University went co-ed, the old man nearly had a stroke.'' Jared's eyes drifted to focus on a memory. ''I think, Lissa, it frightened him that I had the guts to stand up to all my ancestors and say, 'Good for you, guys, but I'm going my own way.' I think it frightened him because he would have liked to rebel, too, he would have liked to be his own person, instead of Isaiah Barnaby's son.''

''How did you patch things up with him?'' Lissa asked.

''Around his seventieth birthday,'' Jared related, ''he finally broke down and talked to me on the telephone. From that point, it took me another three years to convince him to visit me in Colorado. He wouldn't invite me to visit him here. It was a pretty shaky reconciliation at best. Frankly, I'm astonished he named me as his principal heir and executor. I lost count a long time ago of the number of times he ranted that I'd be cut off without a cent, that he'd disown me and so on.... Now he's got me saddled with files and files of transactions, properties, holdings and God knows what, and a big old white elephant of a house and a gas-guzzling Cadillac."

"I bet you can't wait to straighten it all out and return to Colorado," Lissa opined.

Jared gazed steadily at her for a moment before spearing a tomato wedge with his fork. "At first I couldn't wait," he said, refusing to shift his eyes from her. "But the longer I stay here, the better I like it."

Something in his tone made Lissa momentarily believe she was the reason for his altered feelings, but she knew she couldn't be. In spite of the quiet gleam in his eyes, in spite of his subtle hint of a grin, she knew she couldn't be reason enough to make him change his plans, and she was angry with herself for even considering the possibility. "The house," she said, her voice catching as she scrambled toward a new topic. "What's it like?"

"It's big and old and drafty. I've got a strong suspicion that it's haunted," Jared said and chuckled. "You ought to fly over on your besom during the next full moon." Lissa laughed, too, leaning back to permit the waiter to clear their plates. When she glanced at Jared, he was staring thoughtfully at her, his head angled as he stroked his chin. "Here's an idea," he said. "Maybe you could give me a designer's assessment of the house. If I don't sell it, I'll have to overhaul it some-how, to make it bearable for me to live in. Can you do that sort of thing?''

"Overhaul it?" Lissa pursed her lips, suddenly pro-fessional. "I imagine so. I'd have to see it first, but unless it's got cracks in the foundation and termites vacationing in every crossbeam, I'm sure it's salvage-able.''

"It's one hundred eighty years old and the founda-tion hasn't cracked yet, so I don't think it's going to.''

They were interrupted by the arrival of their steaks, which were doused in brandy and then set aflame. People at the adjoining tables turned to watch the spectacle, and Lissa, who hadn't even known what she had ordered, was enchanted by the flamboyant show. When the blaze sputtered and died, she and Jared were served, and she inhaled the rich aroma of the liquor-and-pepper sauce with a happy sigh. She tasted a small chunk of beef and sighed again. "This is good," she told Jared. "What is it?"

He laughed heartily. "Stick with me, woman—I'll keep you well-fed." He tasted his own meat and nod-ded appreciatively. "So will you look at the house?''

"Of course. But you ought to know, Jared, we might have really different ideas, different taste and all.''

"I like your apartment," he pointed out. "And I can quiz you right now. Critique this restaurant.''

Lissa clicked again into her professional mind-set and surveyed the dining room. "Chic. A bit too glossy for me. Also just a touch too gloomy. See the area by the cocktail lounge? It can't seem to make up its mind whether it's high-tech or hotsy-totsy. Carpet's a bit too dark, although that's a practical choice for a restaurant." She turned back to Jared, awaiting his evaluation of her performance.

"Not bad," he said, nodding his approval. "Except that you forgot to mention the biggest drawback: The tables are too large." He stretched his arm across to her, gathered her hand in his and nearly yanked her out of her seat as he drew her fingers to his lips for a kiss. She fell back into the upholstery, breathless and flustered, although Jared gave her a roguish smile. "It's quite a problem, isn't it," he murmured. Lissa busied herself with her steak, her cheeks again reddening uncontrollably. "Do I embarrass you?" Jared asked. "Answer honestly."

She lifted her eyes briefly to his, then lowered them again. "Honestly? No," she muttered. "I embarrass myself."

"What do you mean?"

I mean, thought Lissa, *I honestly mean that I am sitting here letting you get under my skin, falling for every one of your little flatteries, letting you get to me, falling. . . . I'm embarrassed because I feel like a little girl suffering from a big crush, and if you expect me honestly to admit to that, Jared Stone, you've got another think coming.* "I'm just not . . . used to dating," she replied lamely.

Jared mused on this. "Your divorce is three years old. You haven't been sitting around and twiddling your thumbs all this time."

"Yes, I have," she blurted out, then clapped her hand to her mouth, wishing she could stuff the words back into it. Meekly she pulled her hand away. "Well, there's an honest answer for you," she whispered, poking at her food, looking anywhere but at Jared.

He seemed touched by her candor, but Lissa stewed,

furious with herself for having revealed the truth so recklessly. They ate in silence for a while, and when they had both finished, Jared gave her a dark, probing look and reached for her hand again, this time not dragging her from her seat but simply folding his fingers around hers on the tablecloth. "Would you like to see the house tonight?" he asked.

Something hard and tight formed in Lissa's throat, and she struggled to swallow it down. "For a professional assessment, you mean?" she asked, knowing too well that that wasn't at all what he meant.

He continued to study her, his eyes nearly hypnotic in their steadiness. "Whatever you want."

"Because I'm not..." she stammered, struggling against the tension congealing in her chest. "I'm not sure I'm—honest answer, Jared. I'm truly not sure I'm ready for..."

He gave her hand a gentle squeeze. "Whatever you want, Lissa. Okay? I'll give you the grand tour, and you can tell me about how the colors of the walls led to my downfall, and then I'll take you home, if that's what you want. Okay?"

Lissa stared at her lap, her heart rattling loudly in her chest. "Okay," she said hesitantly, unable to look at him. Somehow, though, she knew he was smiling.

SHE WASN'T like the other divorced people he knew. Jared had been surprised—maybe just half surprised, he allowed as he helped her from her seat. He suspected that there had been something between her and Curtis Wade, so that morning he had called an old acquaintance of his father's who worked at City Hall and asked the man to look Lissa up and see what he could find. The news that she had been married to Curtis hadn't exactly astounded him.

But she seemed to lack bitterness. Escorting her outside into the pleasantly balmy late evening, he tried to figure Lissa out. Weren't divorced women supposed to be bitter? Weren't they supposed to wear their divorces on their sleeves like red badges of courage? Someone like Phyllis, for instance...

He cast a quick glance at Lissa. Her hand was hooked gently through the crook in his elbow, her fingers slender and delicate as they curled about his arm. Her eyes were averted, but he could see that her lips were pressed tightly together. She was scared. Not bitter but fearful. He was nearly overcome by the urge to wrap his arms around her, to whisper reassurances that she was safe with him, that he would never hurt her. But he resisted the urge and escorted her down the block toward the car.

She was so unlike Phyllis, so unlike any woman he had ever met before, he thought. He had also done some nosing around about her business, and from all the evidence, Cavender & Morris was an excellent firm with a fine reputation both financially and artistically. Lissa was clearly a successful businesswoman, as well as a lecturer at one of the finest art schools in the country. She had so much going for her, and she seemed to know it, but... but still, Jared couldn't help but see something glinting in her large gray eyes, something troubled and aching that reached deep inside him and held fast, something that made him want to break through to her, win her trust, win her love.

He couldn't say anything about it, of course. She would think he was crazy, talking about love when they'd known each other barely a day. She didn't know how he was with his hunches, and she seemed so skittish. He'd probably frighten her away if he tried to put his thoughts into words.

So he would just take her to the house tonight, and let her look at it. They wouldn't make love—unless she tore off her clothes and begged him, he mused sardonically. No, they would just go to the house and look at it, and maybe she would exorcise the ghosts for him. She was a witch, after all, with her besom, or whatever that thing by her fireplace was called. If anyone could scare away the ghosts of the past, Jared was convinced Lissa could.

Chapter Three

"I didn't know there were any houses a hundred eighty years old on Blackstone Boulevard," Lissa remarked as Jared steered along the broad avenue, with mansion after mansion lining its outer boundaries and a lush narrow park cutting down the center of the road.

"When old Colonel Jeremiah Stone built his house, this was all farmland. His farmland. A large part of the family fortune came from real estate," Jared explained as he turned up one of the driveways, left the engine idling as he sprang from the car to open the wrought-iron gate, coasted onto the property, sprang out again to close the gate and then drove the rest of the distance along the edge of an acre of front yard to a detached triple garage. Even in the dark, Lissa could discern that the squat brick structure had once been a stable. But before she could examine it, her attention was drawn to the building beside the garage—a massive symmetrical Georgian, three stories high, with a double front door and tall six-over-six-pane windows extending on either side. "Good Lord," Lissa said with a gasp.

"A little overwhelming, isn't it," Jared said as he helped her out of the car.

"It's glorious," she disputed, her wide eyes trying to

take it all in: the fan-shaped dormer windows of the top floor, the sculpted shrubs skirting the porch, the intricate brick patterns beneath each windowsill. "They don't build them like this anymore," she sighed.

Jared fumbled with the keys, finally discovering the right one. He swung the door open and led Lissa into a wide, high-ceilinged entry hall from which he vanished into a small cloakroom and switched on the overhead light. "May I take your jacket?" he asked as he removed his own.

Lissa absently handed him her blazer. She was entranced by the intricate woodwork on the parquet floors, the rococo moldings and cornices, the overstated door frames designed to imply columns. Jared emerged from the cloakroom and pushed open a door to a square sitting room. "Front parlor," he announced. "Tell me what's wrong with it."

Lissa laughed at his bluntness, then explored the room. "Not much," she declared with a smile. "The furniture could use some refinishing—cleaning the fabric, polishing—but you don't want something new and flashy in a room like this." She moved to the fireplace, testing its mantel with her knuckles. "Now it's just my opinion, but I'd be curious to see what's under about twenty layers of paint here. It sounds like marble."

"Good guess," Jared congratulated her. "All the fireplaces here are marble."

"Why would somebody paint over marble?" Lissa asked.

Jared grinned. "Maybe some of my forefathers weren't playing with a full deck." He pushed open a door into another parlor and clicked on a light switch. "Back parlor," he stated. "Tell me this isn't the most pompous house you've ever seen."

"I think it's marvellous," Lissa maintained, stepping into the room. The walls held a series of formal oil portraits of dour-looking ladies and gentlemen. "Is this the Stone gallery?" she asked.

"I'm afraid it predates the camera," said Jared.

"Well? Introduce me." Lissa grinned, deliberately imitating his request at her apartment.

He gave her a suspicious glance before allowing a laugh to bubble over his lips. "Okay," he said. "This is Jeremiah Stone and his Laetitia. The colonel was a Revolutionary War hero, and then he made some money doing heaven knows what, and found himself a bride who was a good twenty-five years younger than him and built her this little cottage."

"They don't look very happy," Lissa noted.

"Laetitia was into spending money," Jared explained. "Jeremiah wasn't. Now this," he said indicating a painting of two very mature-looking teenagers, the girl seated on a swing and the boy behind her; they obviously had been rigidly posed. "These are Jeremiah's children. Eugenia Stone was an interesting lady. She never married and was very active in the Abolition movement—quite liberated in her day. And this is her brother Barnaby, who founded a mercantile exchange and made a lot of money."

"That sounds like the primary activity of the Stones," Lissa commented.

Jarted snorted. "Indeed. Now this here is Barnaby's son Daniel Isaiah, my great-grandfather." Lissa studied the sober portrait of the bewhiskered businessman. "Tell the truth, Lissa, doesn't your great-grandmother look nicer than my great-grandfather?"

"She had a softer lap, I reckon," Lissa agreed. "Did you ever meet this man?"

"He died some time before I arrived on the scene. Well, they're a boring bunch of people." Jared ushered Lissa back into the hallway. "You can tell just by looking at them that they wouldn't have enough sense not to slather paint over a marble mantel." Across the hallway he opened the door to a grand formal dining room. "This room, you have to admit, is pretty depressing."

Lissa nodded. "Buff up the floor, paint the walls white, new curtains—cosmetic changes would cheer it up some. Did you actually eat here?" she asked as she strolled down the exorbitantly long maple table.

"Every night, unless my father was going out. Otherwise, it was him and me at opposite ends of this table. Enough to make a kid lose his appetite."

Lissa gave Jared a sympathetic smile; she was beginning to see why he might have felt the need to rebel. He pushed through a back door to a neatly kept pantry, which opened into a vast kitchen. Every appliance was shadowed by its predecessor: a coal stove next to an electric range; and icebox next to a modern two-door refrigerator; a painted work counter next to a Formica counter. "Mercy, this is an antique!" Lissa exclaimed over the wringer-topped clothes washer. "What is all this stuff doing here?"

"This room is so big that people kept replacing broken appliances without removing them first," he said. "It's an embarrassment of riches, isn't it?"

"It's almost like a joke. This room needs major work, Jared, no question about it."

"So far we're seeing eye to eye," he said, smiling. "But your biggest challenge awaits you." Slipping his fingers through hers, he led her back down the hall to a double door that opened at the end of the corridor farthest from the front door. Jared guided Lissa into the darkness, groping for a light switch, and suddenly the room was illuminated.

Lissa gasped again. She had never seen a room this huge in a house; it was the size of a school gymnasium at least, and fully two stories high. Windows lined the two side walls, and the wall facing the room's entry contained three French doors. Each stretch of wall between a pair of windows held a wall-bracket candelabra, all electric, and the floor was scuffed wood. Several pieces of furniture, including an old armchair and ottoman, a cabinet record player, a few scratched tables, some wooden chairs and scores of cartons, were scattered along the room's perimeter; and above the entry extended a balcony, reachable through doors that presumably opened onto the second-floor level of the house. "What is this?" Lissa whispered, awestruck.

"What do you think?" Jared's eyes crinkled as he smiled. "It's the ballroom."

"The ballroom?"

"Of course. Laetitia insisted on it. The orchestra sat up there." He pointed to the balcony. "All the Stone women made their debuts here, and a few of them, including my Aunt Cissy, were married in this room." His voice echoed in the cavernous hall.

"A ballroom," Lissa repeated, sweeping about the room, peering through the windows into the pitch-black night. "It's like something out of a Jane Austen novel." She pivoted to discover Jared leaning over the phonograph cabinet. After a moment, the room was filled with soft, romantic music.

Jared strolled across the floor to Lissa, bowed slightly, and asked, "May I have this dance, Miss Cavender, or is your card already filled?"

"Why, Mr. Stone," she drawled coquettishly. "You knew I'd save a dance for you."

He cupped her right hand in his left one, slipped his other hand about her narrow waist and drew her to him in a leisurely fox-trot. "Any ideas of what I can do with this room?"

"Hang hoops and hold exhibition basketball games," Lissa suggested. Jared laughed and slightly tightened his hold on her, tucking her right hand against his shoulder. "Did they still have balls here when you were a child?" she asked.

"Cocktail parties, political shindigs, things I was usually excluded from," Jared said, letting his fingers wander up her back to twirl through the ends of her hair. "But I bet nobody ever enjoyed this room as much as I'm enjoying it right now."

Lissa said nothing, but as his grip brought her more snugly against him, she allowed her hand to slide around his neck and her head to nestle deep into his shoulder. The kiss he placed on her brow was so gentle it was almost imperceptible, and it suffused Lissa's entire body with a quiet glow. She let Jared press her chest to his, and he released her hand so he could wrap both arms around her. Although his feet still moved in time to the music, his hands began a dance of their own, one stroking up and down her spine in a soothing massage and the other digging deeper into her hair, seeking out her nape and caressing it, until he seemed to have retrained her pulse to his own tempo. She felt as if she were floating away on the music, floating within Jared's arms to another time, another universe.

Jared kissed her brow again, and instinctively Lissa tilted her head up to him. Their lips came together as if magnetized, as if this was the ultimate purpose of the dance. While he rocked her in time to the slow music, his tongue was engaged in a more daring tango, conquering her mouth with intimate jabs and parries. He pulled away to kiss her cheeks, to nibble her earlobe with tender bites, and as if he controlled her completely, she turned her head this way and that, presenting her throat, her jaw, her temple, her mouth again, abandoning herself to the dazzling feel of his lips as they tasted whatever she offered.

She sensed his hand creeping up beneath her sweater to spread along the smooth skin of her back, and his fingers imparted an unfamiliar vibrating warmth to her flesh. It traveled through her bones to her feet and back again, then sank deep into her organs, even deeper than her organs to somewhere intangible, somewhere at the center of her being. Her soul surged with the heat, melted from it; she lost track of her bearings, the music, herself. She was nothing but sensation, nothing but the eddying current of heat and longing that Jared had stirred within her.

Gradually, she became aware that the music had stopped. In its place she heard Jared's muffled sigh as his lips roamed through her hair, and her own erratic breath as she clung to him, trying to recall who she was, trying to determine what was happening to her. She had never felt so totally lost before, so totally willing to lose herself, and opening her eyes to the glaring reality of the room required an excruciating effort. "Jared," she rasped, her voice barely a whisper.

"Mmmm."

"Jared."

Lissa hadn't realized how tightly he was holding her,

but now she felt his muscles begin to soften, his steel clasp begin to loosen so he could pull himself far enough from her to see her face. He contemplated her, his eyes smoky with passion. "Do you want me to take you home?" he asked, and Lissa was certain she heard a faint tremor in his usually confident voice.

Her own voice, she feared, was probably not functional, so she bit her lip and nodded.

"Okay," he relented, allowing himself to keep one hand on her shoulder as he led her to the phonograph, where he switched the power off, and then to the double doors leading out of the ballroom.

Lissa's legs felt leaden, and she tried to reassure herself that she had made the right decision. It was too much, too soon. She had only just met Jared, after all. And she needed time to reaquaint herself with such strong sensations as those he had created within her. Reaquaint herself? No, she admitted silently. These were sensations she had never felt before, not even after months upon months as Curtis's wife. In all that time she had never felt so warm, so fluid, so yearning as she felt after one hushed dance with Jared Stone.

"Jared," she said as he swung open the cloakroom door.

"Yes?"

"The painting." At his bewildered scowl, she clarified herself. "Curtis's painting. Can I see it?"

Jared leaned against the door, studying her, thoughtful. "Do you want to?"

"Well, maybe if I did—maybe I could tell when it was painted, or something...." She tapered off, unnerved by Jared's piercing stare.

After another moment of thought, he released her

from his scrutiny. "It's upstairs," he said, taking her hand and leading her up the broad staircase.

Lissa tried to decipher his sudden strangeness. Was he concerned about taking her to the bedroom level of the house? That didn't make sense; they were both adults, after all, and they had made a pledge of honesty with each other. Besides, she had asked to see the painting. She could never accuse him of using the painting as a ploy to get her into his private chamber.

Many doors opened off the upstairs hall. Jared led her to one and turned on the lamp beside the double bed before letting her enter. She could immediately tell that the room was currently being lived in: though the bed was neatly made, the night table held a book and a pair of reading glasses, and the top of the bureau was cluttered with a comb and brush, after-shave lotion and other toiletry items. The walls were a pale yellow color, the furniture old but sturdy, the carpet worn. "Was this your bedroom as a child?" Lissa asked.

Jared shook his head as he moved toward the bureau. "It's a guest room. At the moment, I feel like a guest here, so..." He slid an unframed canvas out from a crevice between the bureau and the wall and flipped it around for Lissa to see.

Her first reaction was that she was hallucinating. Her second reaction, once she had blinked enough times to know that her eyes weren't mistaken, was shock. She felt herself staggering toward the wall, her thoughts spinning out of control, her throat closing around a low, anguished wail as her mind exploded with the horror that the painting evoked.

It was Lissa—Lissa against a black background. Her naked form was contorted on an invisible surface, one leg extended and the other curled toward her abdomen, her torso writhing as if she were desperate to escape, her face cast downward, her hair cascading behind her sharp profile. It was a stunning painting, a mélange of sharp lines and soft nuances, delicate flesh tones against stark black.

And it was here in Jared's possession. The painting that had destroyed her marriage, that had nearly destroyed her life, that Curtis had sworn he himself had destroyed—here, owned by a man who obviously lusted after Lissa, a man who had undoubtedly been taken enough by the naked model to chase her, to try to seduce her, to experience in the flesh what he had enjoyed on the canvas.

Scarcely able to breathe, she turned on Jared, her eyes inflamed, her body clamoring with rage, and slapped him across the cheek. The slap caused more noise than pain, but Jared reacted swiftly, grabbing her wrists and shoving her back against the wall, nearly as furious as she was. "What was that for?" he growled.

"You bastard!" she howled, half incoherent with anger and disgust. "So this is why you sought me out, is it? The face matches the voice, does it? You liked what you saw and thought you'd try me out in person, is that it? Thought you'd try your luck on a lady who poses naked, huh? Oh, I must be loose, to pose that way—I must be good for a few nights of fun—is that what you thought? Is that why you called me?"

"Stop it." He spoke softly but harshly, trying to shake her out of her hysteria. "Stop it, Lissa. I don't know what you're talking about, and I don't think you do, either."

"You know damned well what I'm talking about," she

whispered, her eyes stinging with tears. "Or is this the first time you've noticed a resemblance between me and... and that?" She could barely bring herself to nod toward the canvas. "Do you expect me to believe—"

"Lissa." His voice took on a husky gentleness as he recognized that her crazed outburst had exhausted her, rendering her harmless. He lowered her hands to her side, relaxing his fingers although he kept them around her wrists. "When I called you at your office, I had no idea who you were or what you looked like. I wanted to see you again because I liked the sound of your voice, and I was intrigued by what you said. When I attended your lecture, yes, of course I realized you were the woman in the painting, and I hoped you'd be able to help me figure out why my father would have it. But when I asked you out for dinner, when I kissed you... that had nothing to do with the painting. Nothing. I won't deny that I'm attracted to you, but that's because you're *you*. It has nothing to do with acrylic on canvas. Give me some credit, Lissa. I'm not an idiot. I know the difference between a painting and a person."

She sucked in her breath and closed her eyes, trying to dam the tears that had accumulated along her lower lids. "I'm sorry, Jared," she whispered. "I'm so sorry. Please forgive me." She dared to open her eyes again and found his face close to hers, watching her with deep concern. "Did I hurt you?"

He tendered a slight smile. "Of course not. You took me by surprise, though."

"Because the painting—" She swallowed, trying to fight back the sobs. "It took *me* by surprise, Jared. I begged him to destroy it, and he swore to me he'd gotten rid of it, he swore... just another broken promise, I suppose...." Her voice faded as the hideous memories took shape once again in her mind.

"Why would you want him to destroy it?" Jared asked. "It's a lovely painting."

"It's the finest piece of work he ever did," she said, moaning.

"So why—"

"Because," she said before he could finish his question, then softened again, wilting against the wall, full of remorse for having spoken so sharply to Jared. "I'm sorry, I shouldn't take this out on you. It's not your fault, and I shouldn't...I shouldn't...." The tears finally crested, racking her with agonizing sobs. Jared pulled her against him, letting her weep into his chest, his arms holding her tight, holding her up. Eventually, he led her to the bed and sat with her, his fingers consolingly stroking through her hair as she cried, offering her the comfort of his shoulder as her body trembled, as she struggled for control over her shattered emotions.

Gradually her tears were spent, and Lissa leaned away from him, pressing her hands to her feverish cheeks, trying to dry them. Jared offered her a linen handkerchief from his pocket, and she gratefully accepted it. "Are you okay?" he asked.

"I'll survive," she managed, attempting a pitiful smile.

"Do you want to talk about it?"

She stared at his handkerchief, smoothing it out with her fingertips, then turned to find him watching her, his brow creased with worry. She attempted another unsuccessful smile. "It's a sordid story, Jared. I don't want to trouble you."

"Trouble me?" An incredulous laugh slipped past his lips. "I'm already troubled by how upset you are. I didn't expect anything like this."

"What did you expect?"

He shrugged. "I thought you might be a little embarrassed when you found out the painting was of you. You had made some comment about 'nude floozies' when I described it, and I figured you'd have to backtrack when you saw it. But it's nothing to be embarrassed about, it's a beautiful picture. Except that you obviously see something in it that I don't see."

Lissa drew away from him to stare at the painting, and a brutal shiver wrenched her shoulders. "Yes," she murmured, almost in a trance as she absorbed the truth of the painting, the things in it that only she could see. She was surprised to hear her voice, surprised to hear herself relate the horror she had never told anyone before, not even Peggy or Paul, who had taken her in that dreadful night. Here, in a quiet, comfortable room, seated beside Jared, his arm wrapped protectively around her, so attentive he seemed to be listening to her with his soul, here she heard herself describing the ugliness that dwelled in the painting. "He did it in one night, Jared," she whispered. "He painted it in one ghastly night, and when it was finished it was as if he'd finished something inside me, killed a part of me."

She sighed, her breath ragged, and let her gaze fall to her knees, no longer able to view the painting without suffering waves of fear and nausea. "I worked in Boston when Curtis and I were first married. I commuted every day while he painted at the house. I'd get home pretty late, and he'd usually be all finished in the studio. It was a garage, actually, but Curtis fixed it up as a studio...." She realized she was rambling and inhaled, focusing on her clenched, icy fingers in her lap. "After a couple of years, I started up Cavender & Morris here in town with Paul—only it was Wade & Morris then, when I was still Mrs. Wade." A bilious taste filled her mouth; she shook her head and swallowed. "I started arriving home from work a lot earlier, because it wasn't a long commute anymore, and I guess Curtis didn't get used to that." She glanced forlornly at Jared. "I don't know if you want to hear this."

He continued to watch her, his dark eyes motionless, his arm securely hugging her against him. "Only if you want to tell me," he said.

She turned away, glimpsing the painting again and shuddering. "Well, you can probably guess. I arrived home early one evening and I saw the lights on in the garage, so I went over to surprise Curtis. He was with a model. He loved working with models; he loved painting nude women. He loved the female form, he said." She grimaced. "He was loving a female form, all right, but it didn't have much to do with painting as far as I could tell. Well, there was a scene. I was shocked and hurt, and after the model got dressed and left, Curtis tried to explain things to me. The way he explained it was that he did this sort of thing with *all* his models, with all the dozens of pretty ladies he had had posing for him. He had to seduce them, he claimed, so he could get to *know* them, to familiarize himself with their bodies, to understand their essence. He had to know them intimately and completely, the way he knew me."

She ran her fingers over the soft material of her skirt, unsure of whether she could continue. The horrible night she was describing to Jared seemed as real to her now as it had been when she was living it, and part of the reality was her disgust with herself for having been so stupid, so naive, so unwilling to see the sort of person Curtis was. She felt Jared tighten his arm reassuringly around her. "You shouldn't take it personally," he guessed at her thoughts. "The guy may have been a jerk, but just because he was cheating on you doesn't reflect on you personally, Lissa."

"It doesn't reflect—? Jared, I haven't gotten to the bad part yet," she said, shaking her head, feeling the color drain from her cheeks as the misery of that night crowded in on her. She again averted her eyes, addressing the floor, her words sounding strangled as she forced them out. "He had to prove to me...his thesis about knowing women, so he dragged me to the garage, Jared, to paint me. He tore off my clothes, and he posed me, and he...he painted...*that*."

Jared studied the painting and frowned, bewildered. "I don't understand."

"Jared." Her hands curled into fists, her fingernails biting into her palms. "He painted me...the way he painted all his models. First, he had to *know* me and *understand my essence* and all the rest of it—only I didn't want to, Jared. I wasn't like the models, I didn't want to. So he...forced me. He said he couldn't paint me otherwise, and he...he forced me. Do you understand now?"

"He raped you." Jared's voice was low and tense, barely disguising his own horror.

"Oh, but you see he was right," Lissa remarked ironically. "Look at that painting and you can see that he truly did understand my essence that night. You can see it if you look closely. I was dying that night, Jared, and it's all there, on the canvas. Curtis was a brilliant painter. You've got to admit it.''

Jared tucked his thumb beneath Lissa's chin and forced her face to his. His eyes were ablaze with indignation. "Why didn't you leave him?"

"I did," she said, sighing. "That night. I was afraid to before he fell asleep; I was afraid because I thought he was crazy—or maybe I was crazy myself. So I waited until he was asleep, and then I ran. But before I left I had to go back and look at the painting. I couldn't leave before I had seen it." Her gaze drifted back to the canvas across the room. "And there it was." She sighed again, her energy sapped yet her spirit surprisingly free and light, relieved at long last to be unburdened. "I talked to Curtis a number of times before the divorce was finalized, and I begged him to destroy the painting, and he said he would. How your father got it I can't imagine."

The room was silent for a long time. Finally, with a parting squeeze, Jared took his arm from Lissa's shoulder and stood up. Without speaking, he strode to the bureau, yanked open the top drawer, rummaged through its contents, and removed a small pearl-handled penknife. Opening the blade, he turned to Lissa. "I'll cut it to ribbons if you want," he offered, his voice husky and his eyes flaming. "I'll tear it to shreds. Just say the word."

"You would do that? For me?"

"Just say the word."

She stared at Jared, weary yet strangely exhilarated. She felt as if a long-festering sore had been lanced and drained, and now she was cured. The wretchedness she had stifled, the despair she had refused to deal with for three long years had finally been vocalized, and she knew the painting could never upset her again. "No, don't," she said. "I'm all right. Just...just put it away. I don't care to look at it anymore."

He returned her stare, measuring her, trying to ascertain that she was as all right as she said she was, and the power of his gaze penetrated her, warming her from across the room. She watched him close the penknife and put it back in the drawer, slide the painting out of view against the wall and approach her. Grasping her by her elbows, he eased her off the bed, his eyes examining her face, searching for lingering traces of pain. "You're sure you're okay?"

She nodded, her gray eyes bright and steady on him.

"Do you want me to take you home?" he asked, his voice low and sonorous.

"No, I..." Lissa was startled by her reply, and shook her head, trying to clear it. All she could think of was that she had to be honest with him. "I don't want to be alone right now," she mumbled, pressing her forehead against his shoulder. "Would you mind if I just... stayed with you awhile?"

He slid his arms around her back and drew her even closer to him. "Of course not."

"I don't want you to think...I mean, I'm not...this doesn't mean I..."

He let his hands move higher, to the back of her head, and tilted it up to meet his. "You need to be held for a while, Lissa. No explanation necessary." He touched his lips lightly to her brow, led her to the bed, and sprawled out on it, kicking off his shoes and spreading his arms to welcome her.

Dazed, fatigued, Lissa stepped out of her shoes and joined him atop the covers. She cuddled up to him and he coiled his arms around her, blanketing her with his quiet strength, swaddling her with his unflagging stability. What was it about him that had made her trust him enough to tell him about the night she left Curtis? What was it that made her feel so close to Jared, that allowed her to open up to him, to share with him her most intimate terror? Whatever it was, she felt it permeating her now, in the soothing warmth of his body, in the delicate breeze of his breath against her hair, in the constant pulse of his heart in her ear, like a secret song of faith, a tranquil promise lulling her to sleep.

SHE FELT SO GOOD in his arms, so right. He watched her face, a picture of gentle repose as she slept, the amber light from the lamp by the bed bathing her smooth, creamy complexion. She had such long eyelashes, he contemplated, such delicate lips.

He knew instinctively that what she had told him about the painting, and about her marriage, was something she had never told anyone before. The nearly violent spate of words had crashed through some emotional dam she had erected around herself, and Jared felt honored that he had somehow managed to break down the dam for her.

If he had been around three years ago, if he had known her then...God, he would have been tempted to kill Curtis Wade. In the eighteen years he had been apart from his father, he had slowly learned how to contain his explosive temper, but Lissa...Lissa was so fragile, so lovely. He could scarcely bear the thought of someone doing such a horrible thing to her.

He closed his eyes, replacing her image in his mind with that of the painting, now carefully out of view. Yes, he had somehow understood the anguish in the portrait, the undefinable pain in the model's averted face, in her writhing body. His immediate impression of the painting had been that the model was gorgeous, but that alone wouldn't have inspired him to seek the truth about its creator. Without consciously having considered it, he had known there was a greater mystery lurking in the canvas. No wonder he had gone after Lissa.

Her breathing was even and deep. Her outburst must have exhausted her, Jared mused, opening his eyes again and studying the play of light through her glorious hair as she slumbered. Maybe he *had* won her trust; the thought encouraged him. Maybe, if she felt comfortable enough around him to share her misery, and now to sleep in his arms, maybe he had gotten through to her. Maybe she was ready for him to explain to her about his hunch, about how appropriate it seemed for her to be here with him, about how, for the first time since he had arrived back in Providence, he no longer felt like a guest in his father's home.

He shifted his arm slightly beneath her, sensing the narrow cage of her ribs against his biceps. Even fully clothed, he found her incredibly sexy. But he didn't want to make love to her, and that understanding surprised him. Not tonight. Tonight he wanted only to hold her.

Maybe tomorrow, he thought, drawing her more snugly into his embrace. *Maybe tomorrow she'll be ready.*

Chapter Four

A motion roused her, a subtle chill on her cheek when Jared slipped away. She opened her eyes, and the amber light from the bedside lamp burned her corneas for a minute until she adjusted. The tall, lean man beside her was trying to uncrick his neck and stretch his legs. Noticing Lissa's fluttering lashes, he smiled. "Hello there."

"What time is it?" she asked, her tongue thick and groggy.

He twisted his arm to read his watch. "A quarter to two."

She scowled and attempted to rub the sleep from her eyes. "Have I kept you up all this time?"

"Mmm. Don't worry about it," he told her.

"Oh, Lord, I'm sorry." She rolled out of his grasp, failing to hide her blush from him. "I just felt so comfortable—"

He cupped his hand over her cheek and urged her face back to him. "My pleasure," he said, cutting off her apology, a tender smile coursing over his lips. "But I *am* kind of tired." His smile faded slightly. "Do you want me to take you home?"

At a quarter to two in the morning? As sleepy as he was? She couldn't ask him to shift into gear and chauffeur her through the chilly night—and she wasn't really sure she wanted him to. "It's a little late for that," she admitted.

His smile returned, stronger than before. "In that case, what do you say we wash up and get some real sleep?" He hoisted himself to his feet, helped Lissa up beside him, and guided her down the hall to a bathroom. "There are fresh towels in the cabinet," he said, pointing out a closet door. "Holler if you need anything," he added as he shut the door.

The bright glare of the lights along the white ceramic tiles screwed Lissa's face into a grimace, and she hastened through her washing, too drowsy to dawdle over the sink. When she emerged, Jared was waiting for her. "There are plenty of bedrooms to choose from," he stated slowly, "if you want privacy."

Lissa tried to read the enigmatic expression on his face. Did he want her to sleep in a separate room? Would that arrangement be easier for him? She knew she would prefer to return to the comforting cradle of his arms, but if she told him that, would he infer that she was inviting him to make love to her?

Maybe he detected her confusion, because he helped her out by offering, "You're more than welcome to share the bed with me."

She tilted her head in appraisal. "Just to sleep?"

He grinned and gave the tip of her nose an affectionate kiss. "I don't know about you, but I haven't got the energy for anything else at the moment." He ushered her back into the bedroom and eyed her outfit. "Do you want something to sleep in?"

"I don't suppose you have any nightgowns lying about," she asked, yawning.

He rummaged through his closet and slipped a plaid flannel shirt off its hanger. "Try this," he suggested, tossing it to her on his way out the door.

She heard the bathroom door shut and undressed quickly, leaving on her panties and buttoning up the oversized shirt. It fell to midthigh, and the sleeves extended several inches beyond her fingertips. She rolled up the cuffs and smoothed out the collar, leaving the top button unfastened so she wouldn't choke herself in her sleep. The sound of Jared's footsteps in the hall alerted her to his return, and she slid under the covers just before he swung through the door.

With a brisk nod, he proceeded to undress. Either he wasn't a modest person or he was too tired to care about modesty at the moment, because as he removed each article of clothing and put it away he seemed oblivious to the woman watching him from the bed. Lissa knew the polite thing would be to avert her eyes, but she was too entranced by the tall, muscular body slowly being revealed to tear her gaze away. As he shook his shirt even on the hanger, she admired his broad shoulders and sun-bronzed back; as he creased his pants and draped them over the hanger she ogled his disproportionately long, sinewy legs. Leaving on his shorts, he crossed to the bed; before he crawled beneath the blanket and flicked off the light she caught a glimpse of the valentine-shaped mat of black hair emphasizing the contours of his chest. He resumed his position on his side facing Lissa, one of his arms cushioning her head and the other slung over her ribs, grazed her cheek with a light kiss, and mumbled, "'Night," before sinking into unconsciousness.

The realization that she was actually in bed with

Jared, actually lying next to his nearly naked and remarkably virile body, astonished Lissa. Her own body,
hidden beneath the baggy flannel shirt, responded to
his closeness as if he were emitting rays of sensuality.
They pierced her skin and shot through her flesh;
twinges of desire ran along her nerves. If not for her
mind, her conscience, her sense of self-preservation,
she would have reached out and embraced him as he
was embracing her; she would have twined her arms
about his luscious torso and press into his solid chest;
she would have woven her slender legs through his and
demanded that he kiss her, kiss her as he had on her
porch, or in his ballroom.... But she wouldn't. She
couldn't. As close as she felt to him, she refused to
blind herself to the situation: He was in Providence
only temporarily, and she was merely someone he had
invited to dinner because he was tired of eating alone,
or because he liked the way she talked...or because he
had seen a nude painting of her.

No, she wouldn't believe that of him. She would
give him the benefit of the doubt. But even if she did,
she would have to be blind to allow herself to succumb
to his charms when she knew he would be leaving soon
enough, returning to Colorado. She would have to be
blind to set herself up for that kind of hurt, and she
wasn't blind. Not anymore.

With a sigh, she let the weight of her head shape the
pillow and allowed herself to drift back to sleep.

It seemed as if only minutes had passed when the
strident clanging of a bell plowed through her skull,
forcing her awake. Opening her eyes, she identified the
sound as a ringing telephone, and gradually the room,

lit by sunshine filtering through the sheer curtains, began to make sense to her.

Jared's eyes twitched open, and his lips instantly formed a grin as his vision fell upon her. While the telephone rang a second time, he drew her toward him for a sleepy, languorous kiss. Even somnolent, he managed to stir her entire body to life. Frightened by her instantaneous response to him, by the hot flood of sensation he created within her, she drew away and muttered, "The phone." On cue, it rang a third time.

"Mmm," Jared groaned, refusing to let go of Lissa as he groped along a shelf of the night table, locating the receiver on the fourth ring. Relaxing against his pillow, he looped his arm around her, cushioning her head against his athletic chest, and yawned before acknowledging his caller. "Hello?" His fingers wove lazily through Lissa's hair as he listened, and then he spoke again: "Hello, Nina—was I supposed to call you? I'm sorry, honey, I forgot."

Nina? Honey? Lissa flinched, shrinking from the man who resolutely held her to him as he engaged in light banter with the woman on the telephone. The nerve of him, the nerve, she gasped, trying to struggle out of his grip as he chatted with some lover of his on the phone. But without much effort, he held Lissa firmly to himself, refusing her the opportunity to escape.

"This afternoon?" he was saying. "Hang on a second." He tucked the receiver under his arm and turned to Lissa. "Do you have any plans for today?"

Too enraged and disgusted to answer, she glowered at him and said nothing.

He ignored her fury. Back into the telephone, he

calmly declared, "I'll be bringing someone with me."
He listened for a moment. "Don't worry, Nina, I'll
bring all the stuff. Around two, two-thirty, then. So
long."

His grip on Lissa eased as he reached over the edge
of the bed to hang up the phone, and she tried to
scramble away from him. "I hope it wasn't me you
were intending to bring with you to Nina Honey's
place," she muttered, her legs snarling in the bed-
sheets.

Before she could untangle herself, Jared sprang with
catlike grace to pin her down. His eyes twinkled mirth-
fully as he forced Lissa to look at him. "Nina is my
cousin," he said, laughing at her jealousy. "And she is
a honey. You'll like her." He hovered above Lissa, gazing down at her, pushing her disheveled tresses back
from her face. As his eyes absorbed her pout, his smile
expanded. "Good morning," he whispered before
lowering his lips to hers.

She was fully alert for this kiss, and despite her pique,
its effect on her was startling. Her hands automatically
slid up around his warm, smooth back, and as his tongue
deepened its probe of her mouth he lowered his weight
onto her, his fingers tracing a tantalizing course along
her neck and behind her ears, his legs embracing hers
with viselike strength. She tried to will herself not to respond to him, but she was powerless against the onslaught of his utter maleness and the rushing heat of her
own long-neglected wants. All she could think of was
how good he felt, how much she desired him.

"Lissa," he whispered, regaining control and lifting
his mouth from hers. He leaned back against his
haunches, continuing to straddle her, continuing to

study her, his fingers moving tentatively along her shoulders, his chest heaving, his lips shaping into a wistful smile. "You're pretty hard to resist, do you know that?"

She twisted her face away, abruptly ashamed of herself for having brazenly encouraged him to indulge in something her own common sense warned against. Jerking her hands from him, she pressed them to her eyes. Jared pried them off her cheeks, impelling her to confront him. "I'm sorry," she rasped.

"I'm sorry I attacked you," he said, grinning sheepishly.

She narrowed her eyes on him. "Jared," she said, a little shy, "you wanted something more last night, didn't you?"

"At a quarter to two in the morning, all I wanted was sleep," he assured her.

She scowled. "You know what I mean. Be honest, Jared."

His grin softened. "Honestly... I'm very attracted to you, you know that. Of course I want to make love to you. But I can wait. I want it to be good for you, so I'll wait till you're ready."

"I'm ready," she whispered, shocking herself. The words must have arisen from her body; she knew her mind couldn't have formed them.

He apparently knew that as well. He gave his head a pensive shake and drew a delicate line with his thumb along her jaw. "You may be willing and able, but you're not ready, not yet," he disputed her, hooking his thumb beneath her necklace. "This is very pretty," he noted, lifting it so its links caught glimmers of light. His eyes darkened slightly. "Did he give it to you?"

"Who?"

"Curtis."

"He never gave me anything," she said, her upper lip briefly curling in distaste. "No, it was a gift from Paul and Peggy — my partner and his wife."

"Good." Jared appeared relieved. "I like it."

Something about his reaction — his tone, the bristling indignation and the pinch of jealousy — touched Lissa deeply. She grasped his hand and drew it to her cheek, then kissed the adventurous thumb and released him. "Why do you want me to meet your... Nina?" she questioned him.

He grinned, heaved himself off Lissa, and swung his legs over the edge of the mattress. "We have to go through some more paperwork while her mother is still in town," he explained as he strode to the closet to fetch a beige terry-cloth bathrobe. "I thought if you came along, you could keep me from burying myself in stock certificates."

Lissa sat up, unsure whether she believed him. "You might have asked me if I wanted to come."

"But that would have given you the opportunity to say no," he pointed out. "Would you like some breakfast? A shower?"

"A shower would be nice," she said with a nod. She still wasn't satisfied with his vague justification for wanting him to bring her to his cousin's house. As she stood up she primly pulled the hem of the flannel shirt toward her knees, figuring that her safest course would be to get dressed before her body could betray her again. Right now, she wasn't sure whom she trusted less: herself or Jared.

He led her out to the hall, but before they reached

the bathroom, Lissa was distracted by what appeared, through an open door, to be yet another parlor. Curious, she opened the door wider and peered inside the room, which was cozily furnished with thick leather and oak pieces, the walls holding built-in shelves crammed with books. "A library," she announced, delighted by the warm sunlight that slanted through the windows onto the plush Persian rug.

"This used to be my nursery," Jared informed Lissa.

"Your nursery?"

"Originally it was Laetitia's bedchamber," he explained, moving into the room. "When the house was built, it was considered proper for an upper-class wife to have her own bedroom. But Jeremiah wasn't a fool." Jared leaned against a door in one wall. It opened into a narrow dressing room with built-in wardrobes, a mirror and vanity, and an entry to a private bath. At the far end of the dressing room was another door, which Jared pushed wide. "This was Jeremiah's bedroom," he said, although Lissa couldn't really see past him into the room. "By designing this connecting passage, the old boy could enjoy his marital visits without all the servants finding out about them. Laetitia's room was my nursery because this was my parents' room—so my mother could come and take care of me when I got to howling through the night."

Lissa examined the beautifully polished grain of the wardrobes in the dressing room. "Was...was the painting in here?"

"In this one," Jared said, swinging a cabinet door open to reveal a rod full of empty hangers. "Standing on its side, awaiting disposition." He shut the cabinet, and when Lissa slipped past him into his father's bedroom he remained behind, letting her explore on her own.

The room, Lissa had to admit, still held the somber mood of death in it, and she understood Jared's reluctance to join her. Although the curtains were open to let in the sunlight, the air felt heavy and cold. The massive canopied bed had been stripped of linens, and the floor was cluttered with cartons, some filled with clothing. The bureaus and highboy had some of their drawers hanging precariously open. "It's a mess," Jared confessed. "I've been going through his things a little at a time. Most of the clothing will end up at the Salvation Army."

Lissa's attention was drawn to an aged gilt-framed photograph of a handsome couple that stood on the bureau. The man, probably around forty, wore a pin-striped suit with a carnation in his lapel; the woman, noticeably younger and nearly as tall as the man, had thick black hair and striking dark eyes. "Are these your parents?" Lissa asked Jared.

"Don't tell me," he answered, anticipating her comment. "I look like my mother."

"She's beautiful," Lissa declared, replacing the photograph on the bureau and returning to the dressing room.

Jared shut the door behind them, choosing to leave through the library. "I lived in here until she became sick," he said. "When I was about four they moved me. It was thought that I shouldn't be too close to a dying woman."

"What was wrong with her?" Lissa asked.

"Cancer. In those days there was no point in hospitalizing her—they had no real treatment. Just mor-

phine. I was allowed to visit her for an hour every afternoon, but my father didn't want me to hear her crying,
so he had me moved to the other end of the house."
Jared's lips twisted into a melancholy smile. "After she
died, he went into deep mourning for a while, and
when he emerged, he decided he preferred to have me
far away so I wouldn't be aware of the women he was
entertaining. At least he *thought* I wouldn't be aware."
They had ambled down the hall, and Jared opened
another door. "Here is the cell of Jared the Rebel."

Lissa was unable to suppress a giggle as she surveyed
what was an archetypical boy's bedroom. The walls
were blue, the furniture dark brown, the hutches filled
with biographies of Knute Rockne and Babe Ruth and
Abraham Lincoln, the wall above the bed decorated
with a large banner from the Moses Brown School, one
of the exclusive preparatory schools in town. "This
doesn't look like a rebel's cell," she said with a laugh.

"I took all the subversive stuff with me when I left
for college," Jared said, winking.

Lissa examined a row of trophies on one shelf: three
for basketball, two for debating. "I reckon you're tall
enough for basketball," she allowed, "but forensics?"

"Captain of the team," he boasted. "I got a lot of practice at home with father. Now, how about that shower?"
He took her hand and escorted her to the bathroom she
had used the previous night. Pulling back the curtain, he
displayed the room's supplies. "Soap, shampoo, tooth-
paste, whatever you need. Scream if the water comes out
brown."

"I'm sure I will," Lissa called after Jared as he disappeared down the hall.

She turned on the faucets, adjusted the water's temperature, and stepped into the tub. She was glad to be alone for a while; she needed time to think. The hot spray pounding against her scalp helped to unscramble her thoughts.

Why her, she wondered. Why, of all the unattached women in Providence, had Jared Stone chosen to occupy himself with her? And what, precisely, was he after? If he had been hoping for a pleasant, no-strings-attached sexual interlude during his stay in town, he had obviously picked the wrong woman.

Well, he seemed fully aware of, and willing to respect, the fact that she was the wrong woman for a quick fling. Yet he had unflinchingly admitted that he did want to have sex with her when she was ready—when *he* decided she was ready. And in the meantime, he had somehow resisted the temptations he must have felt with her in his bed all night.

Maybe company was truly all he wanted—a friendly, intelligent, attractive woman with whom to pass the time while he was stuck in New England. If the circumstances allowed for a bit of physical pleasure, fine. If not, well, that was fine, too.

But it wasn't fine, not for Lissa. Something was bothering her, gnawing at her, and she groped for it, trying to define it. Impatient with her lack of success, she wrung out her hair and turned off the faucets. Leaning out of the tub to grab a towel, she glimpsed herself in the mirror and paused, trying to fathom what was troubling her.

She didn't want to be just company for Jared Stone. She didn't want to be just someone to pass the time with. Last night she had shared with him the truth of her past, the secret devastation she had never revealed

before, not even to her closest friends. What had occurred last night was far more personal, far more intimate than the sexual encounter they had managed to
avoid. Somehow Jared had captured her trust, had
made her willing to be honest with him, and had made
her rely on him to console her. And he had consoled
her. He had held her, simply because she had needed
to be held. No explanation necessary, as he had said.

And he was going to leave. A clammy sadness
gripped her; she tried to dry it away with the towel.
Whatever relationship she might establish with Jared
had a built-in conclusion. Rhode Island was not his
home, and eventually, inevitably, he was going to
leave.

Wrapping the towel around her glistening hair, Lissa
slipped on the flannel shirt and nudged open the bathroom door. The hall was empty, and she heard the
sound of rushing water emerging from the far end of
the house. Apparently Jared was showering in another
bathroom. At least three bathrooms on this floor, she
calculated in an instant of professionalism. At least
three bathrooms, at least three bedrooms—and one
man, one man who had made her trust him, and who
was going to leave her.

Lissa hastened down the hall to the bedroom and
dressed quickly, then borrowed the brush on the bureau to unsnarl her hair. As soon as Jared was dressed,
she resolved, she would ask him to take her home. No
breakfast, no trip to visit his cousin Nina-Honey, no
waiting for Lissa to be ready. The more she considered
Jared, the more she wanted him, and the more she
wanted him, the more she realized she had to get away
from him before it was too late. She wasn't sure what

"too late" implied; all she knew was that merely thinking about him was enough to blind her to the reality of their circumstances, to the foreordained farewell that would end their friendship, to the genuine heartache she would feel once Jared was gone. And she refused to blind herself. She would extricate herself from his invitation to his cousin's house, and she would extricate herself from the hold he seemed to be developing over her. Better to say good-bye now than to prolong things and set herself up for a greater sadness later.

She caught a movement in the corner of her eye and lowered the brush as Jared bounded into the room. His hair shimmered black and wet, and his skin exuded a fresh, spicy scent from behind his closed robe. Smiling broadly, he sauntered to Lissa's side, slid his arms beneath her, and drew her against him in a bear hug. "Much too fancy for a trip to Nina's," he critiqued her. "Once I'm dressed and we've had some omelets and toast, I'll take you back to your place so you can change clothes, and then we'll go. Okay?"

"Jared, I don't know...." She tried to maintain her resolve, but as he tucked her head into the triangle of bared chest above his robe's lapels, she found herself melting, softening. "Maybe we ought to forget the breakfast...." she said.

"Nonsense. Breakfast is the most important meal of the day," he lectured her. "And you haven't lived until you've tried my omelets."

She angled her head away so she could see him, and fought against the quaver in her voice. "I meant, Jared, maybe we ought to... to forget the whole thing."

His brow furrowed as he tried to understand her words. "Forget what whole thing?"

"The... the trip to your cousin's house, and—"

"I want you to come," he declared steadily. "Please." He hooked his index finger beneath her chin and pressed his lips softly against hers. "For me," he whispered.

"Okay," she acquiesced, at once irked and relieved. Irked that she had submitted to his request so easily, after having determined to break things off with him before it was too late, and relieved—relieved because, she acknowledged with a broken sigh, saying good-bye to Jared even now, at the start, would hurt terribly. It would be worse later, she knew, but one more day, just one more day in each other's company, one more day to build up her strength... and then she would face the pain.

HE HAD ALMOST LOST HER, and the thought appalled him. Over breakfast he watched her, hardly aware of the flavor and texture of the plump omelet he forked mechanically into his mouth. All he could think of was that Lissa had almost slipped away.

He would have to explain, he acknowledged. He would have to tell her that he needed her in his house, that he hadn't been able to bear staying in the house until she had entered it last night, until she had entered his room and lain in his arms and infiltrated the atmosphere with her sweetness and vulnerability. He would have to explain to her that she mustn't run away, that she mustn't be frightened of him. *Meeting Nina will help,* he thought. Nina's family was Jared's family, his only family. And when Lissa met them, perhaps she would understand what a home and a family meant to Jared.

Nina would be surprised, he suspected, but pleased.

She'd like Lissa; he was certain of it. He had never introduced Nina to any of his lovers in Colorado—but Lissa was different. Nina would recognize that immediately.

He observed Lissa as she ate her food, praising the omelet even though she was unable to finish it. *She's thin,* he thought. *She could use a few extra pounds.* He would see to it that she ate better. He was a good cook; he would take care of her.

Chapter Five

"Exactly where are we going?" Lissa asked as Jared steered the Cadillac onto the interstate heading east.

"Little Compton," Jared replied.

"That's down by the ocean, isn't it? As I recall, Paul—my partner—told me that the people with money live in Newport but the people with class live in Little Compton."

Jared tossed back his head and laughed. He looked strikingly handsome in a plaid cotton shirt and corduroy blazer above neat khaki trousers. After breakfast, he had taken Lissa back to her apartment to change from her skirt to a pair of gray wool slacks and a fisherman-knit sweater. Jared insisted that she looked perfect, but now that they were on the road, she wondered whether all the Stones were as casual as he was. "When Jeremiah settled on Blackstone Boulevard," he was explaining, "his brother Gideon established a farm near the shore."

"How old is the house?"

"That depends on which room you stand in." Jared chuckled. "The original house was built right after the war—late 1780s or thereabouts. Then a wing was added in the 1820s, another wing in the 1880s, a guest wing in the twenties.... Nina had the kitchen redone a few years ago, but I don't think that counts."

Lissa grinned, unable to resist resting her head against Jared's hand as he extended it along the back of the seat to wander through her hair. "So Nina's you're first cousin, then?"

He nodded. "Her mother is my Aunt Cissy—my father's sister. She's widowed now, and she moved down to Florida a few years ago. But she came north when my father died."

"And Nina's husband?"

"Anthony," Jared said. "He's a professor of history at Brown University."

"That's a long commute for him," Lissa observed.

"Yes, well, these Stone residences have a way of holding on to you. And it's a great place for their kids to grow up. Two," he said, in anticipation of Lissa's question. "Sara is ten and Danny is eight."

Lissa memorized the information Jared had given her, then cleared her throat. "Are you sure I should be coming with you? It sounds like a family affair."

Jared glanced toward her, grinned and patted her shoulder. "I'm sure," he murmured.

They steered off the highway in Fall River, heading south toward the ocean. Little Compton filled the southern tip of a peninsula east of Newport, and many of its neat, well-tended houses predated the Revolutionary War. Jared drove through the center of town and farther south, following a road that ended at the water. He pulled into a driveway only several hundred yards from the dead end created by the beach.

The house before them was a modest clapboard

structure with wings added on to it in an eccentric fashion. Before Jared had turned off the engine, two children darted around the house and scampered to the car. The front door swung open and out stepped a slender, attractive woman in her thirties, dressed in jeans; a beefy, barrel-chested man with red hair and a neatly trimmed beard, also wearing jeans; and a slight, wiry woman with white hair. At least she was wearing a skirt, Lissa noted, relieved by the informality of the hosts.

The younger woman greeted Jared with a warm hug, and then Jared made introductions. "Lissa, this is Nina—my 'honey,'" he teased, causing Lissa to color and Nina to appear mildly perplexed. "This is Anthony," he continued, and the bearded man gave Lissa a crushing handshake. "And this—" Jared escorted Lissa onto the porch to the elderly woman "—is my aunt, Priscilla Bainbridge."

"How do you do," Lissa said, politely offering her hand.

"Priscilla Bainbridge?" the woman said to Jared with a sniff, then took Lissa's hand. "Aunt Cissy to you, dear."

"And this is Lissa Cavender," Jared concluded.

"What about us?" asked the little girl.

"What about you?" Jared growled, easily hoisting her off the ground and swinging her in a circle. "You're half-size. You don't count."

"Me, too. Me, too!" shouted the boy, whom Jared promptly swung as well.

Nina rolled her eyes and ushered Lissa inside. "He spoils them rotten," she confided.

"That's the reason God created relatives," Aunt

Cissy declared. "To spoil children. And in His wisdom, He created parents to undo the damage."

Toting the leather briefcase he had brought along, Jared joined the other adults as they congregated in a snug living room. Its pegboard floor, low ceiling and wide hearth told Lissa that it must have been part of the original eighteenth-century house. "How about some drinks?" Anthony offered as Jared led Lissa to a couch and sat beside her. "Jared, a beer?"

"Fine."

"How about you, Lissa?"

"I believe—a soft drink. Do you have any fruit juice, perhaps?"

"I've got some excellent apple cider," Anthony said as he vanished from the room.

"She said she wanted a *soft* drink," Nina hollered after her husband, then turned to Lissa. "This cider isn't exactly soft," she cautioned. "Sip it slowly."

"Pretend it's applejack," Jared suggested. "You must be used to that."

Anthony returned with a tray, carrying two bottles of beer, two glasses of cider and a glass of sherry for Aunt Cissy. "If you'll forgive a tactless question," Nina said as she approached Lissa with one of the glasses of cider, "where are you from?"

"Tennessee," Lissa answered.

"Nashville?"

Lissa and Jared shared a quiet laugh. "She's from the bustling metropolis of Ouchy Crick. Did I say it right?" he asked Lissa.

Still giggling, she shook her head. "O'cha' Crick. Orchard Creek," she informed the others. "It's a mountain town."

Nina knitted her brows. "How in the world did you two meet?"

"I live in Providence now," Lissa explained.

Jared lounged against the sofa's cushions and sipped his beer. "Lissa is an interior designer—she has a firm in town. She's going to renovate the boulevard house for me."

Lissa flinched. They had talked casually, yes, but she hadn't known Jared was serious. She had assumed he had asked for her appraisal of the house as an excuse to lure her there. She gave him a sharp glance and found him regarding her with sparkling eyes and a content, confident smile.

The others seemed startled, too, but for a different reason. "I thought you were going to sell the house," Nina asserted. "The last time I spoke to you—when was it, Tuesday?—you were planning to talk to some brokers."

Jared shrugged nonchalantly. "I changed my mind."

"Why?" Nina pressed him.

Jared eyed Lissa and his smile expanded. "Lissa managed to convince me that the place was salvageable." Lissa opened her mouth to protest, but Jared stifled her with a knowing wink. She pursed her lips, totally bewildered.

"Well, I for one consider this good news," Aunt Cissy declared. "I like the idea of the house staying in the family. I was married in the ballroom, you know," she told Lissa before turning her attention back to her nephew. "Regardless of the tempestuous nature of your relationship with your father, Jared, he wanted you to have that house."

"He should have told me himself," Jared flared.

"Now, now," Nina interrupted in a soothing voice. To Jared she cooed, "Let the old man rest in peace," and to her mother she added, "Let Jared live in peace. Now why don't we go through this paperwork and get it out of the way so we can all relax. We can use the den. Anthony, you'll keep Lissa entertained, won't you?"

Jared stood, stretched and gathered up his briefcase. "You can swap teaching secrets," he suggested. "Lissa teaches at R.I.S.D., Anthony."

"We'll try to get this over with as quickly as possible," Nina promised as she led her mother and cousin from the room.

"You teach at R.I.S.D.," Anthony mused, sipping his beer. "That's pretty impressive. You look younger than half my students at Brown."

Lissa shrugged modestly. "It's just one course." She heard the sound of a door shutting. "That was awfully diplomatic of Nina, the way she defused that squabble."

"Nina's the family peacemaker," Anthony boasted. "It's thanks to her that J.I. finally broke down and started talking to Jared after all those years. When Jared would phone him at his home, J.I. always hung up, and he instructed his housekeeper to do the same. So Nina got J.I. down here on a visit, got him tanked up and then phoned Jared. They had worked it all out beforehand, of course. Anyway, father and son chatted for about five minutes, and suddenly the old man shouted, 'Hey, wait a minute! I'm not talking to you!'" Anthony chuckled at the memory, and Lissa joined him. "So you're a designer. How did you pick that?" he asked.

Lissa studied the tart drink in her glass. "I originally

thought I'd be an architect," she said. "I was always building things as a child, with blocks and such. My papa built the house I grew up in, and Gramma was always saying I inherited it from him. But when I came up north for school, it occurred to me that people spend more time indoors than outdoors. Pretty buildings are nice, mind you, but I decided I'd rather concentrate on improving the places where people live, where they spend most of their lives. Interior design involves architecture as well as other things."

"You must be very talented," Anthony commented. "Jared wouldn't trust that old fortress to just anyone."

Lissa shifted uncomfortably, still uncertain of what Jared was up to with his sudden announcement. She quickly changed the subject. "I understand that your home is more appendage than house."

"Would you like me to show you around?" Anthony offered. They rose and he ushered her about the house, making her guess which rooms had been added on when and laughing with her over some of the idiosyncrasies that had resulted—the uneven floors, the differing widths of the walls, the varying heights of the ceilings. They ended up in the kitchen, a bright, modern room redolent of a rich aroma that came, Lissa discovered when Anthony opened the oven, from a roasting turkey. Satisfied by its appearance, Anthony shut the oven, topped off Lissa's glass of cider, and took a fresh beer for himself. "Why don't we retire to the patio?" he suggested, leading her through a back door onto a brick terrace overlooking the expansive backyard. "This way we can keep an eye on the monsters." He waved lovingly at his two children, who romped along the edge of the thick forest that framed the yard.

Lissa settled herself on a canvas deck chair and sighed, admiring the splotches of red foliage that proclaimed the New England autumn. "It's really lovely here," she said. "But isn't it a long trip for you to get to work?"

Anthony chuckled. "Well, when you marry a Stone you marry a house. You marry into a different world. It has its pluses and its minuses."

Lissa eyed him with curiosity. "What do you mean?"

He sipped his beer and organized his thoughts. "Before I married Nina, I used to rent tuxedos when I needed them. Now I own three. I have obligations. We have to sit on boards, host charity affairs, attend the appropriate fund-raisers. And there's all this heritage to cope with: the houses, of course, and the myths—the photographs of Cissy and J.I. sitting on Calvin Coolidge's lap, that sort of thing. Ask Jared to show you the handwritten note his parents received when he was born, congratulating them on their new son and signed, 'Your abiding friend, Eleanor.'"

"As in Roosevelt?" Lissa gulped.

Anthony nodded. "It can get to you after a while."

"What are the pluses?" Lissa asked.

Anthony smiled. "The big plus is that I'm crazy about Nina. Besides, as a historian, I find this kind of thing fascinating. But it's tough if you're born into it. I'd like to think that if I were born a Stone I'd have the guts to do what Jared did—light out for the territories. It took an incredible amount of courage for him to do what he did. Nina's brother didn't, and it destroyed him."

Lissa's gray eyes grew round. "Destroyed him?"

"I think it's harder to be a Stone man than a Stone woman. So much was expected of Jonathan, and he wasn't a very strong person. He died in a car accident, but I think it was the pressure that killed him."

Anthony was interrupted by the children, who scampered to the patio. "Can we have cookies?" Sara asked.

"Your mother's making a big dinner," Anthony reminded them. "You don't want to spoil your appetite, do you?"

"But we're starving!" Danny whined.

Anthony scowled and turned to Lissa. "Do these look like starving children to you?" he asked.

"They have a lean and hungry look about them," she returned, grinning.

"All right," Anthony conceded to his children. "But only one apiece." Amid boisterous thank-yous, the children dashed into the house. "You're as bad as Jared," Anthony said, chuckling.

Lissa asked Anthony about his research, and he rapidly warmed to the subject. He told Lissa about the book he was writing on religious refugees in Rhode Island—the Baptist followers of Roger Williams who founded Providence after fleeing the intolerant Puritans of Massachusetts Bay Colony, and the Jews who settled in Newport after escaping the Spanish Inquisition. Lissa listened to his engrossing lecture, happy to learn more about the history of the state that had become her home. After a while, Anthony glanced at his wristwatch and shook his head. "You shouldn't let me go on like that," he scolded Lissa cheerfully. "All you had to do was yawn and I would have shut up."

"I didn't want you to shut up," Lissa said. "I think it's fascinating."

"I wish my students were as fascinated," he grumbled, grinning as he stood up. "What do you say we rescue the Stone clan? Old J.I. sure left a mess of paperwork for them to plow through."

Lissa walked with Anthony back through the house to the den, and he shoved open the door. They found Nina on the floor, surrounded by mounds of paper and envelopes and folders, and Jared and Aunt Cissy on a sofa hunched over a coffee table across which more papers were scattered. When Jared looked up, Lissa smiled, struck by the way his reading glasses, which were aviator-style with thin tortoise-shell frames, made him appear scholarly—studious yet incredibly sexy.

"It's about time you came and saved me," Aunt Cissy snorted, flinging a pen onto the table. "They've got me signing so many documents my fingers are about to fall off."

Jared pulled off his eyeglasses and rubbed the bridge of his nose. "It's good therapy for your arthritis," he reassured his aunt, giving her an affectionate squeeze.

"I was expecting *you* to come and rescue poor Lissa," Anthony chided Jared. "I've been boring her to tears with my dissertation on the First Baptist Church and the Touro Synagogue."

"Shame on you," Nina reproached him, trying to straighten out the papers.

"To say nothing of your children, who are complaining about being malnourished," Anthony added.

"Dinner." Nina shook her head, forcing her attention away from the fiduciary matters with which she had been occupied. "I've still got some preparing to do. Jared, why don't you show Lissa the beach? She deserves a reward for putting up with Anthony."

"I deserve a reward for putting up with you," Jared countered.

"Well, go on, take a walk, show her the ocean. It'll take me a good half hour to get the food on the table."

Jared turned to Lissa, who nodded enthusiastically. "I'd love to see the ocean."

Once they were out of the house, Jared slipped his arm around Lissa's shoulders and strolled with her down the narrow blacktop to the shore. "There's a path through the woods out back," he informed her. "But I'd probably get us lost if I tried to find it."

"Is it a private beach?"

"Technically, but about twelve families along this road share it—they chip in on upkeep. It seemed much too selfish to have the beach all to ourselves, even if it is kind of small."

They reached the white fence marking the end of the road, and Lissa inhaled the pungent fragrance of the water. "It's beautiful," she said, sighing, gazing past the narrow strip of sand to the foamy green sea beyond.

"Take your shoes off," Jared ordered her as he removed his own. They set their shoes and socks neatly beneath the fence, then rolled up their pants and ventured onto the sand. It was coarse with pebbles and shells, and punctuated with large outcroppings of rock. A cool breeze whipped off the water, and Lissa shivered slightly. Jared tightened his arm protectively around her. "You must have thin Southern blood," he teased. "When we were kids, we lived here. Summer, winter, rain or shine. Nearly every weekend my father and I would come down here, and we kids would race through the woods to the beach and play until it got dark."

They strolled along the shore, Jared occasionally picking up a flat stone and skipping it into the water. Lissa watched him, detecting a poignant shadow hovering over him. "Anthony mentioned something about Nina's brother," she said softly.

Jared gazed at her, surprised that she had guessed the cause of his mood. "Jonny."

"What happened to him? Anthony implied that your family somehow...destroyed him."

A pensive smile formed on Jared's face. Noticing a smooth boulder, he helped Lissa onto it and sat down beside her, staring out toward the horizon. "He's probably right," he agreed. "Jonny was as eager to escape being a Stone as I was. Only he escaped with drugs and booze and fast cars." He shook his head. "He's been dead over ten years now, and three weeks ago was the first time I got to see his grave. Aunt Cissy begged me not to come east for the funeral. She said if I came my father wouldn't." Jared's fingers roamed through Lissa's hair, but his eyes remained fixed on the slate-gray water as he remembered. "He was a year older than me, kind of like a big brother. I learned a lot from him—I learned what not to do." He sighed, smiling again. "It pleases me to see Sara and Danny being raised without all the pressure. Nobody will ever tell them what they have to make of themselves. This year Sara wants to be an actress and Danny wants to be a rodeo star, and nobody says they can't because they're Stones."

"What is all the paperwork you've been going through?"

This time Jared's sigh was one of boredom. "We're trying to give the money away. We've got all these stocks and bonds, and we're trying to decide whether to cash them first or donate them intact. And we're arguing over whom we want to give them to. Nina and Aunt Cissy want to give a huge endowment to Brown, but I won a small skirmish, and we're going to donate something to your alma mater."

"The School of Design? Why?"

"Call it a good neighbor policy." Jared grinned.

"Jared, why did you say that about my renovating the house?"

He focused his dark eyes on her. "Don't you want to?"

"Well, we never really discussed it."

"Of course we did," he argued. "I want you to. I figure we can work out the details, draw up a contract or whatever, next week. I'm not asking for favors, Lissa."

"I know that. It's just—I didn't realize you were serious."

"I am," he said.

Lissa felt there was something lurking beneath Jared's words, but she couldn't tell what it was. As he continued to stare at her, she sensed that he had never been more serious about anything in his life. She shivered again, not from the brisk wind but from the smoldering darkness of his eyes; they seemed to dig into her, to cut through her skin and grip her, hold her fast, tug her toward him.

His lips moved against hers, and she felt herself tumbling over the edge, tumbling down into a place far deeper than her intellect could grasp. This was not a kiss of lust or even of friendship; it was a kiss of need, of raw, brutal necessity. When they parted, Lissa was afraid to open her eyes, afraid of what she might see. She forced herself to look, and she found Jared watching her with the same trembling wonder that she was feeling. Neither of them was able to speak. The only sound was the rhythm of the ocean breaking against the sand.

And then another sound: "Jared! Dinner! Mom said to come get you!"

They turned to discover Sara and Danny trotting along the stretch of pebbles from the woods, and Jared slid off the rock to greet the children. "Well, it's about time!" he hooted as Danny tackled him onto the sand. "Since when did you become a linebacker?" he growled as they playfully wrestled.

Sara eyed them with disdain and turned to Lissa. "Boys," she said with a scornful sniff.

Together they trooped back to the road, where Lissa and Jared dusted off their feet and put on their shoes. Danny insisted on racing Jared back to the house, and Jared accepted the challenge, discreetly slowing his pace so Danny could win. They waited, panting and gasping, for Lissa and Sara to join them on the front porch, and then they all stormed into the house, following the delicious scent of hot food to the dining room and taking their seats around the table.

Nina served up a feast of turkey, apple and chestnut dressing, potatoes, salad and wine. "You didn't do all this for us, did you?" Jared asked as he heaped his plate.

"No," Aunt Cissy cackled. "She did it all for me. You can't get good food in Florida. All they eat down there is citrus and grits and an occasional lobster."

"Grits are delicious," Lissa defended her native cuisine.

"If you put enough butter and salt on them," Aunt Cissy retorted. "Then, if you're lucky, they taste like butter and salt."

"Do you really eat all that stuff?" Jared asked Lissa. "Pigs' knuckles and collard greens?"

"Collard greens are quite tasty," Lissa insisted. "Pig's knuckles never did thrill me—too much bone. But sure, I ate all the other stuff. Collard greens, chitlins, corn pone, black-eyed peas—"

"And moonshine fresh from the still," Jared concluded for her.

"Of course," Aunt Cissy complained. "You have to get drunk to eat that ghastly food." Lissa joined in the good-natured laughter.

"Did you like the beach?" Nina asked.

"It's a bit cold down there," Lissa said, "but it's beautiful."

"We saw them kissing," Sara announced.

"Sara!" Nina reprimanded her. "That's not nice."

"It's true. We saw them. Isn't it true, Danny?"

Lissa's cheeks flooded with color, but Jared guffawed, totally, at ease. "Don't yell at her, Nina, she's only reporting the truth. You should encourage your kids to be honest."

"Honesty and tact are not mutually exclusive," Anthony said, frowning at his children. "You shouldn't spy on people," he admonished them.

"I'm sorry," Sara apologized. "We were just curious. We decided you're pretty," she told Lissa.

"Too little, too late," Nina said with a sympathetic smile.

As the conversation veered to other topics, Lissa felt her appetite return. Jared seemed, if anything, exhilarated by Sara's tactlessness, and he regaled the family with news of the West, of the science-fiction movie his sound laboratory was working on and of the rock star who had recently visited his Denver radio station for an on-the-air interview. The enormous quantity of food eventually disappeared, and Nina ignored everyone's claim of being too full for dessert by serving pumpkin pie and ice cream. Amid applause and groans, the family finally pushed themselves away from the table.

"I've got some cleaning up to do," Nina said as she gazed at the empty dishes. "Jared, why don't you and Mother finish up the paperwork on your own?"

"Let me help you, Nina," Lissa volunteered, stacking several plates and carrying them into the kitchen.

Once the dining room table was cleared, Nina gestured toward a stool by the breakfast bar, near the sink. "From here on in," she said as she began to rinse dishes and stack them in the dishwasher, "the biggest help you can give me is to sit put and keep me company." Lissa did as she was told, leaning against the counter and watching Nina efficiently attend to the dishes. "Let me apologize again for my children," she said, pushing a dark curl from her forehead.

Lissa colored slightly but grinned. "It's all right," she said.

"It's just that—well, this is the first time Jared's ever..." She paused to rephrase her thoughts. "I'll be blunt, Lissa. You must be special. He's never introduced us to a woman friend before."

The news jolted Lissa, but she endeavored to maintain her calm facade. "Well, he hasn't been East, has he?"

"Oh, but we go out to Colorado all the time. Once a

year with the kids, and then Anthony and I frequently visit on our own. We're very close—especially with my brother gone." She focused on a knife, rubbing it beneath the faucet as she thought. "I probably shouldn't be saying this, Lissa, but... Jared wouldn't have brought you along if he didn't think you were very special."

Lissa fidgeted uneasily with a salt shaker. "I think he only wanted some company for the drive," she mumbled.

Nina eyed her, then shook her head. "Jared doesn't need company. And he doesn't waste time with people. He gets a hunch and then he sticks with it. He's an arrogant son of a gun," she said, chuckling affectionately, "but he's always right." She turned to Lissa, finally sensing her discomfort. "Like mother like daughter, huh? We both have big mouths."

Lissa smiled in spite of herself. "You're a very honest family, aren't you."

"One of our many shortcomings." Nina grinned. "I'm just about done here. Why don't you go and make sure Mother and Jared aren't eating each other alive?"

"After all that food, I doubt they could manage to eat a thing," Lissa joked as she wandered back to the den. The door was open, and she entered quietly.

Jared and his aunt were once again seated on the couch, Jared wearing his eyeglasses and studying a document. He glimpsed Lissa and smiled, then turned to Aunt Cissy. "The point is, this stock is artificially undervalued at the moment. Probate attached a low fair market value on it. So if we hang on to it now and pay the tax, eventually it's going to recover. Then, in a year or so, if you want, we can donate it to the historical society and take a much bigger deduction.''

Wheeler-dealer, Lissa thought with a private laugh. As Paul would say, you can't deny your blood. And in fact, she realized, Jared no longer seemed interested in denying his blood. Somehow, she sensed, he was coming to terms with his inheritance, not just his monetary inheritance but his spiritual inheritance, too. His decision to keep his father's house symbolized his willingness to accept his own heritage. Perhaps that was the undefinable emotion she had seen in his eyes and felt in his kiss on the beach. Perhaps he was learning that he couldn't find himself by running away; he could find himself only by coming back.

Nina appeared in the doorway and reminded Jared that there was no need to resolve every last detail by midnight. Although Aunt Cissy would be returning shortly to Florida, they could still make decisions over the telephone, and Jared sighed with relief as he gathered the papers back into his briefcase. Anthony had built a fire in the living-room fireplace, and they retired to the cozy room for more socializing. Sara and Danny answered Jared's questions about their schoolwork, and Anthony complained about the distraction of Brown University's impending homecoming weekend, which would mean class attendance would be down and partying would be up. After some minor protests, the children reluctantly said good night and went upstairs to bed; noting the time, Jared suggested that he and Lissa ought to be taking their leave.

"Let us know how the work goes on the house," Nina said as she, her husband and her mother accompanied Jared and Lissa to the car. "We expect to be invited for the grand reopening."

"So do I," squawked Aunt Cissy. "I'd come all the way up from St. Petersburg to see that."

"You're on," Jared said, kissing her cheek. He embraced Nina, who then gave Lissa a warm hug.

"If you can turn that ugly old house into a home," she said, smiling, "it'll be a feat of magic."

"Well within Lissa's powers," Jared teased. "Didn't I tell you she's a witch? She even has a little broom she rides around on."

"Besom," Lissa corrected him, feeling her cheeks redden again.

They waved as they backed onto the road, but once Jared had pointed the car north toward the interstate, Lissa felt her smile wane as she sorted through the day's events. Why had be brought her with him? Was it to keep from immersing himself too deeply in paperwork, as he had claimed? Or was it because he thought she was very special, as Nina had suggested? How could he think she was special when they had only met two days ago?

Two days ago. To Lissa it seemed that more than two days had passed since the afternoon Candy had handed her a sheet of notepaper with Jared's name and phone number on it. Not because the time had dragged, but because so much had happened. In two days Jared Stone had aroused in her body urges she could scarcely comprehend, let alone control. In two days he had made her promise to be honest with him, and he had gotten her to reveal the grotesque truth about the painting, and he had held her through the night and made her believe that her past was truly behind her and that she had emerged from it whole, that she had survived the horror and now could vanquish it. In two days he had made her trust him, depend on him, need him.

She glanced at him, seeing his dark profile come in and out of view as a passing car's headlight's struck his face. Turning swiftly away, she acknowledged the frightening notion that she had gone beyond trusting, depending, needing. Was it possible that she could be falling in love with him?

No. She gave her head a shake, as if that could negate the idea. No, she couldn't have fallen in love with him, not so quickly. It was just that he had been so kind to her, and after what she'd lived through with Curtis, Jared's kindness was blown way out of proportion in her mind. It was just that he was so handsome, so bright, so doggedly persistent, that when he held her and kissed her she felt things she had never felt before. Surely that was all.

If her silence bothered Jared, he didn't show it. He was ruminating, too, driving along the dark highway lost in his own thoughts. At the Gano Street exit to Providence's East Side, he steered onto the ramp and turned north. When he stopped at the red light by Angell Street, Lissa shattered the stillness. "Where are we going?"

"To the house," he replied, vaguely surprised by her question.

"To your house?"

He twisted to face her, his features distorted by the yellow glow of a streetlamp. He seemed astonished by the thought that Lissa might not want to go to his house. A horn honked behind them and he started, realizing that the traffic light had turned green. Coasting through the intersection, he eased to the curb and shut off the engine. "You want me to take you back to your apartment, don't you," he conceded, his baritone tinged with a disturbing huskiness.

"I..." She swallowed, unsure what to say. "Don't you want to?"

He lifted one of her hands in his, studied it, ran his fingers along the slender bones of her fingers. "No, I don't," he finally admitted. "I want to take you home with me. It seemed so obvious to me that I didn't even think to ask you. That's a bad habit of mine. When something seems obvious to me, I assume it's obvious to everyone else." He glanced sheepishly at her. "You don't want to come home with me, do you?"

"It's not that, Jared...."

"You don't trust me?"

"Of course I trust you."

"Then what? Be honest."

She tried to ignore the gentle caresses along her palm and over her knuckles that were creating an eddying warmth up her arm, making it difficult for her to concentrate. "Jared, I just—everything's happened so fast, and I...I don't rightly understand it all. I mean—you asked me to dinner only because you were tired of eating alone. Didn't you?"

He let his head fall back against the upholstery as he exhaled. "That was a lie."

Lissa glanced up at him, shocked. "You lied to me?"

"When I asked you out, it was before we had promised to be honest with each other, remember?" He grinned sheepishly. "I've been down to Little Compton a couple of afternoons, and I've met Anthony on campus a few times, and Bill Driscoll, my father's lawyer—and I had dinner once with my father's housekeeper so we could make arrangements for her pension. . . . No, I wasn't exactly dying for company."

"Then why—?"

"I didn't want you to turn me down. It was a line, and it worked. I don't know, maybe you would have gone out with me anyway." He studied her, waiting for a response.

"Maybe I was the one who was tired of eating alone," she muttered.

Jared slipped his hand beneath her chin and raised her head until her eyes met his. "What's really bothering you, Lissa? Did something happen today that upset you?"

Her lips worked themselves, trying to shape a sentence. "Jared . . . I don't . . . I can't—" She squeezed her eyes shut and shoved out the words. "Jared, I can't just be someone for you to pass the time with until you leave for home."

His fingers slid off her chin and reclaimed her hair. "I *am* home," he said.

"I mean Colorado."

"And I mean here. I've come home."

"But your work, your whole life—you don't plan to uproot yourself. . . ."

"I uprooted myself once when I left here," he said quietly. "But I was just a tumbleweed out there. My roots stayed behind. I didn't know that until I came back. But I know it now."

"What about your work? Your factory and your radio stations?"

"What about them? They haven't gone under in my absence these past few weeks. As Aunt Cissy would say, in His wisdom God gave us telephones and airplanes. And there's more than enough to keep me busy here. My father left me a confounded empire to play with. The only reason I would have returned to Colorado was that I never thought I'd be able to live in that awful house. You showed me I could live there very happily."

"I did?" Lissa asked, overwhelmed. "All I said was that if you painted a few walls and sanded down the fireplace—"

"Lissa," he murmured, leaning toward her and sliding his hand to the nape of her neck, holding her face close to his. "Remember when I told you the house was haunted? It was, it really was. It was haunted by my terrible memories of it. The fights, the misunderstandings...the fear I had as a child of being shunted off just when I needed my father most.... Do you know what he said to me when I left for good? As I was leaving the house, he stood in the doorway waving his fist, and he shouted, 'You'll come back over my dead body.' Terribly prophetic, wasn't he." Lissa opened her mouth to speak, but Jared cut her off. "It was haunted by all those things. Anthony always says how courageous I was to leave, but I think the bravest thing I ever did was to come back. For three weeks I was rattling around in that house, reliving all the old battles, like Eisenhower returning to Normandy. But last night, Lissa, the ghosts disappeared. Just having you with me—you chased them away. Of course I want you to restore the house. You've already accomplished the hardest part."

Lissa's eyes glistened with unexplainable moisture. "I think you're giving me credit for something I didn't do."

Jared shook his head. "No. But I may be giving you a responsibility you're not ready for. I've rushed you. I'm sorry." He switched on the engine. "I'll take you home."

As he curled his fingers around the steering wheel, Lissa reached out and touched his wrist. He turned to her and she whispered, barely audibly, "Take me home, Jared—your home."

He tilted his head to look at her, and although he wasn't smiling, his eyes shone jubilantly. He lifted her hand to his lips for a gentle kiss, then slid his arm around her and drew her close to him as he steered to the majestic brick house on the boulevard.

HE HAD WON. He had broken through to her. As he drove through the night-shrouded, tree-lined streets of the East Side, he felt not the gloating power of victory but a quieter contentment, a sense of satisfaction and accomplishment. Not since he had lost his father's love so many years ago had he wanted so very badly to reach someone, and this time he succeeded. He had reached Lissa, and she trusted him.

The notion filled him with awe. She wasn't just a woman, an attractive lady he had invited back to his place for a night of fun and games. She was Lissa, a witch on a besom, a magician who had already performed a miracle for him without even having been aware of it. Didn't she know her effect on him? Couldn't she tell what she had done for him?

Yes, she must know, he mused as he reached the

boulevard and slowed the car as they approached the wrought-iron gate marking his driveway. He couldn't have expected her to know when he knew, because she didn't know about his hunches. But she had caught up to him, caught on to what was happening. Clearly she understood that when things were right they sometimes happened fast, and the wisest course was to respect them and accept them.

Tonight she trusted him, and he would love her, and she would be his. Tonight she would admit to the truth between them. Tonight he would bring it all home for her.

Chapter Six

Lissa felt her pulse accelerate as she waited for Jared to unlock the front door. Once they were inside he bolted it, then took her hand and led her up the stairs. The stairway seemed much too long; she feared they would never reach the top step. Perhaps Jared shared her fear, because halfway up he paused to kiss her. It was a quiet, subtle kiss, but it expressed a promise—that he would be worthy of her trust, that she would not regret her decision to return to his house.

Somehow they made it to the room they had shared the night before, and Jared clicked the lamp on low. Without a word he enveloped Lissa in his arms and conquered her mouth again, this time his kiss not soft and beseeching but deep and ravenous. His tongue seemed to blaze through her, igniting responses throughout her body. His teeth teased her lower lip with delicate bites, and his fingers plunged into her thick, shimmering mane, trailing over her ears to her throat, to the velvet skin of her shoulders beneath the ribbed neckline of her sweater. Her flesh shivered at his touch. Jared drew his lips from hers, letting his hands slide down the textured front of her sweater, brushing over the tight swells of her breasts. She shivered again, and her fingers clenched at his chest. "Why are you shaking?" he murmured.

"I...I think I'm a little scared," she admitted.

He tasted her brow, then gently grazed her eyes, his breath warming her lowered lids. "There's nothing to be afraid of."

"I know," she said, nodding meekly, her words muffled by his shirt as he pressed her head against him. "Jared, it's just—it was so bad, the last time, with Curtis...."

"Ssh." He drew her face away and traced her trembling lower lip with his index finger. "This time will be good, Lissa. I promise." He let his hand wander back down her sweater to its edge and lifted it over her head and off. She was still shivering as he opened the clasp of her brassiere, but once he removed it and began to sketch ethereal patterns across her skin, up her ribs, along her collarbone, beneath the gold strand she still wore at her throat, down her sternum to her navel, Lissa felt the shivering dissolve into aching. When at long last he lifted his hands to her yearning breasts, she moaned with relief.

"Mmm, you do feel good," Jared said with a sigh as her nipples stiffened against his thumbs. He seemed to wrestle with the urge to continue massaging her breasts forever, but finally tore his hands away and lowered them to the waistband of her slacks. Merely the anticipation of his touch along her hips caused Lissa's knees to weaken, and as he finished undressing her she clung still harder to him, digging her fingers into his shoulders, struggling to remain upright.

Cupping his palms over the soft curves of her buttocks, he pressed her against him, and their mouths again came together, compelled by a hunger Lissa had never known before. Her body was ravaged by glorious sensations, and his kiss gave her the strength she needed to loosen her hold on him, to grope for the buttons of his shirt. This time the moan came from him, and he rapidly offered her the assistance she needed to remove his shirt. As Lissa plowed her fingers through the soft tendrils of hair coating his muscular chest Jared eased off his trousers. He pressed himself against her again, and the contact her satiny skin made with his unyielding flesh shocked her, sending a gust of fire through her. She gasped, trying to contain the conflagration that tore at her soul, then sagged against him, recognizing the futility of her attempt.

Running his hands along her spine, Jared slid his lips off hers and led her to the bed. He arranged her on her back, straddling her, smiling as her fingers drifted through the heart-shaped mat of hair on his chest, down to where it tapered to a point on his hard, flat stomach, then down to his bent knees, which sandwiched her slender hips. Her large eyes shone with fascination and delight as she sensed his skin's response to her delicate touch, and she slid her hands back up along his rock-hard thighs to his ribs to his broad, bony shoulders, where her gaze locked onto his. "Do I meet with your approval?" he asked, aware that she was blatantly assessing and admiring his beautifully sculpted body.

"Yes," she whispered, embarrassed yet unwilling to look away. "The first time I saw you—when you audited my lecture—I wondered whether you might be a model."

"A model?" He laughed.

"I mean for the life-drawing classes at the school. I thought you might be a student. A lot of students model, and I thought...I thought, if you modeled, I would want to spy on you."

His eyes folded into deep laugh lines as he chuckled. "You don't have to spy on me, Lissa. Here I am in all my glory. As for modeling, you have to sit still for that. And I have no intention of sitting still, at least not now."

To prove his point, he lowered his lips to her throat, then shifted his hips down toward her knees to give his mouth access to her breasts. As his teeth moved gently around first one swollen nipple and then the other she cried out, dazed by another fiery gust of longing. Instinctively her hands tensed at the back of his head, holding him to her, and her hips arched toward him. She couldn't rationalize the nearly violent response she had to him, the nearly hysterical yearning he aroused within her, and her desire to figure it out was rapidly dissolving, leaving in its place a deeper knowledge, an unquestioning acceptance of her impulses. "Jared," she called out with a groan, her hips writhing against him. "Jared, I want you...."

"Not yet," he whispered, sliding his lips lower, teasing her navel with his tongue. "Mmm. You taste as good as you feel."

"Jared!" Her need of him was growing desperate, and his head, gliding lower, had slipped out of her grasp. Her hands balled into fists and, as his mouth explored her inner thigh, she pounded them against the mattress, wrestling with the almost unbearable tension that had begun to build inside her. Her fear now was not that she would be unable to respond to him, or that their lovemaking would be overshadowed by her unpleasant memories, but that she would explode from the raging pressure within her.

He took his time, seemingly unconcerned about her anguished state, nibbling at her inflamed flesh and finding great enjoyment in her tortured moans and thrashing motions. At long last he slid back up and locked his lips to hers, and her fists unfurled as she dug her fingers into his taut buttocks, driving herself against him. Her wild eagerness ignited him, and with a groan he acceded to her unspoken demands, entering her and then withdrawing to catch his breath, struggling for his own precarious control. "And you feel as good as you taste," he whispered. "Are you ready?"

"Jared...." Her entire body answered yes. She was more than ready; she was almost insane with readiness.

"I want this to be as good for you as it is for me," he hesitated.

"It is, Jared, it is," she said, drawing him back into her.

He let her lead, he let her choose the path and set the pace, and as the poignant tension twisted through her, it no longer frightened her. Lissa recognized it now: It was hers, a part of her, a gift from Jared, a compass to direct them both higher and higher until it catapulted them, with convulsive fury, to another world, to their own exquisite universe, to the home they had discovered within each other's arms.

Shocked and trembling, she endured the gradual descent back to reality, the fall cushioned by Jared's embrace, by the constant warmth of his body as he covered her with his weight, refusing to release her until his breathing returned to normal and his muscles relaxed. He gazed at her, his eyes radiating a mysterious inner light as they wandered gratefully over her face. "Lissa," he whispered, brushing his hand against her cheek, as gently as he might handle a fragile bit of porcelain. "Have you been saving all that passion just for me?"

She was too stunned by the deluge of sensations and emotions that she had experienced to reply, but her heart knew the true answer: She had been saving all that passion not since her divorce but since her birth—saving it for someone like Jared. Saving it because she hadn't even guessed at its existence. And she might never have known of its existence if he hadn't entered her life, if he hadn't awakened it inside her.

With a contented sigh, he rolled off her and cuddled her tightly to himself, his fingers compulsively losing themselves in her hair. "If you had been here eighteen years ago," he remarked, "I wouldn't have left."

"If I had been here eighteen yeas ago," Lissa refuted him, her voice hoarse but steady, "I would have been a skinny ten-year-old with my hair in pigtails and a Band-Aid on my knee."

"Mmm." He pondered the image. "I would have watched you playing hopscotch, and I would have said, 'She's kind of young, but wow, what potential.'"

"I reckon you would have gotten a hunch about me, wouldn't you," she said, teasing him.

Jared gazed at her, grinning playfully. "If you were here eighteen years ago, you probably wouldn't still be saying things like 'reckon.' You'd be talking like a regular Ro-Diwander." He exaggerated the pronunciation of the state's native residents. He shifted onto his side so he could see her better and said, "Tell me about Orchard Creek."

"What about it?"

"Everything."

She smiled, twined her fingers through his and told him. She told him about the dusty roads and the lush evergreen forests and the clay embankments that glistened red after a summer rain. She told him about the small grammar school she attended, and the regional high school, where she was occasionally treated as something of a freak because she lived with her aunt, who was a pharmacist. Nearly all of her classmates' fathers worked in the coal mines, although an uncommon number of them didn't have fathers because of the hazardous conditions of the mines. Lissa reckoned it was a hard life, but it was the only one any of them knew, so they didn't think much about it. The mine was employment, and the United Mine Workers was the chief social outlet for Orchard Creek. Children simply accepted it. They had the verdant mountains and the pine-scented air and the wild marijuana that grew in everyone's backyard.

It was Lissa's life, but she had been glad to leave it, she revealed. She had always been a daydreamer, always curious about the world beyond her time-forgotten village.

"Weren't your aunt and grandmother disappointed when you left?" Jared asked.

She shook her head. "They wanted me to go; they rather goaded me into it. My grampa died of the black lung, Papa died in a mine explosion, and Aunt Ida's fiancé died in a cave-in, and they said that the only way I could avoid being a miner's widow was to get out of there."

"What did they say when you became a painter's ex-wife?"

She bit her lip. "They were happy when I married Curtis. It didn't matter what he was like, just so long as he wasn't a miner. They...they still haven't come to terms with the divorce. It's kind of a scandal to them. They think the only way a marriage can end is when you hear the wail of the siren at the mine." These were things she had never discussed with anyone before, but the words came easily in Jared's comforting presence. "They're fine people, Aunt Ida and Gramma, but they don't really understand what I've done. They say they love me, but I don't think they approve of me." She sighed, then offered Jared a crooked smile. "Enough of me. Now you tell me everything about you."

He told her. He told her about his own lonely childhood and his belief that he was somehow to blame for his mother's illness. Why else had he been banished from the room next to his parents'? Why else had his father neglected him?

Jared had fought hard to atone for his imagined crime, to regain his father's love. He had willingly obeyed all of his father's orders, complied with all his strange habits. He had spent his allotted ninety minutes with his father each day at the far end of the dining-room table, clad in a jacket and tie, speaking only when spoken to. He had done everything his father asked of him, but nothing worked.

And finally, he had come to the realization that his mother's death was not his fault, and he had revolted. His adolescence had been one long series of battles; the first time he could recall being truly happy was after he had fled to California and put himself through college by working nights in a warehouse in Oakland. "For the first time in my life," he reminisced, "I realized that I could earn money, that I could ignore the only weapon my father had over me. Once I knew I could make it on my own, I was free." His eyes wandered across the attentive, sympathetic face on the pillow beside him. "I've never talked about this to anyone before."

Lissa leaned toward him and kissed him, understanding exactly what he meant. She had never told anyone about the pain of her past until the previous night, when she had shared her anguish with Jared. She was gratified to know that she could unlock his demons and shoo them away, just as he had unlocked hers.

He returned her kiss, and the ardor in it expanded to enompass their entire bodies. Lissa would not have imagined that she had any passion left in her, yet Jared seemed to have tapped a fresh well, and her hunger for him overwhelmed her with as much intensity as it had before. But if the first time their lovemaking had been a discovery, full of fire and fury, this time it was a confirmation, a quiet, profound communion, a shared ecstasy that transcended understanding.

And later, after washing and returning to the bed, shutting off the light and molding their bodies into a comfortable position for sleep, Lissa did understand one thing: It was indeed possible—more than possible—that she had fallen in love with Jared Stone.

They spent Sunday together, Jared insisting that since on Saturday they had done what he wanted, on Sunday they would do what Lissa wanted. She decided she wanted to visit the zoo in Roger Williams Park, and after a leisurely brunch they strolled through the city's eclectic menagerie—the farm animals, the polar bears, the

Harlequin reaches into the hearts and minds of women across America to bring you

Harlequin American Romance.™

FOUR FREE BOOKS... AND FREE TOTE BAG!

Enter a uniquely American world of romance with

Harlequin
American Romance.™

Harlequin American Romance novels are the first romances to explore today's new love relationships. These compelling romance novels reach into the hearts and minds of women across America... probing into the most intimate moments of romance, love and desire.

You'll follow romantic heroines and irresistible men as they boldly face confusing choices. Career first, love later? Love without marriage? Long-distance relationships? All the experiences that make love real are captured in the tender, loving pages of *Harlequin American Romance* novels.

What makes American women so different when it comes to love? Find out with this special *Harlequin American Romance* offer!

Send for your four free introductory books and tote bag now.

Get these Four Books and Tote Bag

FREE!

MAIL TO:
Harlequin Reader Service
2504 West Southern Avenue
Tempe, Arizona 85282

YES! I want to be one of the first to discover

Harlequin American Romance. Send me FREE and without obligation my four free books and FREE tote bag. If you do not hear from me after I have examined my four FREE books please send me four new *Harlequin American Romance* novels each month as soon as they come off the presses. I understand that I will be billed only $2.25 per book (total $9.00). There are no shipping or handling charges. There is no minimum number of books that I have to purchase. In fact, I may cancel this arrangement at any time...and keep the four introductory books and tote bag FREE, without any obligation.

154 CIA NA3N

Name	(Please Print)	
Address		Apt. No.
City	State/Prov.	Zip/Postal Code

Signature (If under 18, parent or guardian must sign.)

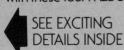

dromedaries—laughing as much over the squeals of the children as over the humorous antics of the animals. Then they journeyed to Providence's proud Italian neighborhood, with its red, white and green line dividing the lanes of the main thoroughfare and its fire hydrants painted to resemble gondoliers. They browsed among the delicatessens with their imported cheeses and salamis and exotic vegetables, and purchased a huge pizza at Lissa's favorite pizza parlor. They brought it back to her house, consumed about half of it, and then Lissa asked Jared to leave. She had work in the morning, she explained. She really needed a good night's sleep.

But staring at her wilting bowl of cornflakes Monday morning, Lissa admitted to herself that she hadn't slept at all. She had hoped that spending the night alone in her familiar brass bed would enable her to regain her perspective, but it hadn't. Never before had she felt so alone, so isolated, as she had last night. The bed had seemed much too big, too cold; the air lacked Jared's warm, musky scent. She had lain awake all night, wishing he was with her.

"Eight-thirty!" She gasped as her eyes drifted toward the wall clock. Bolting from her chair, she dumped the uneaten cereal down the sink and raced back to her bedroom to dress for work. After slipping on a brown wool suit with a pleated skirt, she hurried to the bathroom to pin up her hair. She braided it three times before satisfying herself that the plait wasn't lopsided, then coiled it into a tight knot and pinned it into place. Powdering her nose and touching her lips with a tinted gloss, she struggled to push Jared toward the back of her mind, to keep her attention on the projects awaiting her at work.

Not surprisingly, she arrived at the office ten minutes late.

"Good morning," Candy greeted her, glancing up from the stack of mail that had arrived over the weekend. "How was your big date?"

Before Lissa could reply, Paul pushed through the door, holding the coffee maker's decanter, which he had filled with water in the restroom they shared with the other office suites on their floor. "Well, hello, stranger!" he boomed as he crossed to the conference room. "Where have you been?"

"I'm not that late," Lissa said, following him into the conference room. While he turned on the coffee maker, she sat at the table and wrestled with a yawn.

"I'm not talking about this morning," Paul told her as he flopped into a chair facing her. "I'm talking about Saturday, when Peggy phoned you to hear about your dinner with Bonny Prince Jared."

"I was out," Lissa answered vaguely.

"Peggy surmised as much. So she phoned you again Sunday."

"I was out again."

Paul leaned forward. "Come on, kid, 'fess up. Did dinner turn into breakfast?"

Lissa's cheeks grew hot and she grimaced. "Please, Paul, I'm not in the mood for teasing."

He appraised her somberly. "Good Lord," he muttered. "Are you in love or something?"

Lissa gave him a pleading look. "We—we had a very nice time together," she stammered evasively. "I haven't worked it all out yet."

Her partner continued to study her until the coffee

was ready. He crossed to the counter and filled two cups, handing one to her. "Congratulations," he said, clicking his mug against hers before sipping. "It's about time, lady."

Lissa forced a smile. "Paul—"

"I'm serious," he insisted. "I just hope this guy is worthy of you. Actually, Peggy wasn't calling to check up on you. We had a little news of our own we wanted to share." Lissa glanced up from her coffee. "Somebody around here is running dire risk of becoming a godmother."

"What?"

"Month of May. Make a note of it."

"Peggy's pregnant? Paul, that's wonderful!" She leaped from her seat to give him a joyful hug. "It's about time," she said, mimicking him.

"Now who's teasing?" he said, laughing. "Peggy's driving me crazy. She spent at least ten hours yesterday staring at her stomach and asking me if she looked fat."

"Does she?"

"No, but she will if she eats all the ice cream she made me buy her."

They chatted excitedly about Paul's news for a while before turning their attention to work. Paul told Lissa he had heard that one of the city's hospitals was planning to renovate its pediatrics wing, and they tossed around some ideas for a proposal they could submit. "Everyone's going to suggest primary colors and alphabet blocks," Paul predicted. "I say we take a different approach. I was thinking, how about glass? Give the poor kids a feel for the outdoors while they're stuck in the hospital."

"Lots of plants, too," Lissa concurred. "Let's be outrageous—let's try something greenhouse-y."

Paul nodded, doodling on a pad.

"When are they going to start accepting proposals?"

"November sometime. Do you want to play with it?"

Lissa shook her head. "It's all yours. I've got my hands full with Max's Restaurant this morning. I'm meeting the contractor there and we're going to talk money."

"Good luck," Paul encouraged her as he drained his cup.

Before leaving for the restaurant, Lissa made a quick telephone call to Peggy to congratulate her on her pregnancy. Peggy seemed more interested in hearing about Lissa's date, but Lissa begged off, claiming that she was on her way to an appointment. In truth, she simply didn't feel ready to discuss her feelings about Jared, not yet. Being in love seemed too dangerous, too precious, too new to put into words, even with her closest friends.

The contractor arrived at the restaurant site at the same time Lissa did, and together they presented their bid to Max Michaels. Huddling in his office for two hours, they negotiated over items and fees, finally extracting from him his approval and signature. Lissa and the contractor had lunch together to celebrate, and feeling victorious and ebullient, she returned to her office by one. Swinging through the door to the reception area, she twirled Candy's revolving chair and whooped, "We got Max's!"

"Good for us," Cindy said with a smile. "Somebody came by to see you: Jared Stone."

"He came here?" Lissa asked, catching her breath.

"Since you were out, he decided to talk to Paul instead. He's in there with him now. They said you should join them as soon as you arrived."

Lissa reflexively touched her hair and straightened her jacket. "How do I look?" she whispered.

Candy smirked. "He said he was here on business," she pointed out. Noticing Lissa's anxious expression, she added, "You look fine."

Pursing her lips and squaring her shoulders, Lissa dropped her portfolio and pocketbook in her office, then crossed the reception area to Paul's door. She tapped gently. "Come in," Paul called to her.

As she pushed the door open, the two men rose. For some reason, she wasn't prepared to find them so amiable and relaxed. Jared had been seated on Paul's sofa, dressed in jeans, a clean white shirt, and a herringbone-patterned blazer, and Paul, whose loafers were off and tie loosened, had to swing his feet off the coffee table in order to stand. They had apparently been laughing at something, and Jared's smile widened with surprise as he saw Lissa in her proper business attire with her hair pinned up. Two long strides carried him to her side as she shut the door behind her, and he extended his arm around her shoulders and kissed her cheek.

Abashed, Lissa shied from him and glanced at Paul, who grinned impishly and arched his eyebrows. "How'd it go at Max's?" he asked.

"Fine," Lissa said, still flustered as Jared led her to a seat beside him on the couch.

Paul lowered himself into his chair and propped his feet back on the table. "Just 'fine'?"

"We got the contract," she reported before turning to Jared. "What are you doing here?"

"What do you think? I have a house you promised to salvage—or have you forgotten?"

"It's just—people generally phone first," Lissa floundered, eyeing Paul, who seemed vastly amused.

"Well, I was downtown to see Bill Driscoll, so I figured I'd stop by. I've been describing the house to Paul, and he says he's interested."

"To work on a house like that? You bet," Paul confirmed. "I told him that given the age of the building, we ought to have George Calloway give it the once-over first, check the wiring and structural integrity and so on. We're set for tomorrow afternoon."

"You got George Calloway on such short notice?" Lissa asked.

"When he heard which house it was, he rearranged his schedule."

"I hope he'll do a complete inspection," Jared remarked. "Will he check the plumbing? The water sometimes comes out brown."

"Sediment in the pipes," Paul explained. "If the plumbing hasn't been used regularly it accumulates. Given that just your father and his housekeeper were living there, they probably didn't use some of the sinks. I'm sure that's all it is." To Lissa, Paul mentioned, "I'm going along for the inspection because I want to see this house. But Jared is dead set on having you do the creative stuff."

"We're a team," Lissa sternly informed Jared. "We work on things together. I bounce everything off Paul first."

"Mmm." Jared intoned, grinning slyly. "The mere thought of that drives me wild with jealousy." Paul burst out laughing.

"Honestly!" Lissa said, groaning, eager to change the subject. "What were you all cackling about before I came in?"

"Brown University's homecoming game," Paul replied.

"My father used to take me every year." Jared shook his head and smiled. "He even made me wear a brown sweater and a brown-and-white scarf."

"Your father would have liked my wife," said Paul. "Not only did she go to Brown, but so did her older brother and his wife. They're coming down from Boston for the weekend, and her old roommate and her boyfriend are coming up from New York City, so we're going to have a full house." He studied Jared and Lissa for a moment. "Why don't you guys join us? After the game we're all heading back home for a big dinner party."

"Sounds wonderful," Jared said before Lissa could speak.

She scowled at him, puzzled that such an event would appeal to him. "You'd want to go to a football game?"

"Why not?"

She turned to Paul. "Is Peggy up to entertaining a crowd?"

Paul rolled his eyes. "You and she both act as if she's an invalid. I'll tell her to pick up two extra tickets and we can meet at the stadium before kick-off or something—Lissa and I can work out the details. Meanwhile, we're all set for tomorrow at three, right?"

Jared stood up and shook Paul's hand. "I'll leave the gate open for you. Good meeting you, Paul."

Lissa rose, too, and accompanied Jared to the door.

She cast a parting glance at Paul, who smiled and poked his thumb upward. Lissa tried to look annoyed, but she was too pleased that Jared and Paul had hit it off to mind his gentle kidding. She left the office with Jared, and he nodded pleasantly at Candy as he followed Lissa into her own office and closed the door. Before she could take another step he swept her into a snug embrace, stinging her cheeks with kisses. "I missed you last night," he whispered.

Lissa knew her office was not an appropriate place for the erotic feelings Jared's lips kindled in her, but she was unable to resist the thrilling strength of his arms. "I missed you, too," she confessed. His mouth sought hers and lingered in a long, devouring kiss. It took all of Lissa's willpower to extricate herself from it. "Really, Jared," she scolded breathlessly. "Haven't you any sense of decorum?"

"None whatsoever," he said, easing her away from him and examining her. "Look at you. Right out of the pages of *Dress for Success*."

"I have to dress like this if I want my clients to take me seriously."

"Anyone who doesn't take you seriously is an idiot," Jared declared. "What are you doing for dinner tonight?"

"I was going to heat up the leftover pizza—"

"How about after dinner?"

She smiled and shook her head. "I have to do some preparation for my Thursday night lecture. I usually do that over the weekend, but—"

"Perfect," he said, sidling to the door. "I'll be at your place around five-thirty."

"Jared, I mean it. I have to work tonight."

"No problem," he said, swinging the door open. "Five-thirty." Before she could stop him, he was gone.

Sure enough, he was waiting on the front porch of Lissa's building when she drove home. She honked and waved, then maneuvered the driveway to the lot behind the house and squeezed into the narrow space beside Jared's oversized car. Strolling back to the front of the house, she noticed that Jared had with him a zippered garment bag, his leather briefcase and a paper sack. He approached her on the sidewalk and accompanied her inside. Nodding at the garment bag, she asked, "What's that?"

"That," he said, grinning, "is what I need for tomorrow morning. If you want to kick me out after dinner, I'll go. I'll put up a huge protest, but I'll go. However, being an optimist, I came prepared."

Lissa chuckled. "What do you need for tomorrow morning?"

"My Santa Claus suit," Jared explained as Lissa unlocked the door to her apartment. "I've got to pose for pictures."

"Christmas pictures?"

They stepped into the apartment, and Lissa shut the door while Jared set down his bags. "I'm giving money away tomorrow," he explained. "Brown University, Trinity Square Repertory Company, Women's and Children's Hospital... and they all want a photo of me handing over a check and shaking someone's hand. Can I hang this over a door or something?"

Lissa took the garment bag with her as she moved down the hall to her bedroom. "I'd like to shower and change my clothes. Then we'll eat. All right?"

"Take your time," said Jared, slipping out of his

blazer and rolling up his sleeves. "I'll keep myself occupied."

Lissa hung Jared's suit and her own clothing in her closet, pulled on a robe, and crossed to the bathroom, where she took a quick shower and washed her hair. By the time she had brushed her damp tresses smooth, she could smell the pungent aroma of pizza warming in the oven. Hastening back to her bedroom, she dressed in a pair of jeans and a pale blue velour sweater. She arrived in the kitchen just as Jared was pulling the pizza from the oven. "Smells delicious," she said, grinning.

"So do you." Jared kissed her forehead en route to the dining-room table, where Lissa discovered an uncorked bottle of Chianti.

"Jared!" she chided as she took a seat across the table from him and watched him fill two goblets with wine. "I really do have to work after dinner."

"So do I." He shrugged. "Don't tell me a bourbon guzzler like you can't handle a single glass of wine." He placed a gooey slice of pizza on a plate for her, then took one for himself and bit hungrily into it.

Lissa chewed on her slice, deep in thought. "Do you really want to go to a Brown football game?" she asked after swallowing.

"Of course I do."

"Why?"

"Why?" He leaned back and smiled, his eyes closing. "A college football game in the autumn, the leaves ablaze with color, a nip in the air, a pretty girl by my side...how could I pass it up?"

"But...you said your father—"

"Homecoming," Jared stated with quiet affirmation. "I like the sound of it." He gazed steadily at Lissa. "I

should have asked if you wanted to go before I accepted Paul's invitation. I'm sorry. If you don't want to
go, we'll skip it."

"No, I want to," Lissa assured him, then frowned.
"But you're right. You should have asked me first. I
believe you enjoy trying to guess what's on my mind."

"I don't guess," he said earnestly. "I *know* what's on
your mind."

Lissa snorted. "Oh, do you now? Or are you just re-
lying on your hunches?"

Jared mused. "Maybe they're hunches. It doesn't
matter. I'm never wrong."

Lissa grimaced. "Nina was right. You are an arrogant
son of a gun."

"She said that?" He hooted loudly. "I guess I am."

After they finished eating and cleaned up their
dishes, Lissa informed Jared that she would be working
in her study. "You can listen to music if you want,"
she offered, pointing to her portable radio on the
kitchen counter. "Or if you'd rather, I have a television
in the bedroom."

"There are plenty of things I'd like to do in your
bedroom," Jared noted with a grin, "but watching TV
isn't one of them. Don't worry about me—I've come
prepared." He refilled his glass with wine, scooped up
his briefcase, and moved to one of the cane rocking
chairs. Lissa watched him switch on the lamp, remove
from the briefcase his reading glasses and a thick sheaf
of papers, and sip his wine. "Go ahead," he prodded
her. "Get your work done."

She lingered for a moment, allowing herself to ad-
mire how handsome he looked as he bowed his head
over a document and toyed with a fountain pen. Finally

she forced herself down the hall to her study, settled herself at her desk, and flipped open her folder of lecture notes.

Her fear that she would not be able to concentrate with Jared in her apartment proved unfounded. The knowledge that he was nearby relaxed her, energized her, enabled her to focus on her task. For several hours she reviewed her class notes from her own student days, revising and amending them, adding pertinent information from recent publications and from her own experience. She managed to accomplish more in a couple of hours than she usually completed after a long Saturday afternoon of labor, and at nine-thirty she slammed her folder shut, stretched and wandered back to the living room.

Jared glanced up and closed his pen. "Done so soon?" he asked, a smile forming on his face.

"What all are you working on?"

"Colorado business," he said as he slid his papers back into his briefcase. "My secretary mailed me a package of stuff this morning. Nothing urgent." He removed his glasses and stood up, welcoming Lissa into his arms. "Nothing as urgent as this," he purred, letting his lips meander across her brow. "Are you going to kick me out?"

Lissa answered by lifting her mouth to his. Jared groaned as his tongue found hers, and she felt his entire body harden with eagerness. Lissa thrilled to think that he responded as rapidly to her as she did to him. Her muscles ached in anticipation, throbbed with the longing she had refused to satisfy the previous night. As Jared's hands slid along the soft velvet fabric of her shirt, his kisses grew greedier, and when his fingers kneaded her breasts, her nipples tightened into nearly painful beads of desire. She heard herself sing out his name, and he gathered her up in his arms, swooping her off the floor and carrying her down the hall to her bedroom. "Don't ever kick me out," he whispered into her neck, his breath hot and enticing.

He deposited her across her sunburst quilt. His strong hands tugged at her clothing and removed it, then removed his own. Lissa gazed at his rugged body, its familiarity only making her want him more. "Lissa," he said with a moan as his tongue brushed against her breast's blushing tip. "Can you guess how much I missed you last night?"

"Yes," she said, panting, her flesh seething as a great, moist hunger swelled within her. "I have some idea."

"*Some* idea?" he asked with a laugh, raising his face, leaning back into her hands as she spun her fingers into the dense black waves of hair on his head. "Woman, your whole body is buzzing with ideas. How in the world did I let you talk us into sleeping alone last night?"

She abandoned his hair, delicately tracing his thick shoulder blades, the unrelenting muscles of his back down to his hips, feeling him tense beneath her touch. "Maybe you knew I was right."

He caught his breath, trying to resist the frenzy her fingers stirred in him. "I knew you were wrong," he insisted. "But I figured you'd learn from your mistake. I figured it would make you want me even more." Relishing the gentle friction of her fingers as she drew light patterns against the small of his back, he moaned, then abruptly reached behind himself to pull her hands away.

"Did that bother you?" Lissa asked, surprised by his action.

His mouth grazed her fingers, her wrist, her arm. "It drove me wild," he whispered huskily. "Don't make me lose control, Lissa. I want you to be ready for me."

"I'm ready now."

"Let me make you readier." His lips reached her shoulder, then browsed the length of her body, tasting her collarbone, her ribs, her abdomen, her knees, her insteps and toes. Lissa felt herself incinerating in the heat of his tongue. She groped for him, crying out in exasperation as he coaxed her to an even fuller need, stubbornly refusing to give in to her demands. Finally conceding that she could stand no more torment, he rolled onto his back and drew her onto him, thrusting deep into her with a passion as fevered as her own. His hoarse groans mingled with her ecstatic sobs as their bodies careened wildly to the brink of release. Lissa's body erupted, then Jared's, and she clung to him, gasping from the furious heat of their union, gasping from the devastating glory of sensation that enveloped them both.

They continued to hold each other until the last tremors of love ebbed away, and then Jared eased onto his side, cradling Lissa against himself, his eyes dancing over her with their magical, mysterious glow. "It's... it's different every time," she whispered, astonished by the immeasurable power of what she had just experienced.

"It's better every time." Jared's smile faded as his eyes narrowed. "Why are you crying?"

Lissa hadn't been aware that she was. She touched her cheek, and her fingers felt the dampness filtering through her long lashes. Embarrassed, she tried to twist from him, but he held her firmly. She pawed through her muddled thoughts, trying to make sense of her tears. "It's just—I never knew...I never knew it could be this way...."

He immediately understood what she was struggling to say. Hugging her to him, he cooed softly into her hair. "Forget him," he hushed her. "Forget him. He's gone. He was just a bad piece of history. Now that you know, Lissa, you'll never have to settle for anything less. It will never be less than wonderful for you, Lissa, I promise. Okay?"

Lissa cuddled against him, discovering within his embrace a profound peace, the shimmering tranquillity she had felt the first time he kissed her. Her sadness and confusion evanesced like a mountain mist beneath the strong, steady warmth of the sun. Love would always be wonderful now. Jared had promised.

Promised. She inched away from him, her now-dry eyes searching his face for clarification. "Jared? What do you mean, you promise?"

He contemplated her before answering. "What do you think I mean?"

"I think...." She swallowed. "I think I'm afraid to guess."

He considered her words, then sighed. "Let's wash and get some sleep." He released Lissa and sat up, swinging his feet to the floor.

Lissa stared at him, perplexed. "Why is it, Jared Stone, that I sometimes feel like you're three steps ahead of me?"

He winked and sauntered out to the bathroom. "Probably because I am," his voice trailed back to her.

She pounded her fist against the mattress, then laughed in bewilderment. What had he promised? First he had promised honesty; now he was promising something more. She could guess, if she let herself. She could guess, but if her guess was wrong.... At least she had been honest with him. She was honestly afraid to guess. Better to let him remain three steps ahead of her for now; it was all too possible that if she tried to outrun him, she would wind up running in the wrong direction.

JARED STARED AT HIS FACE in the mirror above her sink. His thick, dark hair was disheveled, a messy souvenir of Lissa's hands. He decided not to straighten it out.

She was so close, he thought, so close... but he was rushing her. He had to stop making assumptions, had to stop believing that she was completely in step with him. Had she really been angry that he had accepted Paul Morris's invitation to the homecoming celebration without consulting her first?

No, of course not. But he had to stop assuming. She had lived a very different life from his. The misery she had suffered was caused by a man. Jared couldn't expect her to hurl herself into a commitment to him. He wanted to explain to her, wanted to tell her that it was a fact, the two of them together, an irrefutable fact, and that she might as well not resist it. But he couldn't. Better for her to discover the truth for herself.

At least she was close. He knew it in the way she reacted to his touch, in the way her body opened to him. Making love to her was far more satisfying than he ever would have imagined. Making love to her was like conquering undiscovered worlds. If he let himself, he could strut about his prowess, but that wasn't what caused her to respond so sensationally to him. It was, he suspected, simply that she had never been loved before, not truly loved. He was the first man who had ever really treated her like a woman.

He thought of her lying on her bed, on that marvelous quilt of hers, waiting for him. He thought of her beautiful body, her soft, tawny skin, the graceful swells of her breasts and hips and her fine, spun-silk hair splayed out across the pillow. He wanted to race back to her, to love her yet again. But he lingered for a moment at the sink, washing his face, then drying it on a handy towel. To love a woman like Lissa was an immense responsibility. He was more than willing to accept the responsibility, but to accept it meant tying up loose ends. He would do that soon, he resolved. As soon as he knew Lissa was ready for him.

Chapter Seven

Lissa was roused by the sensation that she was losing something. She opened her eyes to discover Jared sitting up, pulling away from her. "What time is it?" she mumbled, blinking in the dark.

He kissed her lightly on her forehead. "Ssh. Go back to sleep."

Too groggy to argue, Lissa released him and sank back into the pillow. She watched him stroll naked from the room, and after a minute she heard the rush of water running in the shower. The gentle sound of the water lulled her back to sleep.

The next time she opened her eyes, it was to find Jared clean-shaven and dressed in the trousers and vest of a gray flannel suit, a tie knotted loosely around his neck and his hands balancing a plate of toast and two mugs of coffee. "Good morning, Sleeping Beauty," he said with a smile as he set the breakfast down on her night table and clicked on the lamp.

"Sleeping Beauty is supposed to be awakened by a kiss from the prince," Lissa pointed out.

"Is that so?" he said, laughing, sitting beside her and fulfilling his princely obligation.

Lissa hoisted herself into a sitting position and accepted a slice of toast. "You seem to have made yourself rather familiar with my kitchen," she noted.

"If I can find my way around my kitchen, yours isn't much of a challenge," he explained as he sipped his coffee.

Lissa fingered the material of his vest. "Dress for success," she teased. "Did you develop a sense of decorum overnight?"

"I'm not a total boob," Jared defended himself. "If I showed up at the Brown Development Office in my old dungarees, they'd probably suspect the check was rubber. I should be done making my charitable rounds by noon," he added. "Any chance I can lure you to the house before the others show up?"

"Sorry." Lissa shook her head. "In fact, I may not be done by three—I've got to attend to ordering the carpet and paint and furnishings for a restaurant I'm working on. I figured I'd join Paul and George Calloway at your place when I was done."

"You mean my house is taking a back seat to some restaurant?" He pretended indignation.

"I've got a signed contract from Max's," said Lissa. "What have I got from you?"

"Should I start at the top and work my way down?" Jared leered. He nibbled his toast. "Paul and I did discuss fees—not including cost of materials and furnishings. You two must think you're pretty talented; Cavender & Morris doesn't come cheap."

Lissa's eyebrows inched up. "Did you expect a personal discount?"

"No." He gazed at her. "Your fees do seem to be in line, and I checked your firm out. You've got a topnotch reputation."

"Checked it out?"

"The same day I checked out your marital status. I made some inquiries. Just another hunch I was playing," he explained. He reached for his coffee and sipped it, thinking about and studying Lissa. "Can I ask you something that may not be any of my business?" he ventured.

Lissa smiled at his uncharacteristic tact. "Be my guest," she welcomed the question.

"It's just—given your company's sound bearings—I guess I expected you'd be living in the lap of luxury. Your apartment is nice, Lissa, but it isn't exactly extravagant. Are you saving up for a rainy day?"

Lissa directed her gaze to the strong black coffee in her mug. "I only recently paid off a lot of debts," she muttered. "Curtis left a trail of creditors behind him when he vanished."

"That's right." Jared nodded in recollection of their first telephone conversation. "You thought I was one of them. Did he get you to cosign his loans?"

"He had accounts here and there," Lissa admitted. "Art supplies are expensive—and so are clothes and telephones and everything else. I wasn't legally responsible for all of his debts, but I felt a moral responsibility. It wasn't fair to his creditors to leave them holding the bag."

"It wasn't fair of him to leave you holding the bag, either," Jared observed.

"Yes, well...I reckon it's the price of stupidity."

Jared plucked her mug from her hands and forced her face to his. "Don't say that about yourself."

"Why not?" She exhaled. "I was stupid. You'd have to be pretty stupid to go and marry someone who was busy seducing his models while you were out trying to earn the money to cover the cost of his art supplies. I believe that's the dictionary definition of stupidity, Jared." Her lips curled in a self-deprecating sneer.

Jared weighed her words, then gathered her hand in his. "You made a mistake," he granted. "But it's all over now. You've served your sentence. Don't eat yourself up over it. All people make mistakes sometimes; it doesn't mean they're stupid." His frown softened into a smile. "If you're so stupid, what are you doing here with me?"

"Heaven only knows," Lissa said, sighing.

Jared tousled her hair and stood up. "I don't know about you, lady, but I've got people to meet."

Lissa glanced at her alarm clock and sprang out of bed. Jared considerately kept out of her way as she scurried back and forth between her closet and the bathroom. She grinned when she found his razor and after-shave lotion and comb and brush lined up along her bathroom counter. He certainly had made himself at home, she mused as she pinned up her hair.

They left the house together, strolling to the parking lot to fetch their cars. "Three o'clock or soon thereafter," he murmured as he kissed her good-bye. "I have a feeling I'm going to like this project."

"Time will tell." She laughed ominously. "Have a good time playing Santa Claus."

"Ho ho ho," he said as he slid into his car.

Lissa spent the morning and much of the afternoon engrossed in her work on the restaurant and trying to obtain a blueprint of the hospital that had announced its intention to renovate its pediatrics wing. As Lissa had predicted, she was still embroiled with details when Paul departed to pick up George Calloway and head to

Jared's house, but by three-thirty she had completed her chores and left the office to join Paul. As promised, the wrought-iron gates at the mouth of the driveway were open, and she coasted down the long blacktop skirting the front yard to the garage. Jared answered her ring and greeted her with an ardent embrace. "Jared," she said with a hiss as she wrestled from his grasp. "Please! Where's George?"

"He and Paul are rummaging around in the cellar," he reassured her with a laugh. "Your reputation is still intact."

"No thanks to you," she scolded, following him down the hall to the cellar door.

Before they reached the door, Paul and George emerged, chattering enthusiastically. George was a wizened middle-aged man with whom Paul and Lissa frequently worked, and he clutched a clipboard and pen. "Nice game room," he declared, then nodded at Lissa. "Hi, Cavender."

"Game room?" she asked Jared.

"It's great," Paul concurred. "Big billiards table, built-in bar, fieldstone walls—"

"The foundation looks real good, Mr. Stone," George said as he checked the clipboard. "Three-zone heat—was the heating system recently updated?"

"A few years ago," Jared told him. "I haven't got the date on it. I think my father had the attic insulated around the same time."

"Got to, with a place this size," George said, nodding. "Circuit breakers are also obviously a recent addition. Am I seeing double, or do you really have two stoves in the kitchen?"

Jared let out a hearty laugh. "You're not seeing double, Mr. Calloway. Come, I'd like you to have a look at the ballroom."

"Ballroom?" Paul mouthed silently to Lissa, who grinned and ushered him down the hall. Sure enough, he and George were as astonished by the room as Lissa had been the first time she had seen it. With the bright afternoon light spilling through its many windows, it seemed even larger to her, but less overwhelming than before. While George and Paul lost themselves in its massiveness, Lissa wandered to the French doors and admired the expansive backyard, which offered distant glimpses of the Seekonk River. Paul sidled up beside her, and she smiled at him. "What do you think about this room?"

"I'm in shock," he admitted. "What do you think?"

Lissa's mind replayed their conversation about the hospital wing. "Glass," she murmured. Before she could elaborate, a telephone rang in another room and Jared vanished to answer it. Lissa turned back to Paul. "Lots of glass—kind of a solarium. We could extend the balcony, open up the wall to the second floor, and take advantage of the solar heat."

Paul mulled the concept over. "Southeast exposure isn't optimal, but it's an idea. I like it. A room like this, you've got to do something spectacular. What does Jared think?"

"I'll find out," Lissa said, jogging out of the room.

She followed the sound of Jared's voice to the kitchen, where he was leaning against the counter, the phone tucked beneath his chin as he searched for a pencil. Spotting Lissa, he waved her in as he continued his conversation with his caller. "Oh, it's not so terrible," he was saying. "You just can't survive without me, can you...."

Lissa indicated that she wanted to leave and give him some privacy, but he reached for her hand and pulled her toward him. Tenderly stroking her hair, he spoke into the phone. "I should drop everything and come running, huh," he said, chuckling. "I know...I know... you need me. Well, I can't come before Sunday. Can you wait that long?" He listened. "All right, I'll see what I can arrange. If I fly out of Boston I can probably be in Denver Sunday evening.... No, no need: I'll rent a car and drive myself down. It's silly for you to pick me up when I don't even know what flight I'll be on.... Yes, I'll call you as soon as I get into town. Sunday night—I'll see you then." He hung up and grimaced.

"What is it?"

"A hassle at the plant," he said with a sigh. "A machine is down; someone thinks it's sabotage."

"Sabotage?"

Jared shrugged. "A disgruntled employee. These things happen."

"If it's that important, maybe you should go right away."

"And miss the homecoming game? Not a chance." He thought for a moment, then said, "I'd ask you to come with me, but I want you here working on the house. Do you mind?"

"Do I mind?" Lissa smiled at him, amazed that he would even consider bringing her along. "Of course not."

"Good. *I* mind, but I'll be back as soon as I can. A week at the most. When I get back you can surprise me with all the wonderful transformations you'll have made here."

"Oh, I wouldn't do anything without asking you first."

"Don't be silly," Jared chided her. "I'm putting you in charge. I trust you."

"But Jared—"

He touched his finger to her lips to silence her. "I want you to make this place yours. Free rein, blank check. Surprise me, okay?"

Lissa shook her head, thrilled and frightened by the power he was granting her. "In one week—you'd better not expect miracles."

"I always expect miracles," he said. "And I'm rarely disappointed."

Footsteps and voices alerted them to the approach of George and Paul. "What does he think?" Paul asked Lissa.

Lissa scowled. "He wants to be surprised."

Paul looked dubiously at Jared, who confirmed Lissa's statement. "That's right. I want to be surprised."

Paul guffawed in disbelief. "Either you're crazy or you're insane."

"A little of both," Jared admitted with a laugh as he led them to the stairway to explore the second floor.

"WHY DID HE GIVE ME such responsibility?" Lissa groaned the following morning as she and Paul hunched over her workbench, sketching various possibilities for altering the ballroom. They both favored a design that involved reconstructing the roof as a plane of glass, two stories high above the balcony, sloping down to one story high by the outer wall, which would in turn be rebuilt almost entirely of glass. ''I hate the idea of tearing apart his house without his knowing about it.''

"He's going to know about it as soon as you start dismantling the roof," Paul remarked.

"Not if we do it while he's gone. He'll come back and find a gaping hole where his ballroom used to be. Do you suppose we ought to wait until the spring, when it's warmer?"

"Not necessary," Paul argued. "The guy gave you *carte blanche* because he wants you to do it."

"It seems awfully risky to me," she demurred.

"It's his risk," Paul said. "Look, Lissa, he's practically dared you. He wants his house remade, and he's dared you to remake it. So do it. What have you got to lose?"

Lissa turned her glistening eyes to her friend. "Him," she replied, suddenly aware of exactly what she was risking. "If he hates it, he'll hate me."

Paul leaned back against the workbench's stool and took Lissa's hand reassuringly in his. "I've only just met him—I hardly know him—but I think you're underestimating him. If you're right—if he's the sort of guy who throws down the gauntlet, and you pick it up, and then he turns around and says, 'I hate you'—then good riddance to him."

Lissa shuddered. It was easy for Paul to speak that way; he wasn't in love with Jared. He couldn't begin to understand how crushed Lissa would be by such a scenario. She herself could barely understand how she had become so enamored of Jared, so dependent on him, in so short a time. If he rejected her design, it would be a rejection of her. And if he rejected her, she would feel no less demolished than the ballroom's ceiling.

"Listen to me." Paul spoke quietly and solemnly. "He's the one who's taking the big chance. Not you—him. Think about it. You should be flattered out of your skull that he's willing to take such a chance on you."

"I am," Lissa confessed tremulously. "But I'm also scared."

"Taking a chance is scary," Paul agreed. "And I know you don't like to take chances, especially after what happened with Curtis. But Jared Stone is taking at least as big a chance with you, kid. You don't want to let him down, do you? If you let him down, maybe he'd feel as bad as you felt when Curtis let you down."

"We're talking about Jared's *house*," Lissa reminded Paul.

"Are we?" Paul asked pointedly.

Swallowing, Lissa forced her eyes back to the drawings on her bench. "I just...I just wish I knew he was ready for something like this," she murmured. "I want him to think it's good...." A pallor rinsed her cheeks as she heard herself echo Jared's words about making love to her: "I want it to be good.... I want you to be ready...." Had he been as anxious to satisfy Lissa as she was to satisfy him? Could it be that he was as eager to make her happy, as worried about fulfilling her expectations? Of course he had been confident about the beauty of sexual pleasure...yet certainly Lissa was as confident about her professional abilities. She had never paled before a challenge like this, she had always welcomed the jobs with the greatest risks. And for Jared, his house was as haunted as Lissa's own body had been; his house was as troubled and tortured by memories as was Lissa's spirit. Jared had had the courage to conquer Lissa's past. The very least she could do was try. "All right," she resolved in as firm a voice as she could muster. "Let's do it. Let's break down the walls."

After taking care of her obligations to Max's Restaurant, which required little attention now that the contractor had begun construction work and the furnishings had been ordered, Lissa spent the remainder of the day planning work on Jared's house. Most of the renovations would be cosmetic: painting or papering the walls; sanding and polishing the floors; having the rugs and nicer furniture cleaned, replacing other pieces room by room; removing the heavy enamel paint from the fireplaces and balustrade. For the ballroom's reconstruction, she set up an appointment with a glazier to analyze the feasibility of her design. Then she worked with Candy on amending her standard private-house contract to reflect Jared's specifications. "He really wants hands off?" Candy asked incredulously.

"Put in a clause that says he'll be required to approve expenditures. He said he's giving us a blank check," Lissa explained, "but I don't want him suing us for overcharges after I've run through his bank account."

"He wouldn't sue you, would he?" Candy said, smiling impishly. "He's too sweet to sue anyone."

"Sweet?"

"When he was in here on Monday," Candy reported, "he asked where you were, and when I said you were out, he pouted. I think that's sweet."

Lissa colored and shook her head. "Don't let him fool you," she said as much to herself as to Candy.

"Behind that pout is a Stone. A wheeler-dealer by birth."

"I'll put the clause in," her secretary promised.

At Jared's insistence, Lissa returned to her apartment after work only to change her clothes, then drove on to his house for dinner. As she approached the welcoming gates, she tried to pretend the house truly was her own. If it were, she would love the spectacular solarium she was planning for it. The freedom Jared had given her was indeed awesome, but once Lissa had made up her mind to accept it, once she had decided to rise to the challenge, she no longer felt overwhelmed. Paul was right; the risk was Jared's. Obviously he believed she could do for him what he had done for her. The trust he had placed in her made her feel heady and brave.

He greeted her at the doorway with a quick kiss before hurrying back to the kitchen. "I've got something burning in the oven," he explained as she followed him down the hall.

"Stuffed clams!" she squealed as he placed a steaming platter on the table in the kitchen. "I'm duly impressed."

"Quahogs, my dear," he corrected her. "Clams in forty-nine states, but quahogs in Rhode Island. Don't you Appalachian mountaineers know anything?"

"One thing I don't know is how to stuff them, whatever they're called. When did you become a culinary artist?"

"At a very early age," he told her as he poured her a glass of Chablis. "For most of my childhood I was closer to our cook than to my father. I'd do anything just to be able to keep her company—peel potatoes, grate cheese, knead bread. I picked up a few things here and there.''

He set the table with dishes, silverware and, from the refrigerator, a large tossed salad, then gestured to one of the two chairs, taking a seat across from her. He lifted his glass in a toast to Lissa, spread his napkin across his lap, and nudged the salad bowl toward her. "I hope you don't mind eating in the servant's quarters," he apologized. "The dining room still gives me the willies.''

"It won't when I'm done with it,'' Lissa swore.

Jared touched his finger to his mouth to silence her. "Surprise me.''

"Okay,'' she said, laughing. "But understand, Jared, when you come back next week, you're going to find a big mess. Nothing more.''

"If it's your mess, I don't care. Remind me to give you the keys so you can get in here while I'm gone.''

"You'll also have to sign a contract,'' Lissa informed him. "Candy should have it typed up by tomorrow.''

"No problem. Why don't I stop by tomorrow afternoon, look it over, and then take you out to dinner?''

"Only if you take me someplace where they serve food as good as this,'' Lissa said after tasting the savory clam stuffing. "But afterward I have to teach.''

"Can I sit in on your class?'' he asked.

"If you won't be bored by it.''

"Bored?'' Jared's eyes closed as he laughed. "I'll be listening for hints about what you're going to do to the house.''

"I thought you wanted to be surprised!''

"I do,'' he insisted. "I do. But a few hints wouldn't hurt.''

"Do you want a hint?" Lissa grinned slyly. "I'll give you a hint. What I'm planning is bold."

"Bold." He sipped his wine, his dark eyes glowing. "I'm going to love it."

When they were through eating, they cleared the dishes together, and then Jared asked Lissa whether she had brought along clothing for tomorrow. "No," she replied. "Was I supposed to?"

"Of course." He frowned. "Well, we'll drive over to your place to pick up some stuff and then come back."

"Jared," Lissa wailed, flinging her dish towel onto the counter. "Why do you always *tell* me what I'm going to do? Why won't you *ask* me?"

He absorbed her words, considered them, and offered a sheepish smile. "Why should I ask when the answer is written all over your face?" He sighed deeply, then dropped to his knees on the scuffed linoleum floor. "Miss Cavender, would you honor me with your presence in my bed tonight?"

Lissa laughed. She reached down and took his hand in order to help him to his feet. Instead, he pulled her onto the floor, his arms snaking around her as his tongue thrust into her mouth. Lowering himself onto his back, he eased her on top of him, his hips arching up against hers, his fingers sending warm pulses across her skin as he slid them up beneath her sweater. "Jared," she whispered, her body moving with his in a shared rhythm. "The floor is so hard."

"And you're so soft," he said, groaning.

"You can't be comfortable—"

"With you in my arms, I'm comfortable."

"We could go upstairs—"

"People in bold houses should do bold things," he murmured, losing his lips in her hair.

He's daring me, Lissa thought, drawing herself up, her knees straddling his waist. He was challenging her, and she accepted the challenge. When he reached for her shoulders, she wrestled his hands away, wedging them beneath her knees. His eyes hardened with surprise, then grew darker and fuller as Lissa slowly unbuttoned his shirt. At each button she paused, kissing the newly exposed stretch of chest, finally reaching his belt and spreading the shirt away. She would make him crave her as he had made her crave him. Gently, she moved her lips across every inch of his warm, furry chest, exulting as she felt him writhe beneath her. "Are you ready?" she purred.

"Yes!" It was a tortured gasp.

"I believe I'll just make you readier," she drawled, sliding down to his belt buckle, unfastening his jeans, inching them off. She tasted his ankles, his shins, his knees. His hands finally free, he groped for her, but she ducked out of reach.

His fingers clenched into fists and he fought against his ragged breath. "Lissa, you're driving me crazy."

"That was my intention," she said, her voice soft and husky.

Swinging his arm around, he caught her shoulder and dragged her face back up to his. A hoarse growl rose from his throat as his lips collided violently with hers. His fingers tore at her clothing, abandoning her sweater up around her neck, shoving her pants as far as her knees and then kicking them off, scorching her with his feverish probing. He entered her with a savage power, nearly lifting them both off the floor. Lissa was overcome by a cataclysmic throbbing, a deluge of fiery sensation, and he pushed further, seeking to reach beyond her body to her soul. And then he found it, igniting it, setting off a chain reaction, one luscious spasm of ecstasy after another until she was too weak to cry.

His head dropped back to the cold floor, his skin damp, his eyes smoldering, two still-glowing embers burning into her. "Lissa," he said, his breath still coming in gasps, his hand reaching up to touch her face. "God, what you do to me...." He shut his eyes and hugged her. "If we never moved from this spot for the rest of our lives, I'd die happy."

"Doesn't the floor hurt your back?"

"What floor?" he asked with a laugh and gently smoothed out her bunched sweater.

Lissa nestled against him and smiled, knowing exactly what he meant. He was her floor, her foundation. He was her roof, the walls around her. Lying in his arms, she knew the meaning of home.

SHE FELT SO LIGHT in his arms, light yet solid. His hands moved consolingly up and down her back, tracing her feminine curves. If he were an artist, he wouldn't paint her. He would sculpt her.

But he wasn't an artist. He was a businessman, with a mess to resolve back in Colorado. The memory of the problem awaiting him at his factory caused anger to flare up inside him. Lissa's adventurous assault on his body had temporarily eradicated the memory. But only temporarily.

When Jared's pulse finally subsided, he and Lissa picked themselves up off the floor, gathered their clothing, and dressed. They drove together to her house so she could fetch a dress-for-success suit and a pair of shoes to wear to work the next morning and then returned to his home. They climbed the stairs to the guest room he had made his own, and he wheeled in a portable television set so they could watch a movie while snuggled together in bed.

He tried not to think about what was brewing back in Colorado Springs. Listening to Lissa's comments on the movie, her soft, mellifluous drawl stretching her words and her large gray eyes lifting to his whenever she addressed him, he was able to shunt the situation at the factory to the back of his mind. She was so beautiful, he thought, curled up against him like a cat, warm and comfortable and purring. Tame, he thought, stroking his hand through her hair in a gentle pattern, tame and domesticated. Who would have thought that a mere hour ago this sweet, soft-spoken lady had been attacking him with utter abandon on the floor of his kitchen?

Simply recalling her astonishing passion aroused him, and he subtly shifted his legs against the mattress. He didn't want to go because he didn't want to leave her. Not even for a week.

But he had to go. He had made countless telephone calls during the day, trying to find out what exactly was going on. But nobody was willing to say anything. At least not over the telephone. He had to go there and deal with it in person.

Maybe, he thought, his fingers twirling through the downy golden hair at the nape of her neck, maybe it was for the best that he should return to Colorado for a while. He had been giving his enterprises out West only the most superficial attention during the past week.

Debbie was a superb assistant, but she couldn't run everything herself. He had responsibilities out there; no matter how immersed he was in reacquainting himself with his old home—and acquainting himself with Lissa—he couldn't just ignore his businesses. So he would go and fulfill his obligations. He would be a boss. He would set things straight.

And he would see Phyllis. He had things to set straight with her, too, and that had to be done in person. His fingers paused in their exploration of Lissa's hair as he considered the woman he had been dating with some regularity in Colorado Springs. Phyllis was a vivacious person, bright and funny, occasionally a bit headstrong. Divorced and fiercely single. Actually, Jared was pretty sure Phyllis was dating other men besides himself. She ought to be; she was certainly attractive enough. It wasn't a subject she and he discussed, because there was no need. They were friends, good friends, that was all.

He would have to tell her about Lissa, about how Lissa had somehow managed to turn his house into a home for him. He would have to tell her he was learning that Providence had always been his home, even when he was busy denying it. He would have to tell Phyllis that somehow, without even realizing it, Lissa had made him recognize that he belonged here, in his family's house, accepting the fact that he was the son of Joseph Isaiah Stone.

He had to tell Phyllis all these things—in person. That was only right. She would understand. And then, when he came back to Providence, when he came back home to Lissa... Maybe by then he wouldn't have to worry about rushing her. Maybe after a week away from him she would understand what was going on between them.

"I believe that was a decent film," she said with a sigh, turning from the television screen to face Jared. "What did you think?"

His eyes flickered between the television and Lissa. She looked so earnest, so interested in his opinion, that he couldn't resist a sly smile. "I think," he told her, "that I'd much rather be on the kitchen floor with you than watching a television movie."

She opened her mouth to protest, but before she could speak, he kissed her. And then it all went away again, the difficulties out in Colorado, the trip he didn't want to make—it all went away, and only Lissa existed for him. Only Lissa's arms gathering his body to hers, welcoming him once again.

Chapter Eight

As work progressed on the restaurant, Lissa was able to turn her attention fully to Jared's house. She spent most of Thursday and Friday there wandering from room to room, taking inventory of the furniture, deciding what to keep, what to restore, what to discard. She met with the glazier, and she and Paul examined the construction of the ballroom, locating struts and beams and chuckling over Jared's bemused expression as he watched from the doorway. She made arrangements with McReed's, the firm she frequently hired for custom refinishing of furniture, and with a flooring company that could handle reclamation of the dulled parquet floors. She pored over fabric samples, wallpaper swatches, lighting fixtures. At night, she cuddled against Jared's warm body and prayed that she would satisfy him as much as he satisfied her.

"A small hint," she said Saturday morning as they sat in the kitchen eating breakfast. "Some of the furniture I'll be replacing has some value. I know an antique dealer who'd pay a pretty penny for a few items."

"For instance, the dining-room furniture?" Jared

accurately guessed. "If you want to make a deal with him, fine. But don't knock yourself out."

"It's your money," Lissa said with a shrug.

"I'm sure you'll find a way to spend it," he said, laughing. "I still don't understand why you put that clause in the contract about my approving all expenditures."

"I only intended to make an unusual arrangement as standard as possible," Lissa explained.

"And this way I'll have to call you for an accounting every day while I'm in Colorado," he teased. "I was planning to do that anyway."

When they were through with breakfast, Jared dressed in new jeans and a cable-knit sweater, pulled a down parka from his closet, and led Lissa into his father's bedroom. "I've got something to keep you warm," he murmured as he studied her outfit: a gray turtleneck and navy blue corduroy slacks.

"To keep me warm?"

Jared rummaged through the drawers of his father's bureau. "At the homecoming game."

"Jared, it's a sunny day. I'm sure my tweed blazer—"

"For a football game?" He shook his head. "You'll need something warmer. It can get pretty cold in the stands. When was the last time you went to a football game?"

"High school," Lissa admitted.

"Down South," he scoffed. "Trust me. You'll need a warm jacket. Aha!" He retrieved from a drawer two long brown-and-white striped mufflers. "The official homecoming scarves."

"Is this truly necessary?" Lissa asked, laughing as Jared wrapped the bulky muffler about her neck.

"When you do a thing, you do it right. We can stop by your place and pick up a warmer coat." He walked with her back to the room where he had left his parka, shrugged it on, and slung the other scarf around his neck.

"Jared, it's early. We're not supposed to meet Paul and Peggy until twelve-thirty."

Jared stared at her, pretending to be amazed. "Lissa Cavender, don't you know anything? It's homecoming weekend. We have to do the whole routine."

"What whole routine?" she demanded to know.

Jared refused to enlighten her. "Come on, honey, let's go bundle you up."

They drove to her apartment and she exchanged her blazer for a wool pea jacket. Then they steered south to the Brown University campus, struggling to find a parking space along the crowded curbs where returning alumni had parked. Jared finally located a spot several blocks from campus. Taking Lissa's hand, he marched her down a side street to a small liquor store. "Jack Daniel's Green Label," he told the clerk. "In the flask bottle." Lissa laughed as Jared handed the clerk some money and slipped the flat bottle into a pocket of his parka. "We've got to do it right," he said, giving Lissa a mirthful squeeze.

"Now where are we going?" Lissa asked as he continued toward the campus.

"Wriston Quad," he informed her, leading her through an iron gate in the brick wall surrounding the university's fraternity quadrangle. "You always have to visit the quad before the game. It's part of the routine."

"Pardon my ignorance," Lissa said with a sniff as they

wandered up the sloping path to the grassy lawn about which the fraternity buildings stood. As they arrived at the lawn Lissa gasped in astonishment. Every fraternity had constructed a huge outdoor statue in praise of the school's football prowess. The game was to be played between the Brown Bears and the Princeton Tigers, and each wire-and-cloth sculpture symbolized Brown's trouncing of Princeton. One statue featured an eight-foot-tall brown bear with a tiger's tail hanging from between its grizzly jaws; another had a bear stomping its paws on the crushed back of a tiger; yet another showed a tiger hanging from a noose with a bear pulling the rope tight. "Good Lord," Lissa muttered. "Rather gory, isn't it?"

"Every year the fraternities try to outdo each other," Jared explained with a low laugh, pointing out the Greek letters painted onto the bears' chests. "I'm glad to see the tradition is still alive. My father and I always checked out the sculptures before the game."

Lissa shook her head. "It's a far cry from the School of Design. We didn't even have an athletic field, let alone a team."

"Your high school must have done school-spirited things."

"A bonfire before the big game," Lissa allowed. "But nothing like this."

"Welcome to the Ivy League," Jared remarked with a grin. "I must admit, even Berkeley didn't go to this extreme."

They strolled hand in hand among the sculptures, analyzing each, stomping on the crisp leaves raked into heaps along the paths, smiling at the crowds of students and alumni. Friends greeted each other with shouts about eating tigers for breakfast, about conquering the Princeton "Pussycats." Lissa found the mindless enthusiasm delightful.

Eventually she and Jared made their way back to the car and drove to the stadium. The field abutting the stadium was jammed with more cars, and hundreds of ticket-waving fans swarmed around the entry gate. Lissa clung to Jared's hand, afraid to lose him in the crowd as she searched for Paul and Peggy. After a few anxious minutes, she located them at the appointed meeting place and raced over. Flinging her arms around Peggy, she hooted, "Hello, Mama! How're you feeling?"

Her tall, stalky friend hugged her back. "It's awful. Paul refuses to pamper me."

"Are you nauseous?"

Peggy shook her head no. "Starving all the time. Do I look fat?"

Paul grimaced and Jared laughed as Lissa touched Peggy's flat tummy. "In another week, you'll be ready to join the circus."

Peggy groaned and turned to Jared, carefully appraising him. "So you're Jared Stone," she said, contemplating him and nodding. Then she tilted her head toward Lissa and mouthed, "Wow."

Lissa blushed furiously, hoping that Jared hadn't been able to read Peggy's lips, and Paul helpfully led him away to introduce Peggy's brother, sister-in-law and friends.

"Honestly, Peggy—" Lissa scolded.

"He's *gorgeous*, Lissa. Paul didn't tell me that part. All he said was he was a nice guy."

"He *is* a nice guy," Lissa argued.

"With looks like that, 'nice' becomes irrelevant. No wonder you're head over heels."

Lissa's protest was stifled by the pressure of Jared's arm about her shoulders. "I hope you're impressed by our official scarves," he addressed Peggy with self-mocking boastfulness.

"They're all the rage in Providence this fall," Peggy joked as the group moved through the gates into the stadium.

The game was played with rambunctious spirit, and the crowd responded loyally to the home team. Since Lissa hadn't attended a football game in years, she frequently had to ask Jared for explanations of what was going on. Each time Brown scored points, the school's cheerleaders raced across the field and bowed salaams before the goal post, and during halftime the school's marching band put on a show comprised of haphazard choreography and off-color humor.

Lissa was glad Jared had insisted that she dress warmly. The brisk autumn air held a distinct chill, and she let Jared warm her hands in his and warm her throat with nips from his flask of bourbon. "Was that part of the routine, too?" she asked at one point as Jared tucked the flask back into his pocket.

"Always," he replied. "Although my father had a sterling silver flask with his initials engraved on it. I think it's downstairs in the game room someplace. But bourbon was definitely part of the routine."

"But you were just a little boy!"

"I was allowed three sips: one after the first score by Brown, one at halftime and one at the start of the final quarter. I used to think the stuff tasted vile," he confessed with a rumbling laugh. "But I was a man about it."

The game ended with a resounding ten-point victory for Brown, and after filtering through the cheering hordes back to the field where they had parked, Lissa and Jared arranged to meet their friends back at the Morris house. "Where are we going?" Jared asked Lissa when they were settled into his car.

"Lincoln," Lissa told him. "Do you know how to get to Route 146?"

"More or less," he said, waiting patiently for the traffic to ease up.

Lissa studied him as he gazed through the windshield, his fingers curled loosely about the steering wheel and his eyes foggy with thought. "Jared," she whispered. When he didn't respond, she repeated herself more loudly. "Jared."

"Hmm?" Breaking from his trance, he inched the car out into the road and glanced at Lissa.

"Are you okay?"

He considered her question, then grinned and squeezed her knee. "Yes, I'm okay. Just remembering." He drove without speaking for a few moments. "There were good times, too. With my father, I mean. I used to love the homecoming games because it was just him and me. One of the few things we shared as a father and son. I had forgotten.... I deliberately forced myself to forget the good times—it hurt too much to remember them." He eyed Lissa, a poignant smile playing across his lips. "But now it's time to remember. I'm glad I went."

"I am, too," she murmured, twining her fingers through his.

They drove through the Lincoln State Park, its trees blazing with vibrant autumn color, and Lissa gave Jared directions to Paul's house, which was tucked into a heavily wooded hillside. The dirt driveway was already filled with cars, and when they strolled up the slate path to the front door, they heard music and laughter oozing from inside.

Paul swung open the door for them, a beer bottle clutched in his hand. "Join the party," he welcomed them. "Thank goodness Brown won. If they hadn't, this would have been a wake. Can I get you something to drink?"

Jared asked for a beer and Lissa a glass of wine as they removed their coats and scarves and hung them on the polished wood coat hooks that lined the hall. Lissa admired the improvements Paul had made on the house since her last visit—fresh paint on the walls, the downstairs powder room completely refurbished. "Now they've got to make a nursery," she told Jared after describing to him the run-down condition of the house when Paul had bought it last spring.

Mellowed by their drinks, the lively jazz music and the aromatic fire in the living room's wood-burning stove, Lissa and Jared relaxed and chatted with the others. Lissa hadn't seen Peggy's brother and sister-in-law or her college roommate in a long time, and they had a great deal of catching up to do, but Jared soon felt comfortable enough to engage in conversation as well. When Peggy's brother asked him about his famous father, he answered the questions without rancor, and deftly managed to steer the discussion to other topics.

Lissa smiled inwardly as she watched him gracefully divert the spotlight from himself, querying Peggy's brother about his work as a lawyer in Boston.

"Come give me a hand," Peggy mumbled, and, assured that Jared could hold his own in the living room, Lissa followed her friend to the kitchen.

"What do you want me to do?" she asked as Peggy shut the door.

"Talk to me!" Peggy squealed girlishly. "He's wonderful. How long have you known him?"

"Barely a week," Lissa admitted.

Peggy shook her head in disbelief. "I keep telling myself that, but seeing you together—Lissa, it's like you've found your Platonic Other."

"Don't get bookish," Lissa said, laughing at her friend.

"All right," said Peggy, moving to the stove and checking various pots that simmered with food. "I won't get bookish. Plain talk, girl: Paul says you're spending lots of time with him. How serious is this thing?"

Lissa shrugged. "I don't know."

Her friend gripped her shoulders. "I'm Peggy." She spoke quietly. "Talk to me. It's obvious you love him. Does he love you?"

"I don't know," Lissa said with a sigh. "He...he seems fond of me."

"Oh, don't be a blushing Southern belle. He must be doing something right, you're glowing like a lighthouse. It's all over your face. I don't think I've ever seen you this—no, happy isn't the word. Blissful. Whatever's going on, Lissa, don't let it slip away."

Lissa gave Peggy an impulsive hug. "I'll do my damnedest," she swore.

"That's the spirit. Now help me set the table."

They consumed a hearty meal of goulash, noodles, salad and Portuguese sweet bread, and then retired to the living room for tea, fruit, homemade brownies and more conversation. At around nine o'clock, Jared caught Lissa's eye and angled his head toward the door. She responded with a subtle nod, and Jared stood up. "I hate to be bowing out so early," he apologized as Lissa rose from her chair, "but I've got to catch a flight to Denver tomorrow."

"He wants to run for cover before Lissa starts working on his house," Paul kidded as he headed for the hallway to fetch their coats.

Amid thank-yous, hugs and handshakes, Lissa and Jared departed from the house. Jared opened the car door for her, then climbed in behind the wheel. "I hope you don't mind leaving while the party is still in full swing," he said while searching for the right key.

"Not at all," Lissa assured him. "I'm pretty weary, actually."

He turned on the engine and backed into the road. "Watching a football game can sometimes be almost as tiring as playing one."

"Are you tired?"

He shook his head. "I just wanted to have some time alone with you." He arched his arm over her shoulders and drew her cozily close to him. "I wish I didn't have to go. I'm going to miss you, woman."

"You'll probably be too busy to miss me," she said modestly.

"No," he disputed. "But that's a reasonable strategy. I'll try to keep myself busy. Will you miss me?"

"Not a chance," she drawled. "I'll be too busy without even trying."

"Liar," he said, sliding his hand up along her neck and stroking her earlobe with his thumb. "Fortunately, I can read your mind."

"And it says that I'll miss you?"

"It says—" he grinned mischievously "—that you wish I'd push a little harder on the accelerator so we could get home and into bed sooner."

Merely hearing the words and feeling the gentle caress of his fingers along her neck elicited a sharp pang of desire in Lissa. She closed her eyes and sighed, momentarily overcome, then opened her eyes again. "I'm going to miss you something terrible, Jared," she confessed. "Honest answer."

"I'll get back as soon as I can," he vowed. "Maybe less than a week. We'll see how it goes."

They spent the night locked in each other's arms, loving each other until their muscles ached, until their mouths were dry, trying to compensate for their impending separation. Lissa would drift off to sleep only to dream of Jared's lips on the nape of her neck, his hand cupping her breast, and she would open her eyes to discover she hadn't been dreaming at all. "Lissa," he would whisper, and she would answer with an insatiable kiss, her body shedding its drowsiness, flowering awake for him. Then he would doze, and she would find her fingers sketching mindless patterns through the hair on his chest, and he would groan and reflexively lift her onto himself. Sleep seemed useless to Lissa; she would have plenty of opportunity to catch up on her rest after he was gone.

They were subdued over breakfast. Lissa suspected

that Jared was preoccupied with the difficulties that awaited him in Colorado Springs, but she allowed herself the meager pleasure of believing that he was as saddened as she was about saying good-bye. He refused her offer to drive him to Boston's Logan Airport, insisting that he would prefer to leave his car in the long-term parking lot so it would be waiting for him when he returned. "Who knows what flight I'll wind up taking back?" he pointed out.

He presented Lissa with a silver key ring containing five keys. "I haven't gotten all of them figured out yet," he admitted. "This one I know opens the front gate, and these two are for the front door, though I can never remember which goes into which lock. One of these is for the garage, and one is for the outside cellar door. Let me give you some phone numbers, too." He located a pad and pen and jotted the numbers down. "It probably makes more sense for me to call you, since I'll be coming and going, but if you can't wait to hear my voice..." He glanced up at her, his eyes sparkling. "This first number is my house, and this one is Debbie's number."

"Debbie?" Lissa asked as Jared made note of the name on the pad.

"My secretary, assistant, right-hand lady at the plant. She can usually track me down."

"All right." Lissa stuffed the paper and the keys into her pocket. She accompanied Jared upstairs and helped him pack, although he needed few clothes, having left most of his wardrobe back in Colorado when he had come East for what he had thought would be a brief stay. Together they climbed back down the stairs, Jared deciding to take one last look at the house as it was. "When I come back, it'll be entirely new."

"It will not," Lissa countered with a chuckle. "It'll be the same old place with new paint on the walls."

"For what you're charging me, you'd better do more than that," he said with a good-natured scowl. "I guess it's time to hit the road."

He tossed his suitcase into the trunk of the Cadillac, opened the door for Lissa, then drove down the driveway, locking the gate behind him before turning onto the boulevard. They traveled in silence to Lissa's street, and Jared parked in front of the yellow house. Sliding across the seat, he took Lissa in his arms. "I'll call you as soon as I get to my house, okay?"

"Okay." Lissa returned his tender kiss. "Have a good trip. I hope it all gets smoothed out."

"Never fear," he boasted with a wink. "I'll whip everyone back into line."

One more kiss, and Lissa left the car, forcing a wide grin as she waved him off from the porch of her building. As soon as his car turned the corner, she felt the air around her grow noticeably colder; she pivoted and scampered inside to her apartment.

She settled at her desk to work on her lecture notes and wondered why she felt so lonesome. She had survived twenty-eight long years without Jared Stone in her life, and had spent only ten days with him. Why should his departure leave her feeling as if she had lost a limb? He would be back soon. And he would be telephoning in a few hours. Trying to shrug him out of her thoughts, she bent over her folder and sorted through her notes.

The silence in her apartment grated on her. When Lissa was done with her class preparation, she organized her plans for the next morning at Jared's house:

the removal of much of the furniture, and the arrangements with a construction firm to begin work on the ballroom. She was mildly surprised when, by six, her telephone hadn't rung, but she assumed Jared had gotten tied up somewhere. She ate a light supper of soup and salad, took a bath, turned on the television, and found herself eyeing her alarm clock and her telephone. The hands of the clock swung steadily through the hours; the telephone remained silent.

At ten, she clicked off the television, crawled beneath her quilt, and shut the light. She was sure Jared had a good reason for not calling... but her throat clogged with sobs and her fingers flexed into fists. *There must be a good reason; he must be busy,* she thought, but the tears welled up in her eyes and her mind filled with all the gruesome possibilities of why he had failed to call her. After all, he had another life out there, another home. Following the advice she had playfully offered last night, he had decided to keep himself too busy to miss her.

Angry and hurt, Lissa dozed fitfully. In her sleep she reached for Jared, and his absence stirred her awake. She rolled over, reshaped her pillow, dozed again. And then, abruptly, the telephone rang. She eyed the clock: eleven-thirty. Grumbling, she lifted the receiver. "Huh?"

"Did I wake you?" Jared's voice pierced through her grogginess. "I'm sorry—it's only nine-thirty here. I just got in."

"What—" Lissa shook her head clear. "Was there a problem with your flight?"

"No," he explained. "Debbie was waiting for me at my house. She barely let me drop off my suitcase before dragging me to the plant."

"But Jared, it's Sunday. Wasn't it closed?"

He chuckled. "I have a key. Then I was whisked away to my foreman's house for dinner and powwowing." He sighed. "I'm pooped. How are you?"

Lissa smiled, scolding herself for having distrusted him, for having been angry. "All right," she told him. "Scheming to transform your palace on the boulevard. How was your plant, Jared? Is this sabotage thing for real?"

"Hard to say. The machine that was damaged is up again, but we're a week behind on orders as a result. I'll have to spend tomorrow apologizing to all our customers for the delay. Then I'll have to start nosing around to find out what's really going on. It may take longer than a week," he said and sighed.

Lissa bit her lip. "Well, I suppose it's got to be resolved."

"I know. Look, I don't want to keep you up all night. I'll have a better idea tomorrow of what I'm facing here. So close your eyes, kiss the pillow, and pretend it's me, okay?"

"It's a poor substitute," Lissa said with a laugh.

"It's the only substitute that won't make me jealous. Take care, honey. I'll talk to you tomorrow."

"Good night, Jared."

She lowered the phone, closed her eyes, and sank into the pillow. A warm, peaceful contentment washed over her, and in no time she was fast asleep.

JARED PROWLED the modern A-frame house that he had considered his home for the past several years. The sleek leather-and-chrome furniture in the cathedral-ceilinged living room, the deck with its view of Pike's

Peak, the efficient, well-applianced kitchen seemed vaguely familiar to him, but he still felt like a visitor, a stranger. It wasn't home anymore.

He opened a can of beer, took a deep swig, and returned to the living room, where he flopped onto the down-filled sofa and closed his eyes. Things were worse than Debbie had let on over the telephone a few days ago. Some sort of feud was brewing between the older workers and the newcomers at the plant, something, Debbie hypothesized, to do with the fact that the senior workers held more stock in the company than the more recent employees. Personality clashes. Ill winds.

And more—a problem at the radio station. Debbie had briefly filled him in as they drove to George's house. The big Vail promotion his station had been in the process of organizing was about to fall through. Arguments over money. The man Jared had hired as station manager was excellent when it came to budgets, but his thrift in negotiating the Vail promotion was about to undermine everything.

Jared felt guilty. He felt guilty about shortchanging his Colorado businesses. And he felt even guiltier when he confessed to himself that, even facing the responsibilities he had here, he would rather be in Providence with Lissa.

He took another long draft of his beer, then rose from the couch and ambled to the kitchen, where he dialed Phyllis's telephone number. "Jared!" she greeted him boisterously once he had identified himself. "You're home?"

He swallowed before speaking. "I'm in Colorado," he clarified, wondering if she detected his subtle correction of her statement. "Can we get together?"

"I'll erase everything on my calendar," Phyllis chirped. "Are you free tomorrow?"

"I...don't know." The sooner he saw her, the better. But as long as he didn't fully know what was going on at the plant, he was reluctant to commit himself. "I've got a lot of business to attend to," he explained slowly. "But...perhaps I can give you a call when my schedule is a little clearer."

"Of course," Phyllis obliged him. "I've just stopped erasing. I've missed you, you bum. You might have called, you know. Last I heard, they had telephones in New England."

"I'm sorry." He fingered his beer glass, tracing lines through the condensation on the surface with his index finger. "I thought it would be better to talk when I saw you."

"Well, I'm glad you're back. I've got lots to tell you, too. You know the Shipley account I was fighting for when you left? I won it."

"Good for you," he praised her. Phyllis was employed by a large advertising firm in the area. They had met through their work. Jared knew she was ambitious—her ambition, she often bragged, had contributed to the collapse of her marriage. "You can tell me all about it when we see each other." Suddenly he was impatient to get off the phone.

"Fine. Give me a call when you can squeeze me in. Bum," she said, teasing. "I'll change the sheets."

He opened his mouth and then closed it, struggling to sort out his thoughts. Maybe telling Phyllis about Lissa, about the home that awaited him in Providence, wasn't going to be as easy as he had imagined. Everything seemed easier when he was with Lissa, detached from the complications of his life out West. "I'll call you," he promised softly. "Take care."

"See you soon, lover-boy," Phyllis cheerfully bade him farewell.

He hung up the phone and roamed aimlessly back to the living room. He crossed to the broad, triangular window that opened onto the deck and stared out at the starlit night. The sky was clearer in Colorado than in the industrialized Northeast. He could easily decipher the Big Dipper, Cassiopeia, Polaris. It was the same sky arching over Providence, he thought, arching over the genteel yellow Victorian-style house in which Lissa slept. He pictured her in her cozy brass bed, beneath her beautifully crafted quilt, fast asleep, her pillow tucked comfortably beneath her head. Thinking of her soothed and strengthened him. Sighing, he turned from the window and climbed the stairs to his bedroom.

Chapter Nine

Monday arrived, bringing with it a full schedule of responsibilities. Lissa put on a neatly tailored suit and an air of professionalism as she headed directly to Jared's house to await the cadres of workers she had arranged for. The truck from McReed Furniture Refinishing arrived simultaneously with a squad of house painters; the flooring specialists drove up soon after. Lissa directed the laborers in the removal of the house's furnishings, and when she had a moment, she telephoned Candy at the office to check on the weekend's mail and the morning's messages.

A construction contractor arrived at ten, and Lissa showed him the ballroom and the architectural plans she and Paul had drawn up. He studied the design, nodded, and said, "We could get the exterior done in two months."

"One," she demanded.

He eyed her gruffly. "Beginning of December."

"Thanksgiving."

"Double overtime on Saturdays?"

Lissa offered a sugary smile. "By the book."

The contractor exhaled. "I don't know about you,

Miss Cavender,'' he said and chuckled. ''You bargain like a man, then you turn those big gray eyes on me. All right, we'll aim for Thanksgiving.''

Satisfied, she turned her attention to the task of setting a value on the dining-room furniture and the antique appliances in the kitchen. The antique dealer arrived at noon, and he was clearly impressed by the items Lissa wanted to sell him. He offered a fair sum, but Lissa dickered with him on principle and got him to agree to a higher price. ''This stuff is in great shape,'' he said, admiring the dining-room pieces. ''How come you're ditching it?''

''It's full of bad memories for my client,'' she explained.

While the first floor emptied, Lissa sorted and packed the knickknacks that decorated each room. She removed the Stone gallery of portraits from the rear parlor and lugged them upstairs, having already resolved to leave the bedrooms and third-floor servants' quarters untouched for now. The third floor—which contained two suites of bedrooms, a sitting room and a bathroom—had been well maintained by Jared's father's housekeeper, and as for the second floor, Lissa wanted Jared to discuss his preference with her. His father's bedroom was clearly the nicest room on the floor, and she suspected that he would ultimately choose to make that room his own, but she was loath to revamp it before Jared was ready to cope with his father's ''ghost.'' If any room was truly haunted, she suspected it was the master bedroom.

By four-thirty, when the last of the workmen had left, the house was a shambles. Lissa strolled through the rooms, her footsteps resounding in the emptiness. The floors were unevenly faded from the rugs, and the ugly linoleum kitchen flooring had been stripped off. Drop cloths had been laid by the painters in some rooms. Two metal rods had been rigged against the doors to the ballroom to secure the house in preparation for the next day's demolition of the ballroom's roof.

Satisfied and weary, Lissa locked up the house and drove downtown to her office to pick up her mail. Working to make Jared's house the home it had never been for him, she decided, was almost as good as being with him. He had never been far from her thoughts all day; she had been constantly conscious of him, constantly wondering what his reaction would be to the alterations his house was undergoing, constantly asking herself whether by clearing the junk from the kitchen or scraping the paint from the staircase's balustrade she was vanquishing another ghost for him. Paul's pep talk and Jared's boundless faith in her encouraged her. He would be pleased, she assured herself.

Since the city was beginning to empty of workers trying to beat the rush hour by leaving early, she was able to find a parking space on the street not far from the building that housed her office. She strolled down the block toward the concrete skyscraper but froze several yards from the building's entry when she spotted a painfully familiar figure slouching beside the revolving door.

Curtis. A slowly spreading nausea consumed her as she remained glued to the concrete beneath her feet, gaping at the slim, brown-haired man leaning against the plate-glass wall of the building. He lifted his hangdog eyes to her, straightened up, and waved.

Abruptly, she felt an unaccustomed bravery steeling

her spine and propelling her forward. She had nothing to fear, she realized. Curtis couldn't hurt her anymore. Jared had promised that love would always be beautiful for her, and there was nothing, nothing Curtis could do to destroy her. She marched toward him in resolute strides, stopping when she reached him.

"You're looking good" were his first words.

Her eyes took him in, and she became aware that she couldn't say the same for him. His cheeks looked gaunt, his eyes underlined with gray shadows. The sleeves of his wool blazer were slightly frayed. He was still handsome, still an undeniably attractive man, but he looked oddly bedraggled to Lissa. "What are you doing here?" she asked softly.

"I came to see you." He provided the obvious answer. "I went up to your office but your secretary told me you were out. She's new, isn't she? I didn't remember her."

"She's been with us for two years," Lissa told him, wondering why in the world she was standing on a busy street in downtown Providence making small talk with a man she loathed.

"I was going to wait for you up in your office, but Morris threw me out. He's still a prig, isn't he."

"He's one of the finest people in the world," Lissa said, haughtily disputing Curtis. *Lord, he looks skinny,* she thought, unable to tear her eyes from his sunken cheeks. Dissipated. He looked burned out.

"Can we talk?" he asked.

She pressed her lips together and inhaled. Her gaze dropped to his shabby jacket, his patched jeans, his scuffed hiking boots. "Come on up," she conceded grimly.

They strolled through the building's airy lobby to the elevator and rode upstairs to her office suite. They entered to find Paul conferring with Candy in the reception area. Paul's eyes instantly hardened as he took note of Curtis. "It's all right," Lissa said hastily, allowing Curtis to follow her into her own inner office. She felt Candy's and Paul's stares on her as she held the door for Curtis, and once he had entered, she called out again, "It's all right," before shutting the door behind them.

Curtis immediately made himself at home on her sofa. For safety's sake, she kept her distance from him, taking a seat at her desk and folding her hands primly above the smooth teak surface. "Things are going well for you, I take it," Curtis politely noted.

"Very well," she replied in a clipped tone. "What do you want?"

"Don't be so snippy," he scolded her, settling more comfortably into the upholstery. "I come as a friend."

"I'll bet."

A tense silence permeated the room. She wanted to demand of Curtis that he state his business and then remove himself from the premises, but she stubbornly refused to ease him into conversation. Let him speak when he could bear the silence no longer, she decided. She was certain she could outlast him.

"I'm broke," he finally announced.

Lissa's face reflected no surprise at that bit of news. "Still playing poker, I reckon," she muttered.

"Don't start in," he said, stopping her.

She suppressed the surge of anger that consumed her. Her teeth gnawed at the inside of her lip, but she said nothing.

"I'm staying up in Boston. Remember Ed Kelly?" Curtis's tone was friendly and conversational, which irked Lissa. "He graduated with me. Remember him? Photography major." At her nod, he continued, "He's a staff photog for some alumni magazine for one of the colleges there. Can you believe it? That's what I call selling out."

"That's what I call being a responsible adult who means to support himself," Lissa retorted.

Curtis cast her an impatient glower. "Well, he's putting me up, so I can't complain," he granted. "I don't know how long I can stay there, though. I'm sure I'm beginning to stink like three-day-old fish."

"It's unlike you to be so sensitive," Lissa observed dryly.

He glared at her again. "Anyway, I guess I've got to move out sooner or later. I wish I had the cash—"

"If you came here for money, you wasted your time," she cut him off.

He weighed her words for a moment, then shifted in his seat. "Before I was in Boston, I was down South," he revealed. "I've been traveling around a bit lately... looking for inspiration. I've been thinking of experimenting with some landscapes."

"Oh? Landscapes don't have sex with painters," Lissa caustically pointed out.

Curtis flinched, then shifted again. "I stopped by and visited your folks when I was in Tennessee," he announced.

Lissa grimaced. It was bad enough that Curtis was inflicting himself on her; he didn't have to be badgering her poor grandmother and aunt as well. "Lord help you if you asked my aunt for money," she grumbled quietly.

Curtis offered a surprisingly easy smile. "Your aunt wasn't home," he told her. "But your granny was. Sitting on the porch in her rickety old rocker, piecing together a quilt. God, Lissa, it was like two parts Grant Wood, one part Norman Rockwell. I almost laughed out loud."

Lissa's fingers began to curl into fists, and she hid her hands in her lap. "Say one bad thing about my gramma, Curtis Wade," she warned him tautly, "and I'll claw your eyes out."

Her blunt threat caught Curtis unprepared. His eyebrows shot up, pleating his brow into a series of parallel creases. "I wasn't going to say anything bad about her, Lissa," he claimed. "As a matter of fact, I was going to say some very nice things about her. I like your grandmother. I like the way she thinks."

"Do you?" Lissa's voice had to wrestle its way past the clenched muscles in her throat.

"She said she hoped we would get back together," Curtis related. "She said we were two sensible, talented, well-educated people and there was no reason on earth why we should be divorced."

"That," Lissa rasped, "is because I was kind enough not to tell her the truth about you."

Curtis let this insult pass. "She advised us to have a baby."

Lissa's jaw dropped. She was rendered speechless.

"The way she explained it," Curtis went on, "the way things are done where she comes from is that when a couple is having its problems, they have a baby and it takes their minds off themselves. Lots of good ol' mountain wisdom in that gray-haired lady, Lissa."

"You're insane," she said through gritted teeth.

"We aren't even a couple anymore, or haven't you noticed?"

"Yeah, well, look," he said, straightening up, apparently deciding to get down to business. "I'm broke, and I need some money. Which you seem to have in abundance," he added, his eyes sweeping over her well-appointed office.

"You aren't helpless," she countered. "Why don't you sell some of your damned paintings?" And then she paused, recalling the painting Jared had found in his father's closet, the best painting Curtis had ever done. He had sold that, hadn't he? He wasn't helpless. The one painting she had begged him to destroy he had managed to sell.

She opened her mouth to ask him about it, then hesitated. Something blocked the words from emerging. If she mentioned the painting, she would have to tell him about Jared. Not that she had any concern about sparing Curtis's feelings, but...but she couldn't bring herself to say Jared's name in Curtis's presence. She felt too protective about Jared. It would be an insult to him, an affront to him, to discuss him with someone as venal and selfish as Curtis. So she remained mute.

"I haven't really got anything I could sell at the moment," Curtis was commenting. "The bad stuff is worth less than the canvas it's painted on, and the good stuff...I don't know. If I had enough good stuff, maybe I wouldn't feel so possessive about it. I mean, they're mine, my creations. I can't just part with them, Lissa, you know that."

"You did once," she let slip, then felt her back stiffen as she awaited Curtis's reaction.

He seemed perplexed as he shook his head. "No I didn't," he maintained. "What are you talking about?"

What was the point? He would only lie to her if she reminded him of the final painting he had done of her. He would lie, and she would once again be swamped by memories that Jared had managed to conquer. She couldn't stand the idea of reliving the horror of the painting yet again.

"Lissa." Curtis leaned forward, his eyes imploring her. "I think your grandmother was on to something. I've tried being away from you, and it just hasn't worked. Why don't we make another go of it?"

"Nothing in the universe would make me get back together with you," Lissa murmured stonily.

"You must have loved me once," he pointed out.

"I must have been a blind fool once," she shot back hoarsely. "But I'm not anymore. Neither blind nor a fool."

His expression registered his own recollections. "You mean because I got involved with my models?" he guessed. "Lissa...come on, grow up. All men mess around—all normal men. At least I had a reasonable justification for what I did. It was necessary for my painting. It contributed to my art."

"Spare me." Her voice dripped with bitterness.

"Men are different from women," he defended himself. "They're built differently."

"Oh, is that what they taught in the life-drawing classes?"

He ignored her sarcastic tone. "Men have different needs. I've never yet met a man who was completely faithful to his woman."

"Oh? Well, I have," Lissa announced.

Curtis's eyebrows arched again, and then his face relaxed into a smug grin. "Oh, I'd bet my last dollar that he's cheating on you," he remarked. "All men do it. No one woman can satisfy a healthy man." He ruminated for a moment. "Who is he? Somebody I know?"

She considered once again asking Curtis about his connection to Jared's father, but thought better of it. He had sold a painting once, that was all. He had told Lissa he would get rid of the painting and he had, in the most profitable way he could think of. The details weren't important, not important enough to expose Jared to Curtis. For that was what she would be doing if she breathed his name. Curtis was sneaky and untrustworthy; who knew what he'd do if she provided him with information about her new lover? "I reckon it's none of your business," she said coldly.

His eyes brightened. "Is it Morris?" he asked. "You and he have always been tight. And his wife isn't much to speak of. Kind of flat-chested, as I recall. Not worth painting."

"Get out." Lissa's voice grew even icier. "Get out of here, Curtis."

"So that's who it is," he said, chuckling, mistakenly proud of himself. "I should have known. You and he were probably already at it when we were still married. No wonder he took you into his firm, no wonder he brought you along for the ride—"

"You make me sick," she spat out. "Get out of here."

He stood up, his smile more conceited than before. At the door he paused, and when he turned back to Lissa the smile was gone, replaced by a beseeching look. "I haven't got the fare back to Boston," he confessed.

She shut her eyes and moaned. Anything, she thought, anything to get him away from her before she went mad! Groping for her purse, she yanked out her wallet and handed him a twenty-dollar bill. "Here," she growled, extending the bill to him, unable to look at him. "Take it and go. And so help me, if you ever bother my gramma again—"

"I'm on my way," he swore, accepting the bill and then moving back to the door. "Thanks for the bucks."

She refused to open her eyes again until she heard the door close. When she found herself alone, she heaved a shaky sigh. She was astounded by the sheer depth of her rage. She had thought Jared's sweet influence had cured her of such powerful feelings of animosity, but it hadn't. Curtis could still evoke unfathomable hatred within her. She prayed he was gone for good.

Her gaze fell from the door to her telephone. She would have to call her grandmother to apologize for Curtis's intrusion. And to explain that her marriage was irrevocably destroyed. There would be no reconciliation, no babies. She dialed the long-distance number and took several deep breaths to steady herself.

"Hay-lo," her grandmother's distinctively twangy voice buzzed through the line. Whenever Lissa spoke with her relatives in Orchard Creek she was reminded of how much her own accent had been diluted by her years spent in New England.

"Gramma? It's Lissa," she identified herself.

"Lissa! Wayl, Ah b'lieve this is somethin' of a surprise."

"How are you, Gramma?" she asked. Her voice was still shaking. She swallowed to stabilize it.

"Gettin' on, gettin' on," her grandmother replied. "And how's yerself?"

"Gettin' on," she echoed her grandmother's familiar drawl. "Gramma, I just talked to Curtis. He says he paid you a call."

"That he did, darlin'," her grandmother acknowledged noncommittally.

"Gramma, we're not getting back together. He only came to see me because he needed money," Lissa explained.

A long pause ensued. "Lissa, Ah reckon Ah don't duly understand," her grandmother said with a sigh.

"I know you don't, Gramma, but it's done. It's over between us. I'm sure he was a fine, charming gentleman when he called on you, but he isn't really. Not to me." She hoped her grandmother wouldn't ask for more of an explanation.

To Lissa's relief, she didn't. "Ah don't s'pose it makes no sense to me. You all are livin' a life Ah don't rightly understand, but that's your affair, not mine." She sighed. "Ah do hope you all are farin' well."

"I am, Gramma," Lissa honestly admitted. "Gramma, I've . . . I've met someone else. Another man. He's a very good man, Gramma. You'd like him."

"Uh-huh."

"He's a fine man, Gramma. I love him."

Her grandmother said nothing for a minute. "Wayl, if yer happy, that's what counts. Yer Aunt Ahda and Ah do so worry about ya."

"I know you do," Lissa conceded. "I love you both, and yes, I'm happy with him. He's very good to me."

"Then Ah wish you well," her grandmother said.

Lissa exhaled, her tension seeping from her. Merely thinking of Jared placated her. Her fury with Curtis slowly waned, a warm swell of love for Jared taking its place. "I'll talk to you soon," she promised her grandmother. "So long."

"Take care o' yerself," her grandmother admonished her before hanging up.

Jared. That was all that mattered. Jared, his house, his love. As her grandmother would say, that was what counted.

She stood up, righted her shoulders, and left her office, discovering that Candy and Paul had already departed. Exiting the building, she strode briskly to her car and headed up the hill to the East Side. Once home, she bathed, slipped on a lounging caftan, and prepared herself a supper of broiled chicken and salad. As she was lowering herself into her chair at the dining table, her telephone rang. She raced to her bedroom to answer it.

"Working late?" Jared greeted her through the wire.

The sound of his voice was like a magic spell, filling her veins with affection for the man, the only man who counted. "Keeping busy so I don't miss you," she rejoined lightly, too embarrassed by her overpowering feelings to reveal them to him.

"I tried you earlier," he informed her. "I can't talk long, I'm supposed to meet the program director at my radio station for dinner. How's my house?"

"A total mess," Lissa reported, laughing. "How's everything at the plant?"

"I don't know." Jared sounded grim. "There's something afoot here—some bad feelings between two groups of employees that erupted while I was otherwise occupied. I've been trying to get to the bottom of it, but it's hard. Nobody wants to rat on anyone else. It's silly—if something hurts the company, it hurts everyone here, since they're all part-owners. I'm going to have to charm some answers out of somebody."

"You'll have no difficulty doing that, I reckon," Lissa said. "Charm is one of your long suits."

"Not everyone succumbs to it as easily as you, sweetheart. Did you spend all my money yet?"

"I'm working on it," Lissa said, reaching for the notes she had brought home with her in anticipation of his call. She rattled off a few expenditures, as well as the price she had gotten from the antique dealer.

"He paid that much for junk?" Jared asked, surprise in his voice. "What did you do, seduce him? Uh, hang on a second." Lissa heard the phone click as she was momentarily put on hold. Jared's voice soon returned. "Gotta run, Lissa. My program director is pacing the floor. Take care, woman. I'll talk to you tomorrow."

Hanging up, Lissa realized that she had been hoping he would say something more romantic, but she couldn't be angry. It seemed he was facing difficulties in Colorado that he hadn't anticipated, and he was blunt enough not to hide them from her, to waste time in idle sweet talk. Shrugging, she returned to her cooling supper.

WHAT WAS IT about her voice, he thought, staring down from his window to the teeming street below him. She had sounded edgy, almost manic. He supposed everything must be going supremely well for her, that was all. He was glad he hadn't burdened her with the trying details of his work. She was happy; things were going well in Providence.

But...no, there was something else in her tone, something he couldn't put his finger on. The cheerfulness seemed forced. It *wasn't* all going well. Yet she hadn't chosen to go into detail with him, either. He hoped it didn't have anything to do with the house.

Now that's a selfish thought, Jared mused, angry with himself. If Lissa had a problem, he shouldn't be more worried about the creaky old mansion on the boulevard than he was about her. Yet he knew, he knew why the image of his house had leaped into his mind. Because it wasn't just his house anymore. It was her house, too, the house she was going to make into their house. He wanted it to be perfect for her. He wanted it to be the most fulfilling job she had ever done. He wished he were with her, diving into her deep gray eyes, feeling her arms around him, feeling her breath across his shoulder as she told him how perfect the house was for them both.

"Jared?" Debbie's voice cut metallically through the intercom. "Shake a leg, boss. People are waiting."

He pushed his thoughts of Lissa from his mind. It was just the distance that had made her sound strange to him, the miles that had been temporarily interposed between them. Right now he had to contend with the Vail promotion. Shaking his head clear, he strolled from the office.

Chapter Ten

Tuesday morning was as hectic for Lissa as Monday. After the front parlor was painted, one of the painters began work on the fireplace, armed with a sharp blade and a bottle of solvent. The flooring people laid down the no-wax tiles she had ordered for the kitchen, and she negotiated with one contractor over delivery of a new aluminum double sink, to replace the deep ceramic basin sink, and with another contractor about a butcher-block counter to provide more efficient work space in the oversized kitchen.

In the afternoon, leaving the painting foreman in charge, she escaped to check progress on Max's Restaurant and to visit several furniture showrooms in search of new dining-room pieces. She eventually found what she was looking for: a sleek oval table of polished cherry, a matching buffet and a simple white globe lamp for overhead. At a hardware store she picked up a dimmer switch. When she was done with it, the room would have a clean, fresh look to it, decorated with several plants and little else. She was certain it would restore Jared's appetite.

He sounded ebullient over the telephone later that

afternoon. "Did you solve the problem at the plant?" she asked.

"No, but I solved a problem at the radio station," he boasted. "It's a big promotional deal with a resort in Vail. They were quibbling over nickels and dimes, and one of our competitors was waiting in the wings, ready to steal the promotion from us. I cut through the garbage and worked out a nice arrangement."

"Wheeler-dealer," Lissa blurted out with a laugh.

"Business as usual," he calmly responded. "Anyway, I have to have dinner with the folks from Vail tonight so we can slap each other on the back a few more times. Any figures you want to pass along?"

Business as usual. Lissa sighed once she had hung up the telephone. Well, the sooner he was finished with his business as usual, the sooner he would be returning to Providence. And anyway, she decided, it was just as well that he kept his telephone conversations with her short and to the point; that way she wouldn't be tossing and turning all night, dreaming about him, missing him.

The work continued apace on Wednesday. Lissa allowed herself a respite from her overseeing chores and wandered downstairs to the cellar to explore the game room. It was massive, with raw brick constituting one wall and a lavish bar of fieldstone and mahogany built into another. The bulk of the room was consumed by a beautiful billiards table, draped with a protective canvas sheet; plush leather chairs stood invitingly along the perimeter. She swung open one of the paneled closet doors, blinked in the darkness, and when her eyes adjusted, discovered a set of wooden chairs and a folded octagonal table. Dragging it toward the illuminated doorway, she realized that the table's surface was covered in green felt. "A card table," she mused. "A poker table."

Poker! J. I. Stone must have been a dedicated poker player if he owned a table like this. Why not? And if he was a poker player, wasn't it possible that he might have met Curtis over a game?

It seemed unlikely that a kingmaker–financier would have played poker with a young painter, but Lissa knew Curtis had engaged in some unlikely games. She had learned as much when some of the people to whom he owed money had contacted her after the divorce to collect on his IOUs. Curtis had traveled in unexpected circles. He had befriended an odd assortment of people. Some of them were probably intrigued by the notion of sharing the acquaintance of an artist. For successful businessmen, such a friendship must have seemed exotic.

Of course, playing poker with J. I. Stone wouldn't explain the painting, but it might explain how they met. Lissa's curiosity was piqued.

Racing up the stairs, she glanced at her watch and calculated the time difference between New England and the Rockies. In all likelihood, Jared would still be at work, but she was too impatient to wait for his evening call. She could try his house, and if he wasn't at home she could try his secretary.

Attempting to stifle the construction noises, she closed the kitchen door and reached for the telephone. She dialed the series of numbers and waited for him to answer. "Hello?" came a soft woman's voice.

Had Lissa dialed wrong? "Uh...is this Jared Stone's house?"

"Yes," said the woman.

Lissa scowled, then shrugged. It must be Debbie, his secretary. "Is Jared home?" she asked.

"He's just outside. I'll get him—oh, here he comes now. Jared?"

Lissa heard the muffled sounds of the phone changing hands, and then Jared's familiar baritone: "Jared Stone here."

"Jared?" Her own voice sounded feeble to her.

"Lissa!" he boomed in surprise. "Hang on...." Pulling the phone from his mouth, he shouted, "Make yourself at home, Joyce, this may take a while." Back into the phone he asked, "What's up?"

"Joyce?" Lissa swallowed.

"Shop steward at the plant," he explained smoothly. "We weren't getting anywhere in my office with everybody eavesdropping, so we cut out and came here to talk. How's everything going?"

"Fine," Lissa mumbled, her mind reeling. For some reason, all she could think of was *charm*. He was going to charm some answers out of somebody. She felt her eyes burn and her fingers grow icy around the smooth plastic of the receiver. "If...if you're busy," she stammered, "this can wait."

"No, it can't," he gently insisted. "If it could, you wouldn't have phoned me."

"I just..." She swallowed again, trying to overcome the gagging sensation in her throat. "I found a card table downstairs in the cellar, and I was wondering if you father was a poker player."

"One of his passions," Jared confirmed.

"High stakes?"

"Whatever the market could bear," Jared told her. "Why do you ask?"

"Because Curtis..." Her vision blurred, and she fought against the lump in her chest. "Curtis was a gambler, and he played in a lot of games. I thought that there was a possibility...."

"The painting?" Jared assisted her.

"Maybe. Maybe they met through a game, and Curtis had promised to get rid of the painting, and knowing him, he probably figured to get some money for it. He was always so desperate for money.... It's a possibility, anyway. I don't know," she concluded lamely.

"It's a definite possibility," Jared supported her theory. "Maybe my father thought it was a worthwhile investment. It's a damned good painting."

"Well, I just thought...I just thought I'd ask," Lissa mumbled. "I won't keep you. I know you're busy."

"Keep me," Jared murmured. "I'm never too busy for you."

"No, really," Lissa muttered, barely assuaged by his words. "I'm busy, too."

"I'll talk to you tonight, then," he said.

Lissa replaced the telephone and surrendered to a wrenching shiver. Of course, he could be conferring with his shop steward at his house. If she could believe that J. I. Stone played poker with Curtis, she ought to be able to believe the far more logical idea that Jared would be meeting with an employee at his home.

She tried to consider the situation rationally, but instead her skull filled with the soft, sensuous purr of the woman's voice, and with a memory of the conversation Jared had had in this very room, on this very telephone, when he had been summoned to Colorado: "You can't survive without me.... You need me.... I should drop everything and come running...." Words spoken to a co-worker, or to someone more intimate?

"Miss Cavender?" The painting foreman barreled into the kitchen. "We're ready to pack up for the day. Wanna see the fireplace?"

Lissa pushed aside her troubled thoughts to survey the workers' recent accomplishments.

WHEN JARED PHONED HER later that evening, full of self-satisfied assurance that his gambit with the shop steward had been successful, that after a couple of beers Joyce had opened up to him, Lissa tried to blot out the image she had of a tall, virile boss and his underling—the debonair, dark-eyed man extracting from a whispering woman the truth behind his plant's problems with liquor and maybe a relaxing massage and a few well-placed kisses. "It'll still take a few days to iron this thing out," Jared informed Lissa. "And I've got to smooth the ruffled feathers of our customers. But I should be back sometime next week." All Lissa heard was "next week." Later than he had predicted.

Of course Jared had a life out there; of course he had business acquaintances; of course he would be dining out with people, inviting people to his house. Why should any of this take her by surprise? Why should she be rankled by it? Who ever said she owned exclusive rights to Jared Stone?

Nobody had ever said it, yet that was what Lissa had wanted, what she prayed for. She loved him, loved him exclusively, loved him with more intensity than she had loved the man she had married. And in her love for Jared she had blindly refused to acknowledge that exclusivity was one thing they had never promised each other. She had given herself completely to him, yet she had never allowed herself to entertain the possibility that he had not given himself completely to her. Perhaps she was the only woman he wanted to be with in Providence, but he hadn't ever claimed that Providence was the *only* place he wanted to be. Yes, he had said it was home, but Colorado hadn't evaporated in the meantime. So he wanted a woman in every port. Given how handsome, how powerful, how sensual he was, who could expect otherwise?

Lissa's memory played with the ghastly meeting she had had with Curtis on Monday. What had he said? All normal men cheat on their women. No one single woman could ever satisfy a normal man. And Jared surpassed "normal." He was so sexy, so passionate. If she hadn't been enough for Curtis, why should she assume that she was enough for Jared?

Maybe Curtis was right. Maybe this was the way all men were. She hadn't realized the truth in her marriage until it was too late, until the hurt of her husband's betrayal had nearly demolished her. But she had learned things from Curtis, ugly things, true, but important things. Perhaps his surprise visit to her two days ago had been an act of fate, designed to remind her about the ways of men, and their needs and hungers, about how one woman alone could never satisfy them.

She continued working on the house, but the work no longer filled her with joy. She admired the freshly polished parquet floors with a cold detachment; she arranged the new dining-room furniture with professional precision; she browsed through a nursery looking for plants with the eye of a designer, not a lover, and selected a jade plant and a philodendron, hearty species that would require little attention. She couldn't permit herself to indulge in the fantasy that she would be at Jared's house often enough to care for them.

The week dragged, long and lonely. Lissa spent day after day at the house with the builders, viewing the rubble that had once been the outer wall of the ballroom, seeing it as a symbol of the rubble that had once been her spirit. When Jared phoned, full of pride over his accomplishments, Lissa responded numbly. If he detected the listlessness in her tone, he didn't question it.

No wonder he was proud. He had it all. He had the wealth to spread his women around, thinking that they would never find out about each other. Curtis hadn't been so lucky. When Lissa had been working in Boston, he had been able to indulge in his extracurricular activities without her finding out about them, but once she had moved her career to Providence, closer to home, he had been caught. Clearly Jared didn't expect to be caught. He was a Stone, a prince. His empire spread across the nation. He could keep his royal consorts in blissful ignorance if he chose.

Except that Lissa had called him. She had heard Joyce's voice. And she wasn't a fool. She would never let herself be betrayed again. Once was enough.

LISSA WOULD BE TEACHING NOW, Jared thought as he steered his Porsche along the winding drive that cut through Phyllis's condominium development. It was Thursday evening, and Lissa would be at R.I.S.D. He pictured her at her lectern, in a tweedy pair of slacks, perhaps, lecturing in that intoxicating mountain drawl of hers. He wondered if any of her students had crushes on her. If he were a student in her class, he would be smitten.

Well, he was smitten. As old and supposedly sophisticated as he was, he was smitten. And he was worried. Things weren't going smoothly for her, he knew, but she wouldn't share it with him. He heard it in her voice, in the pauses between her words when he spoke to her every night. Something was bothering her, but she wouldn't discuss it with him.

Evidently it was something she preferred not to talk about over the telephone. Certain things had to be discussed face to face, a fact acutely pertinent to him as he parked in front of Phyllis's angular modern townhouse and ambled to the door to call for her.

A tall, slender woman with thick auburn hair, Phyllis looked absolutely radiant. She greeted him with a warm hug—no, warmer than warm, he thought as he quietly extricated himself from her embrace. "Hello, lover-boy," she purred in that husky voice he had once found so seductive. "Let me get my coat and then we'll go."

They went to one of the newer restaurants in town, its paneled dining room festooned with hanging ferns and its waiters attired in foppish bow ties and slenderizing black trousers. They ordered drinks and steaks, and then Jared settled back in his chair and listened to Phyllis as she babbled enthusiastically about the Shipley account she had recently won. "It means a promotion for me in the not-too-distant future," she crowed ecstatically. "This is it, Jared. I've made the big time. I'm on my way."

Good, he thought. She was in such high spirits, he

was certain she would take the news about his moving back to Providence in stride.

He waited until they were served their food before broaching the subject. "I'm having my father's house rehabilitated," he began.

"Oh?" Her eyebrows lifted in curiosity.

"It's a big, drafty mansion," he told her, "an enormous brick monster of a house. I grew up there, me and my father and a few servants. It's one of those sorts of buildings, like a setting for a bad gothic novel." Why was he wasting time talking about the house?

"So you're having it rehabilitated?" she asked. "To make it easier to sell?"

"I don't think I'm going to sell it," he stated slowly, measuring her reaction.

She didn't seem to react at all. "Makes sense," she replied with a light shrug. "May as well have a place to stay on the East Coast. What the hell, Jared. You can afford it."

"It's more than just affording it," he admitted, picking at his salad. "No, what I'm saying is it's more than just a place to stay. It's my home, Phyllis, do you know what I mean?"

"Where you grew up," she concurred. "Of course I know what you mean. I still have a special place in my heart for Los Angeles. Always will."

He chewed slowly on a forkful of lettuce. It was tasteless to him. He studied the smooth, polished lines of Phyllis's face and, taking a deep breath, pressed on. "I met a woman in Providence."

Finally he saw that his words had struck something in Phyllis. She lowered her fork and angled her head at him. "Oh?"

"She's... an interior designer."

"Working on the house?" Phyllis guessed.

"As a matter of fact, yes," he replied.

"That's nice. Someone you trust, I hope," Phyllis prattled. "You don't want to go back and find out she's painted the ceilings black and spread the floors with Day-Glo rugs."

"She's an interior *designer*, not a decorator," Jared corrected Phyllis. "There's a world of difference." He was tempted to slip into a dissertation on everything he had learned from Lissa about her profession, but he refrained. "She's done wonders with the house already, Phyllis. She's... she's an incredible woman."

"I'm sure she must be," Phyllis acknowledged. "To restore a big old mansion like that...."

"She's turned it back into a home for me," he explained.

"Good for her," Phyllis said cheerfully.

Did she understand? Maybe. He couldn't tell. What seemed obvious to him often didn't seem at all obvious to others. "Phyllis, what she's doing—what she's *done*—it's very special. It means a lot to me. It wouldn't have been a home without her." At Phyllis's helpful nod, he paused. "Am I making sense to you?"

"She's a special woman and she's making the house into a home," Phyllis dutifully repeated.

"I mean... I'm really taken with her."

"I'm sure you are," Phyllis noted.

What had he expected? Perhaps Phyllis was accepting the news much more readily than he had been prepared for. Perhaps he didn't have to spell things out further for her. Phyllis was a sharp, independent woman. She understood what was going on.

His confidence was jarred when, at the conclusion of

their meal, the waiter returned to their table to ask if they were interested in coffee and dessert. "Why don't we go back to my place instead?" Phyllis suggested, winking at Jared.

He felt his jaw stiffen slightly as he shook his head and sent the waiter for the check. "I don't think so, Phyllis," he said, softly and gently.

Something flickered in her almond-shaped green eyes. "Something wrong?" she asked.

"I just...I just think it would be better if I didn't come home with you," he attempted, then sucked in his breath for fortitude. "Phyllis, I've tried to explain...this woman in Providence is someone special."

Phyllis fingered her napkin, heaped at the side of her plate, and contemplated the dark, handsome man across the table from her. "What, did you exchange vows with her already?" she asked snidely.

"No," he honestly answered. "But I just don't think it would be right for me to spend the night with you now. Not with things as they are."

"I see," Phyllis muttered frostily. She remained mute as Jared signed for the check and pocketed the receipt. "Tell me, Jared," she ventured quietly as he stood up. "Are we still friends?"

"Of course." He smiled. "We'll always be friends, Phyllis."

"Now that's a consolation," she said, feigning overwhelming relief. Her grin turned genuine. "You had me scared there, lover-boy. I do enjoy your company, you know. Even out of bed."

"Glad to hear it," he said, matching her smile. She understood. They could part as friends. He knew she'd take the news without a fuss.

He drove her home, walked her to her door, and

offered a light kiss on her cheek before saying good night. She was an incredibly sexy woman, he thought as he walked in solitude back to his car. It felt weird to be heading back to his house alone, but he had felt strangely lonely all week long, without Lissa. Even if he had succumbed to Phyllis's unquestionable attractiveness, he would have felt lonely with her. It was an unfamiliar sensation for him, loving a woman enough to renounce all others, loving a woman so much that no other woman could satisfy his needs.

Soon, he thought, as soon as he unraveled this stupid feud at the factory enough for him to feel it safe to return to Lissa, he would be back with her, back home for good.

Chapter Eleven

By Monday, Lissa was convinced that Jared had invented the problems at his plant just to create an excuse to return West for a few days. Or if not invented them, exaggerated them. He had waited until he was certain of his hold on her, and certain of her willingness to renovate his house for him, and then he had taken off to visit Debbie, Joyce and all the others.

In fact, Lissa was less than surprised when instead of hearing Jared's voice on the telephone Monday evening she heard a woman's voice. "This is Debbie Parsons, Jared Stone's assistant," the woman identified herself. "He asked me to call you because he's in Denver tonight. He had to take care of some business with his radio station up there, but he wanted you to know he'll be flying back East tomorrow. He should be in Providence by early evening."

"Okay," Lissa replied woodenly, thinking he must have a honey in Denver, too. Probably one in Phoenix and one in Los Angeles as well. A warm bed not far from any of his enterprises.

"He also asked me to give you this message," Debbie continued. "It doesn't make sense to me, but he said you'd understand. 'Keep busy, kiss your pillow, and rah-rah homecoming.'"

"Oh." Lissa felt the iceberg that had taken up residence in her abdomen begin to thaw. "Yes, I understand. Thank you." Hanging up, she relished for a moment the melting sensation, the tenuous warmth that Jared's private message imparted. Then she steeled herself against it. He was only priming her to be ready for his return, she thought resentfully.

Paul stopped by at the boulevard house on Tuesday to show Lissa some drawings he had executed for their bid on the hospital job, as well as to poke around the house and see what Lissa had accomplished. He studied the metal girders shaping the new outlines of the ballroom, and enthused over the new dining room with its white walls, elegant furniture, soothing light, and touch of greenery by the window. "Curtains?" he asked Lissa.

"I'll get to it," she said with a weary sigh.

"Very impressive. Now I know why I haven't seen much of you these days. You look exhausted, kid. Knocking yourself out for him, aren't you?"

"Knocking myself out for the job," she retorted.

"Well, he's sure to be pleased," Paul said, assuming her petulance was due to fatigue. "When's the old boy coming back?"

"Tonight," Lissa muttered, wrestling with her anxiety over his return.

"Give him my regards," Paul said as he swung open the front door. "Maybe we'll all get together or something when things calm down."

Fat chance, Lissa grunted to herself as she waved Paul off. She wasn't sure exactly what was going to happen when Jared arrived, but she suspected it wouldn't be pleasant. The last time she had been involved with a man, she had been oblivious to his other women, and as a result she had been made to feel utterly foolish. This time, she had almost stumbled into the same mistake. The fact that Jared's other women might be two thousand miles away didn't make Lissa feel much better. Yet he hadn't deceived her; he hadn't been dishonest. She couldn't be angry with him. All she could do was protect herself, defend herself against the pain Jared had unwittingly inflicted.

She remained at the house until the workmen left, then scrubbed her hands and face in the downstairs powder room. She located her blazer and purse in the kitchen and stalked out of the house, locking it up behind her. As she inserted her key into the slot of her car door, she saw two headlights cutting through the hazy pink twilight at the far end of the driveway. She sucked in her breath and bit her lip while the large black car coasted down the macadam, easing to a halt beside her.

If Lissa was apprehensive about seeing Jared, he was ecstatic about seeing her. Dressed in his down parka and jeans, he leaped from the car and captured her in a crushing hug. "Lord, have I missed doing this!" he crooned into her hair.

Although her mind tried to resist the onslaught, her body disloyally softened against his familiar chest. Her nostrils filled with his warm, masculine scent, her hands curled around his rigid shoulders, her lips rose to his in a long, exquisite kiss. She felt Jared trembling against her—with cold or with heat, she wondered as a scorching gust roared through her own flesh. She fought against it, panicked by the thought that he could come back and reclaim her the way he had gone to Colorado and reclaimed the women he had left there.

Easing out of the kiss, she averted her eyes and gulped down her tears. "Would you... would you like to see the house?" she mumbled at the ground.

"I'd rather see you," Jared said, slipping his hand beneath her chin and forcing her face back to his. "What's wrong? Aren't you happy I'm back?"

"Yes," she said. "Yes, I—" And then the tears broke loose, cascading down her cheeks in a great release of bitterness, doubt and fear.

Jared pulled her against him, offering his shoulder for her to press her head against. "Hmm," he intoned dubiously. "Any happier and you'd be suicidal. Come on, let's talk." He guided her toward his car.

"Don't you want to see the house?" she said between sobs.

"Not while you're like this." He swung open the passenger door for her, then took his seat behind the wheel. Instead of starting the car, however, he simply cuddled Lissa against himself and let her weep, his hands weaving in a consoling pattern through her unraveled chignon. "I knew something was wrong." His voice was gentle. "You were so strange on the phone. But you didn't seem to want to talk about it.... Will you tell me about it now?"

Lissa mopped her wet cheeks with her palms. "There's nothing to tell."

"Be honest with me, Lissa. You're not the sort of person who cries without a good reason."

Through her tears, Jared's face appeared sharper and darker to her. She blinked and looked away, staring through the windshield at her own car, feeling Jared's fingers tangle through her hair. "It's none of my business," she whispered hoarsely. "You have women in Colorado, and it's none of my business."

His fingers paused, and she could sense Jared's frown without seeing it. "Do I now?" he said more than asked.

"I know I have no right—"

"Whoa, Lissa, let's back up a few steps." Again with his thumb on her chin, he urged her to face him. "I *had* women in Colorado. Past tense. I'm not exactly cut out for celibacy, as you've probably noticed. In fact, celibacy was particularly rough on me this past week, because I kept thinking of you. You've spoiled me, Lissa." Not sure whether to believe him, she tried to twist away, but he held her firmly. "I saw a woman I had been involved with—when was it, Thursday night?—yes, it was Thursday, because I kept thinking of you teaching your class. We had a drink and dinner, nice and friendly, and I told her I was planning to move more or less permanently back to Providence, and she took it in stride. That's it. And you do have a right to ask."

"What—" Lissa choked. "What about Debbie?"

"My secretary? Sharp lady. Didn't she give you the message I left with her yesterday?"

Lissa conceded with a nod. "And Joyce?"

"Joyce?" Jared guffawed. "Joyce is fifty-nine years old. Also a terrific woman, but I'm not interested in hooking up with her bratty grandchildren."

Lissa searched his eyes in the thickening darkness, seeking proof. "Honestly?"

Jared exhaled and released her. "I can't make you

trust me, Lissa. Either you do or you don't. I'm not going to beg you to have faith in me."

"I'm sorry, Jared...." She reached out for his hand, gripping it as if it were a lifeline back to the tranquillity she had known a few weeks ago. "It's difficult for me. I was deceived once."

"Not by me," he reminded her. "Never by me." He studied her face, dabbing at stray tears, and offered a reassuring smile. His lips approached hers again, and when his tongue probed her teeth she opened up to him. The tranquillity she had hoped for came, but it was washed away by a more volatile desire. As her mind had been torturing itself these past few days, her body had been enduring a torture of its own. Her fingers clawed beneath his parka for his chest, her legs contorted themselves trying to drive against his, her muscles flexed with need. She felt Jared's arousal in his frenzied hands, in his limbs, in his tongue as it savagely pursued hers, in the agonized groan that scraped across his throat. He broke from her, breathing heavily, mildly dazed. "Can we go inside?" he asked, laughing.

Too drained by her emotional turmoil to join his laughter, Lissa nodded and shoved her door open. Jared met her by the front bumper, lugging his suitcase and briefcase from the backseat, and sauntered beside her to the front of the house. He fiddled with his keys, fitted the appropriate one into the lock, and gave Lissa a glance of trepidation before opening the door. "Do you want to warn me about anything before I go in?"

"Don't expect miracles," she replied.

He entered the foyer and reached for the light switch. The hallway was illuminated by a naked bulb; Lissa had removed the dowdy old fixture when the painters began work on the ceiling. But the fresh white walls and the natural grain of the banisters, which still required varnishing, provoked a grin from Jared. His eyes traveled to the highly buffed parquet floors, and his grin deepened.

Lissa urged him toward the front parlor. "The furniture isn't back yet," she apologized. "But you might like the fireplace."

He strode across the room to examine the smooth roseate marble that had revealed itself after steady applications of paint solvent. He ran his hand across the glossy surface and nodded. "Beautiful." He sighed.

"Not much to see in the back parlor," Lissa said as she prodded him back out to the hall. "But I think you'll like this." She inched open the door to the dining room and rotated the dimmer switch until the room was filled with a soft, soothing glow.

Jared entered timidly, as if waiting to be besieged by the memories of the unpleasant dinners of his youth. Instead, he was greeted by the graceful dining-room table and its uncluttered chairs; the rich cherry sideboard; the clean, nearly stark walls; and the lush jade plant, in an ornamental urn, resting on a small cherrywood plant stand by the center window. He circled the room, studying it from different angles, finally returning to Lissa's side. Folding his arms about her, he planted a kiss on her forehead and murmured, "Perfect. I love it."

Lissa smiled proudly and led Jared to the kitchen. "Now this needs some work yet—there's a butcherblock counter going in here...."

"I'll see it as it happens," Jared silenced her, kneeling to get a closer look at the new flooring. "This is pretty," he said. "But the other floor had a special memory for me." He stood and arched an eyebrow slyly.

"I reckon you can create a new memory on this floor if you have a mind to." Lissa said with a scowl.

"I have a mind to," Jared reached for her. "But first let me see the ballroom."

Lissa gnawed on her lower lip. "I don't know that you want to," she cautioned him as he started toward the double doors at the far end of the hall. "It's really an awful mess—"

"What's this?" Jared pointed to the bars Lissa had wedged into the door-frame to hold the doors shut. With a sharp jerk, he removed them and walked into the room. A cold blast of air struck him as he groped for the light switch. "What the— Lissa!" Only some of the candelabras were still connected, but they cast enough light for Jared to see the steel skeleton where the rear wall and ceiling used to be. The few furnishings in the room had been removed and the floor covered by a protective tarpaulin, but Jared remained beneath the balcony near the doorway, shaking his head in amazement.

"It's...it's supposed to be bold," Lissa told him hesitantly, afraid that Jared's silence wasn't one of approval.

He wrapped his arm over her shoulders as he peered into the night sky. "I'll say," he muttered.

"Please Jared, don't pass judgment on it, until it's completed."

"I already have passed judgment," he said, his eyes wide with delight. "I love it. A bit chilly, though, isn't it?" he said, chuckling, as he switched off the light and shut the doors.

"You're easy to please," Lissa remarked after the ballroom doors were secured.

"No, I'm not," he countered. "It's just that you know how to please me. Come show me what you've done upstairs."

"I haven't done anything upstairs."

"Well, how about doing something now?" Jared suggested, his eyelids lowered and his eyes brooding with desire. Lissa's lips twitched into a smile. How could she resist such blatant sexuality? How could she have ever imagined she could resist it? Taking his briefcase in one hand and his elbow in the other, she climbed the stairs with him.

"THERE'S SOMETHING ELSE I have to tell you," Lissa murmured.

They were cuddled in the bed. Jared had found an extra blanket and spread it over them, but the room was still chilly from the wintry night air that seeped in through the demolished ballroom to infiltrate the entire house.

He liked the cold because it drew them closer together. He liked depending on Lissa's body for warmth. Holding her, kissing her, loving her had been like drinking a glass of fresh, clear water after ten long days in a desert. He had never wanted—or needed—a woman as much as he wanted and needed Lissa, and now, after so many nights alone, he was satisfied.

He rearranged himself beside her, adjusting his head against the pillow so he could peer into her face. She seemed troubled, her beautiful gray eyes veiled with shadows, the anguished shadows he had seen in them the first time they had met. He braced himself. Not more doubt, he prayed. Not more distrust. Not after he had won her faith again.

"While you were gone," she drawled in a soft, hesitant voice, "I saw Curtis."

Something resembling fierce jealousy shot through him. He was startled by it; he had never been a particularly jealous sort of person, and he logically knew he had nothing to feel jealous about when it came to Lissa's ex-husband. But he couldn't seem to control the surge of angry emotion that filled him. She gazed across the pillow at him, as if searching his face for strength. It bothered him to realize that what she would see in his expression wasn't strength but his own unjustified measure of doubt. "Did you?" he managed.

She nodded, lowering her eyes to his mouth.

"Why?"

"He showed up at my office last week."

"Why? What did he want?"

"I don't rightly know," she allowed.

Jared trailed his fingers through her silky, tawny hair. Curtis had come to see her; she hadn't sought him out. His unreasonable jealousy slowly abated, and he found solace in the luxuriant texture of her hair, in the gentle caress of her breath against the line of his jaw.

"He mentioned something about our getting back together," she explained in a muted voice. "He talked about having a baby."

Jared's hand froze. "What?"

"I don't believe that was his idea," Lissa hastened to add. "It was my gramma's idea. He was down to visit her in O'cha' Crick."

Jared suffered another unexpected rush of jealousy. He shut his eyes and tried to contain it, to interpret it.

He didn't like the notion of Curtis Wade's behaving as if he were still connected to Lissa's family. That her grandmother had once been Curtis's in-law was an undeniable fact, but it irked Jared. The mere thought of Curtis fitting himself into the world of the Cavenders under the heading of family was infuriating.

He swallowed and opened his eyes again. Lissa was staring at him, awaiting a response. "Do you want to get back together with him?" he asked, trying to smother the edge of panic in his tone.

"Lord, no!" she exclaimed. "I gave him some money and sent him on his way."

"You gave him money?" His panic subtly increased.

"He was broke. He claimed he didn't even have enough to get himself out of Providence."

"How much did you give him?" Jared asked.

"Twenty dollars."

His hand began its exploration of her hair again. Twenty dollars. How could she give that vile man anything, he wondered.

She appeared to sense his dissatisfaction. "Jared," she whispered. "I would have given him a thousand dollars if that would have taken him farther away. I'd rather he be going to Kathmandu than to Boston."

"He's living in Boston?"

"At the moment."

Jared exhaled. "Lissa, why didn't you tell me this when it happened?"

She remained silent for several minutes. "I'm sorry," she finally spoke.

"Sorry that you didn't tell me?"

She fell silent again, working through her thoughts. "Jared, he said such terrible things about...about men, and how they're compelled to cheat on their women. He told me it was normal and natural, and that no one woman was enough—"

Jared cursed. A hard, ugly word escaped his mouth as he drew back from Lissa. "And you believed him? That's why you thought such ridiculous things about what I was up to in Colorado? Dammit, Lissa—" He tried to bite back his rage, but it spilled over to encompass her. "You'd believe him before you'd believe me? Dammit, how could you?"

His fury obviously hurt her. He saw her eyes closing over with moisture, and she turned away. He fought to regain his composure. It wasn't fair to blame her for accepting Curtis's lies. She was still so vulnerable, still so easily shaken. How could he fault her for her insecurities? She had known Curtis a long time, and Jared less than a month. And now she was seeing his temper for the first time, the temper he had worked for years to master. He wrestled it back into its cage, deep in his soul, and sighed. "I'm sorry," he murmured, daring to touch her shoulder.

"Jared, I can't help..." Her voice faded, choked by a sob.

"I know," he purred consolingly. "I know. You still have scars."

She said nothing. He let his hand wander gently over her back, tracing the delicate angles of her shoulder blades, feeling her flesh trembling beneath his fingertips. "I want to trust you," she said after a lengthy silence.

"You have to trust me," he amended.

She wasn't looking at him, but he saw her head move in a small nod. "Jared..." The word was muffled by the pillow. "Jared, I didn't ask him about the painting. I...I wanted to, but I couldn't bring myself to."

"That's all right," he placated her.

Slowly she turned back to him. "I ought to have, I suppose," she admitted. "But I couldn't. It hurt so much just to see him."

"I know." He brushed his lips against her brow. "Don't worry about it." Mollified, she snuggled to him, her legs weaving through his, her head nestling onto the firm muscle of his shoulder.

He held her close, feeling his anger replaced by the consolation of knowing he could soothe her, knowing she would turn to him for comfort and find it in his embrace. "I'd like to meet your grandmother," he ventured.

Her breath was warm and uneven as it fell along his coppery skin. "You would?"

Her surprise gnawed at the sense of contentment that inhabited him as he held her. If she were ready, if she were completely ready to abandon herself to his love, she wouldn't have been startled by his comment. "Yes," he emphasized. "Very much."

Her head moved more cozily into the crook of his neck. "Then I reckon you will," she granted.

Not "I'd love for you to meet her," but "I reckon you will." As if it was only his desire, not hers, that he meet her family. Jared wasn't pleased, but he realized that he couldn't expect more from Lissa right now. He mustn't let himself forget what she had been through in her life, in her marriage. He mustn't let himself forget that his hunches weren't hers, that her faith was still a very fragile thing. He would have to accept what she gave him until she was ready to give him more. He would have to be patient. Patience wasn't an asset he had in abundance, but he would have to make do with what he had for the time being. At least he had Lissa. He had her body, and he was pretty certain he had her love. In time, he knew, he would have her trust as well.

Chapter Twelve

With Jared's return, Lissa felt reborn. From the intense joy of their first days together to the intense depression of their time apart, Lissa had felt herself always hovering on the edge of hysteria, fighting—often without success—for control. It had been a kind of emotional vertigo: part of her struggling to maintain her balance, part of her desperate to fling herself over the edge. But now, as her time with Jared passed in a natural flow, the dizziness subsided, the giddiness replaced by the snug comfort of Jared's love. When she was with him, she was happy. When she wasn't with him, she was serene.

With him back in Providence, she no longer had to spend all her time at his house but could attend to other projects. Jared accepted the comings and goings of the laborers without a fuss, although he occasionally found the noise too intrusive and carried his work up to the servants' quarters in the attic, installing a telephone with a portable jack in the sitting room. If he had to run errands, he let Lissa know in advance, and she arranged her schedule to be at the house in his absence.

As the furniture deliveries continued, Lissa presided

over the rearrangements of the parlors, and Jared offered a few initial suggestions about the bedrooms, although, as Lissa had suspected, he wasn't quite ready to deal with his father's room yet. But the upstairs hall was painted, and two of the bathrooms fitted with modern plumbing. Lissa drew up plans for opening the back wall to the balcony in the ballroom, but she didn't want to begin that phase of the reconstruction until the ballroom was once again enclosed. October was sliding into November, and the breezes held a threat of winter. No need to make the upstairs as drafty as the downstairs, she reasoned.

On particularly cold evenings, Lissa and Jared retired to her apartment so they wouldn't have to tolerate the ballroom's leaking cold all night. They spent every night together, and even on those nights when their work rendered them too exhausted to do anything but curl up in each other's arms and sleep, Lissa felt herself thrive in the conviction that Jared was hers as much as she was his. How could she not have trusted him? How could she have let Curtis shake her trust in Jared? How could she ever have been jealous of a fifty-nine-year-old shop steward? How could she have failed to see that Jared seemed to depend on her as much as she did on him?

He had told her he wouldn't beg her to have faith in him, and he didn't have to. Faith spread through her like a flourishing plant with runners, budding and blossoming with new strength every day.

"I like this quilt," Jared commented one evening in Lissa's bedroom while she was brushing her hair out before bed. She turned to discover him seated beneath the covers, his broad, muscular shoulders hunched as he examined the intricate starburst pattern spread across his knees.

"Do you?" She grinned. "I sewed it myself."

"You did?"

"Quilting was one of the big activities in O'cha' Crick. It's rather relaxing. I wish I had more time for it." She set down her brush and joined him beneath the blanket.

He reached for the lamp, then paused, watching Lissa as she fluffed the pillows. "I've been thinking," he began, and Lissa stopped to pay attention. "I know the house is your pet project, but you asked me to consider the bedrooms, and I've been toying with a few ideas."

Lissa glanced past Jared to the alarm clock on her night table. "It's after eleven," she protested. "Can't this wait till tomorrow?"

"No." He gave her an earnest stare. "One of the ideas I had was that maybe, in the master bedroom, there could be a brass bed with a hand-stitched quilt. Would that be really out of line?"

Lissa scowled, trying unsuccessfully to decipher the undercurrent in his words. "No, if that's what you'd like. I reckon I could speak to some crafts people at the School of Design—I don't know any quilters in these parts, but I'm sure there must be some."

"I wasn't thinking of just any quilt," Jared said quietly. "I was thinking of this quilt."

"If...if you want it that much," Lissa said with a shrug, "sure, you can have it."

Jared's eyes coursed over Lissa's puzzled face for a moment, then softened as he smiled. "Thank you," he said, clicking off the lamp and nestling into her eager arms.

During the first week of November, the Thermo-pane glass for the ballroom–solarium began to arrive, and on Saturday, Lissa remained at Jared's house to observe while the first few panes were slid into place The eerie girders began to make sense to Jared as he stood beside Lissa, watching the glaziers wield the large transparent squares of material. "It's a greenhouse, isn't it?" he guessed.

"Something like that." Lissa smiled. "It took you long enough to figure it out."

"Oh, I figured it out ages ago," Jared retorted.

"Liar!"

"Lahr!" he mimicked her twangy drawl, then grinned sheepishly and kissed her cheek. "Well, maybe not ages ago. I can smell a good deal a mile away, but design was never my forte. I excel at appreciating it, not at imagining it. That's what I keep you around for."

Deferring to the brisk late-autumn wind, they ducked inside, shutting the ballroom doors behind them. "I was wondering why you kept me around," Lissa said in a sniff as she shrugged her cardigan around her shoulders. She was dressed casually, in jeans and an old shirt, because she was planning to do some grouting work on one of the upstairs bathrooms. Jared had complained that he could take care of the grouting as well as she could, but she insisted that she liked to get a little dirt under her nails every now and then—it reminded her of her origins, she joked. "And I won't charge you any extra," she had sworn.

She followed him down the hall to the entry, where his briefcase awaited him. "I hate to kill a Saturday afternoon at Bill Driscoll's office," Jared said as he zipped his parka shut. "But he said he's found a mysterious folder in a file cabinet. It contains some obscure records of my father's, and maybe together we can figure it out.''

''Well, if he's nice enough to meet you in his office on a Saturday afternoon,'' Lissa pointed out, ''you ought to be nice enough to go.''

''Believe me, I'd rather be spreading putty into the bathtub crevices.''

''I'm sure,'' Lissa scoffed sarcastically as she nudged him to the door. ''Now go on, get on with you. I've got work to do.''

With a good-bye kiss, she waved him off, shut the front door, and bounded up the stairs to the bathroom she and Jared usually used. Yanking off her sneakers, she climbed into the tub armed with a tube of caulking and a stack of old towels. She applied the white sealant meticulously, taking pride in her mindless labor and admiring the slick veneer of the tiles. When she had nearly completed the job, she was interrupted by the sound of the door chime. Springing from the tub, drying her hands on a towel and ignoring the small white smear of caulking on her chin, she padded in her socks downstairs to the entry and opened the door.

Facing Lissa was an attractive, well-groomed woman a few years her senior. She stood several inches taller than Lissa, her height augmented by high-heeled leather boots. Her tailored suede coat fell to midcalf, and her thick, auburn hair was swept dramatically back behind one ear. On the brick front step stood a cowhide suitcase, and Lissa noticed a cab cruising down the driveway toward Blackstone Boulevard. ''Is this Jared Stone's residence?'' the woman asked Lissa, her lips neatly outlined in a dark red gloss.

"Yes," Lissa said as she surveyed the woman, bewildered, instinctively trying to block the doorway with her petite body.

The woman peered beyond Lisa. "Is he here?"

"Not right now."

"I'll wait for him, then," said the woman, easing her way past Lissa into the house.

"I don't know when he'll be back," Lissa informed the woman. "Why don't you go home and I'll have him call you when he gets back."

"Home?" The woman chuckled. "Home is Colorado Springs. I'm here for a visit."

Lissa felt her throat constricting, but she kept her pitch low and even. "Then why don't you wait at your hotel? I truly don't know when he'll be—"

"What hotel? I'm staying here," the woman stated.

"Is...is Jared expecting you?"

"I'm surprising him. He didn't exaggerate about this place," she muttered, gazing curiously about her. "Although if he did go and hire a servant like his father, I would have expected he'd find someone with a clean face. Could you bring in my bag, please?"

"No, I could not," Lissa growled through clenched teeth. "I am not a servant and I will not bring in your bag. If you're determined to wait here for Jared, you may as well sit in the parlor. Kindly stay out of the way of the workmen out back." With an indignant huff, Lissa spun around and marched back up the stairs, leaving the glamorous woman and her suitcase to fend for themselves.

Storming into the bathroom, she slammed the door with a vicious bang. The gesture didn't temper her anger, however, and she sank onto the edge of the tub and fumed. Who the hell did that woman think she was, barging in and treating Lissa with such supercilious disrespect? So she was going to stay here, was she? So she had come all this way just to surprise Jared? The surprise would be on her, Lissa harrumphed as she climbed into the tub to finish her task.

She was tying the laces on her sneakers when she heard activity at the front of the house. Dashing out of the bathroom to the top of the stairs, she listened to the welcome sound of Jared's key in the door. As she descended the first few steps, Lissa saw the woman emerge from the parlor, her coat shed to reveal an impeccably tailored woolen suit. The front door opened, and Jared had scarcely stepped inside when the woman flung her arms about him and purred, "Surprise, loverboy!"

"Phyllis?" Jared's voice was muffled by the woman's passionate kiss. Lissa watched furtively as Jared's arms relented, then moved tentatively around the woman to her shoulders. Lissa couldn't see his face, but eventually he extricated himself from the kiss, his arms remaining around the woman as he said, "What are you doing here?"

"I thought I'd surprise you," she said with a laugh.

"I'm surprised."

"I wanted to see your new home, darling. I was in New York on business—I got the promotion! And since I was so close to Providence, I decided to come up and spend some time with you. You aren't mad, are you?"

"No...I'm..." He eased away from the woman as Lissa slowly plodded down the rest of the stairs, her jaw set to smother the trembling that threatened to overcome it. "I'm...surprised," he concluded vaguely, turning to Lissa. "Have you two met?" he asked, his eyes glued to her.

The metallic rasp of her voice surprised her as she spoke. "Yes. Your friend plans to stay here, Jared. I've finished upstairs." She pushed past him to the cloakroom for her pea jacket.

Jared moved as far as the closet door, but one acid glance from Lissa prevented him from coming any closer. "Lissa," he whispered, the woman lurking nosily behind him.

"I'm sure you two want to visit," Lissa stated dryly, resisting the urge to gag, to scream. "Good-bye." Flinging her coat over her shoulders, grabbing her purse, she flew from the house.

She refused to look at Jared, who hovered in the doorway as she got into her car and sped up the driveway to the boulevard. She virtually refused to look at the road, and barely missed being sideswiped by a car as she emerged into the traffic. She continued north until Blackstone Boulevard ended at the Providence town line, and crossed into the next town, finally braking to a halt in the parking lot of a small shopping center. Crumpling against the steering wheel, she released the torrent of tears that she had managed to suppress until now.

If he had done anything, anything besides what he did! She sobbed, her shoulders heaving spasmodically. If he had shoved the woman away instead of embracing her! If he had denied her the kiss! But he hadn't. He had submitted to it. He had given the woman the greeting she had been waiting for.

So he had told his lady friend he had made Provi-

dence his home. Evidently he hadn't told her *why* he
had made it his home—that he had decided to create a
home with Lissa. Maybe that wasn't the real reason,
after all. Maybe all he had told the woman was that he
had a new address and that she should stop by anytime
and make herself comfortable.

Curtis was right; men weren't to be trusted. And
Lissa had trusted Jared not once but twice. As a result,
she felt doubly destroyed. It was only his presence, his
irresistible warmth and virility that had made her believe she could trust him. If she saw him, she knew, he
would try to make her trust him again, and she
wouldn't be able to stand it. She couldn't survive
another time.

Hiccuping in the last throes of her anguish, Lissa
struggled to clarify her thoughts. She couldn't go to
her apartment; Jared would find her there. Shifting
the car into gear, she steered west, toward Lincoln.
She had fled to Paul and Peggy once before, and she
knew she could rely on them to see her through her
agony again.

She tested the speed limit, blind to the picturesque
scenery of Lincoln State Park, intent on reaching their
house before she became too devastated to focus on
the road. She prayed her friends would be home. She
prayed they would be willing to offer her their love and
support.

"LISSA!" Paul answered her knock with a broad smile
that rapidly faded as he surveyed her wretched expression. "What happened?"

Peggy appeared in the kitchen doorway as Lissa
stumbled into the house. Paul shut the door behind her

and removed her jacket as Peggy approached, her face creased with worry. "Are you all right?"

Lissa shook her head. "Can I stay here for a while?" she pleaded hoarsely.

"Of course. You don't have to ask." Peggy led her to the living-room sofa and helped her to sit down. "What happened?"

"I . . . I can't talk about it," Lissa said shakily, waiting to be besieged by fresh tears. None came. Her eyes ached with dryness. Sandwiched between Peggy and Paul on the couch, she stared blankly at the floor. Paul rested a brotherly hand on her shoulder.

"Did you and Jared have a fight?" Peggy softly questioned her.

"Yes. No." Lissa bit her lip.

Peggy eyed Paul above Lissa's bowed head. "Would you like me to phone him?" Paul offered.

"No!" Lissa reacted vehemently. "No. It's done. It's over." An arid sob escaped from her throat. "I can't go through it again. It's all over."

Paul waited for a further explanation, but when none was forthcoming, he squeezed Lissa's shoulder and stood up. "Would you like a drink?" he asked. She nodded. "Peggy?"

"Just a glass of milk," Peggy told her husband. "While you're in the kitchen, honey, check the meat loaf, okay?"

Lissa turned to Peggy. "Are you about to have dinner?"

"It can wait," Peggy insisted.

"No . . . no, don't let me interrupt you. Eat your dinner. I'll be okay."

"Would you to like to join us?"

Lissa shook her head. "I'm not hungry."

"Then come and sit at the table with us," Peggy commanded her, helping her off the sofa and into the kitchen, where Paul had filled two glasses with bourbon and a tumbler with milk.

Lissa stared at her drink without touching it. Her friends moved silently around the kitchen, setting the table and carrying food from the oven. They took seats, and Peggy patted Lissa's fisted hand before serving herself.

"Was it something with the house?" Paul attempted. "He didn't like the ballroom?"

"Leave her alone," Peggy cut off her husband. "She doesn't want to talk."

Lissa raised her eyes gratefully to Peggy. "Thank you, both of you. You always put up with me and my stupid crises."

"We love you," Paul reminded her. "Why shouldn't we put up with you?"

"And your crises aren't stupid," Peggy added. "I wish you'd stop using that word in reference to yourself."

"If you want to talk about stupid crises," Paul tried to cheer Lissa up, "I could tell you about the job I did on the carpet in the nursery. I measured it wrong. How long have I been doing this sort of thing professionally? I can't believe I measured it wrong."

"Forget it," Peggy said, laughing. "An area rug is almost as good as wall-to-wall carpeting."

Lissa sipped her drink and paid as much attention as she could to their banter. She knew they were discussing the nursery for her sake, and she appreciated their effort. But nothing could mollify her right now. She felt worse this time than she had that hazy early morning she had sought refuge from Curtis. Then she had been frightened and frantic. But she had been young and ignorant. This time she should have known better.

And that last time, she realized with a horrid chill, she hadn't been as much in love as she was this time. Then she was grieving over her marriage. Now she was grieving over herself, over her love, over the man who had seized her heart, her mind, her soul.

When the telephone rang, she flinched. Paul and Peggy exchanged a silent glance before Paul strode to the phone and answered it. "Hello?... Oh, hello, Jared."

Lissa flinched again, giving Paul a fearful look and shaking her head.

He frowned but obediently turned back to the phone. "No, she isn't here." He listened for a moment. "Okay, if I speak to her, I'll let her know. So long." He lowered the phone with a quiet click and eyed Lissa. "He wants to see you."

"I don't want to see him."

"I'm just passing the word along."

"No." Lissa said, shaking her head for emphasis.

The evening stretched into night. Lissa requested that her hosts do whatever they had been planning to do, but they insisted that their only plans had been to watch some television. Paul turned on the set in the living room, and he and Peggy sat on either side of Lissa, mutely watching a string of situation comedies. The bourbon slipped tastelessy past Lissa's throat, and before her glass was half empty she grew tired of it and pushed it away. She couldn't drink. She couldn't think. All she seemed capable of doing was wallowing in despair.

At eleven, Paul shut off the television. "Please spend the night," Peggy invited Lissa. "I don't want you going home alone."

Lissa nodded and thanked Peggy.

"Cut the gratitude stuff," Paul scolded her. "We're your friends and we're here to help. Peg, you've got a nightgown or something Lissa could borrow, don't you?"

As if she were an invalid, she let Peggy tend to her, helping her out of her clothes and into a floor-length gown of thick white flannel. Peggy even stayed with her as she washed her face and brushed her teeth, then ushered her into the guest room, which contained only a bed and a small table. "We were going to finish this room," Peggy apologized, tilting her head toward the stark, curtainless window, "but the nursery suddenly took priority." She gently tucked the wool blanket about Lissa. "If you want anything, just give a shout."

"I'll be all right," Lissa said quietly.

"I mean it," Peggy reiterated. "Even if you wake up in the middle of the night and want to cry, I've got two shoulders and Paul has two more." She turned to leave, then came back to the bed and touched Lissa's cheek. "I don't even want to guess what's going on," she whispered. "But I bet Jared is as heartbroken as you are."

"That's a bad chance to bet on," Lissa retorted morosely. "Maybe he's disappointed, nothing more. He'll survive." With his chic lady friend from Colorado Springs, she added to herself.

Peggy switched off the light and shut the door. The room filled with the moon's silver radiance. Lissa twisted her head away from the window to stare at the

eerie shadows of tree branches weaving across the
floorboards. She knew she wouldn't sleep, and she was
afraid even to close her eyes. When she did, they filled
with the image of Jared folding his arms around his
Colorado woman, Jared leaning into her kiss, Jared insisting he wasn't mad.

So he had tried to find Lissa here, so he had told Paul
he wanted to see her. Of course he did—he wanted to
patch things up with her. After all, his other woman
would be here only a few days, and Jared would need
Lissa to keep him company until Debbie or Joyce or
some other woman appeared on his doorstep. He
wasn't cut out for celibacy. Why should he go through
the effort of finding a new Providence woman when
had had Lissa handy? Lissa, ready, willing and able,
Lissa like a loyal dog, waiting effectionately at the foot
of his bed.

A sob wrenched her, and she felt her hands curl into
fists. Oh, she had resented Curtis for being a gambler.
Not until their divorce had she realized the extent of
his gambling, and as she met with his creditors she
shook her head in disbelief at his ill-conceived ex-
cesses. How could anyone have been stupid enough to
gamble on cards, she had wondered. How could anyone
have bet against such ridiculous odds?

Yet she had been the most foolish gambler of all. She
had challenged far greater odds, and she had staked not
money but herself, her sanity, her spirit. And she had
lost. She hadn't known her opponent, she hadn't read
his bluff, and she had been forced to fold.

She heard Paul's muffled voice downstairs, and she
realized that he and Peggy must still be awake, worry-
ing about their demoralized friend upstairs. She felt

guilty for troubling them, and she pushed herself into a sitting position, trying to clear her head. She would go downstairs and tell them not to fret. Their cozy house and their generous friendship were all she needed from them.

Swinging her feet to the cold floor, she pulled down the hem of the nightgown. Footsteps thudded up the stairs, and she paused, assuming Paul and Peggy might be on their way to bed, in which case she wouldn't disturb them. A narrow strip of light sliced across the floor as her door was inched open, and Paul's silhouette filled the crack. "Lissa?" he whispered. "Are you asleep?"

A taller silhouette materialized behind him, and Lissa knew immediately that it couldn't belong to Peggy. She shrank back against the wall and tried to shake her head. "Lissa," came the soft, sensuous murmur she knew all too well. "Let me talk to you."

Before she could respond Paul had vanished from the doorway, and Jared had slipped into the room and closed the door.

SHE LOOKS SO TINY, he thought, her small body hidden beneath an oversized white nightgown. He had never seen her in a nightgown before, he realized, and the high-necked, long-sleeved garment made her appear almost childlike.

He drew in a deep breath as he crossed the room, his hand tightening on the paper-wrapped parcel he carried. He was too weary to feel angry anymore. He had spent his anger that afternoon, after driving Phyllis to a hotel, making certain she could find a room for the night, and returning to the house alone. Then had been

the time for anger, and he had expended it in a storm
of rage, prowling through the vast rooms, pounding his
fists against the marble fireplace mantels, fuming at the
stark greenhouse that had once been the ballroom.

And ultimately he had found himself upstairs in the
room he had so often shared with Lissa, the room she
belonged in with him. And he had found the painting.
In his bitterness, he had nearly torn the damned painting to shreds with his bare hands, with his teeth. He
would have—he would have destroyed it. But he
couldn't. Not until he had seen Lissa one last time. Not
until he had tried one last, possibly futile time to make
her see sense.

She recoiled from him when he reached the bed,
clutching at her pillow as if it were a shield against him.
"Go away," she said in a choked voice.

He lowered himself onto the bed, as far from her as
he could be without falling onto the floor. Lissa curled
into the angle of the walls behind the bed and hugged
the pillow to herself. As his vision grew accustomed to
the room's darkness, he noticed that she had jammed
her eyes shut, refusing even to look at him. "Please
don't do this," he pleaded. "Just listen to me."

"How did you find me?"

"I knew you'd be here, even when Paul told me you
weren't. Aren't these people your closest friends?"

"If you knew I'd be here, you sure took your time
coming to fetch me," she hurled at him. "Were you
busy getting in a few rounds with your floozie?"

Her bitterness astonished him, cutting through him
like a stiletto. "Lissa," he snapped in a quiet fury, then
let his voice go gentle. "I was afraid if I came while you
were still awake you'd run away again." He swallowed.

"My floozie, as you call her, is spending the night at the Wayland Manor Hotel. She'll be leaving for Colorado tomorrow morning. She's not a floozie," he added. "Just a woman who had misunderstood what I was trying to tell her when I saw her last."

"Misunderstood the part about me, I reckon," Lissa snorted. "She knew all about your house."

"People tend to understand what they want to understand. They believe what they want to believe. I had told her I met a special woman who was working on my house. Apparently she listened selectively—she heard only the part about the house."

"Why did you kiss her?"

"Kiss her?" Jared scoffed in disbelief. Is that what Lissa thought she saw? Just like Phyllis, Lissa had understood only what she wanted to understand. "I was trying to push her away without knocking her over," he explained.

"I'm supposed to believe that?"

"If you want." He exhaled. He couldn't stand the hurt he felt emanating from her. He couldn't stand the realization of how much she hated him. "It's the truth. That may or may not mean anything to you, but it's the truth. I swore to be honest with you, and I've never broken that promise. I don't think I'd be able to even if I tried." He paused to collect his thoughts. The paper parcel rattled at his feet as he shifted his legs. "Phyllis asked me to apologize for her. She said she acted rudely to you, and she's sorry."

"Is she heartbroken?"

"No," said Jared. "She's a lot tougher than you are."

"I suppose she is. I'm just a stupid old fool."

Jared reached across the bed and yanked Lissa's hand away from the pillow. He had to touch her, had to reach her. Even if he couldn't save their relationship, he had to make her stop tearing at herself. If that was all he could ever give her, it would almost be enough.

"You're not a stupid old fool," he refuted her. "You've been through a lot, and I knew it would take you time to open up to me. The thought that I had succeeded, that I had broken through, made me happier than anything else in my life." His fingers tightened passionately around her slender hand. "It's not the sort of success I'm used to. The only other person I've ever wanted to break through to was my father, and I failed with him." He heard the catch in his voice as his throat tightened. Didn't she see how much he needed her? Couldn't she feel it? "Please, Lissa, please tell me I didn't fail with you."

"Of course you didn't," Lissa wailed wretchedly. "If you had, I wouldn't be hurting so badly now."

"Lissa..." Her pain sliced through him. "Lissa, I'm not going to beg you to forgive me for something that isn't my fault. If you aren't ready to come home with me, all right. I... I brought you something." He reached between his feet and lifted the flat, rectangular parcel from the floor. "I don't know why—I thought you should have it. If this is really the end of the line for us...." Please, he added silently, please say it isn't. "It belongs to you."

He handed it to Lissa, and she tore off the paper to reveal a plane of stretched, painted canvas. She didn't have to look at it to know that it was the painting of her, the painting that had brought them together. "Why?" she asked.

"After I took Phyllis to the hotel, I returned to the house. And I found this. I kept staring at it, Lissa, staring at it and thinking of you tormenting yourself here...and tormenting me.... I couldn't destroy it, Lissa. But I couldn't live with it, either. It's yours."

Lissa blinked, unable to speak.

"I thought you might want to know that the papers Bill Driscoll had discovered in my father's files were an accounting of his poker earnings. He was a law-abiding citizen, and he had kept a record of his gambling accounts for tax purposes. He had listed the painting in settlement of a five-hundred-dollar debt. Was Curtis in that heavily?"

Lissa nodded.

"I think my father got the better end of the deal," Jared commented softly.

"Jared," Lissa said, her voice a groan. "Jared, I haven't cried since I got here. May I cry now?"

He answered by pulling her toward him, offering the solid expanse of his chest as a receptacle for her tears.

She wept freely. His arms closed around her as she shuddered. He felt as if he were holding her pain itself in his embrace, that if only she could trust him, he would wrap it up and dispose of it for her. "Lissa," he whispered, her hair soft and cloudy against his mouth. "What should we do?"

"You're the one with the hunches," she mumbled into his shoulder. "You tell me."

"Are you really willing to trust my hunches?" he asked.

"Do I have any choice?"

He allowed himself a slight smile. Maybe she did understand, after all. Maybe she finally did understand the way it was. He raveled his fingers through her hair as she leaned into him, her shoulders quivering with a few lingering sobs. "I want you with me. I knew it from the moment I heard your voice, and the feeling only gets stronger. I know I rushed you; I kept trying to hold back, but—I've been trying to tell you this for so long now."

"Tell me what?"

"Lissa, I want you with me forever. I want you to marry me. I knew it the day we went to Nina's house in Little Compton, when we were on the beach. If I'd said anything then, you would have thought I was crazy. You hardly knew me, and you had no idea how accurate my hunches are." He kissed her brow before continuing. "I almost asked you that first night in your apartment, when I promised you that love would never be a painful thing again. I was waiting for a sign from you that you understood what I was trying to say, but you didn't, so I let it lie. I figured you weren't ready yet."

"Jared—"

"And the other night, when I asked you about your quilt.... I love your bed and your quilt because they're yours, because you come with them. When I said I wanted the quilt in the master bedroom, all I needed was one small sign that you were ready for what I had to say. But I was afraid I was rushing you, always rushing you. Three steps ahead of you, I think that was how you put it. I was waiting for you to catch up to me."

"Jared, if you had only told me...."

"I was telling you every way I knew. You know I have a habit of assuming that when something is obvious to me it's obvious to everyone. I was going crazy, sitting on my hands, waiting for it to be obvious to you. I didn't want to rush you after what you'd been through the last time you were married. I only wanted you to be ready, to recognize it on your own. I asked you to make my house yours, Lissa, because it *is* yours. It means nothing to me unless you're in it. Don't you see that?"

Lissa cuddled against Jared, apparently stunned by what he had said. She clung to him, her hands tracing the familiar strength of his body through his cashmere sweater; she clung to him so tightly that he suspected only a surgical knife could separate them.

"I take it your silence is one of acceptance?" he asked hopefully.

"I love you," she whispered.

He let her words sink into his body, into his soul. She loved him. She had said it; she had admitted it. She accepted it. His elation rendered him momentarily speechless, and when at last he found his voice, he said, "Lissa, there's something I want you to let me do."

"Anything, Jared," she vowed.

He took her acquiescence as an expression of her love for him, but he knew that what he had to ask, wouldn't please her. "Lissa, I want to contact Curtis Wade."

She twisted her head to face him. "Why?"

He labored over his words. He couldn't very well admit what he really wanted to do to Curtis—flay him, for starters, perhaps pull out his fingernails.... He inhaled and chased his wild imaginings from his mind. "I want him to know that he's never to bother you again. He's never to ask you for money. He's never to discuss getting back together with you. I want him out of our life."

Lissa said nothing. What was wrong, he wondered. Had he come across as an overbearing, overprotective man? Had he sounded too possessive?

Or was she unwilling to relinquish her relationship with Curtis, no matter how torturous it was? Was it possible that she still harbored a love for her former husband? As Lissa's silence stretched from one minute to two, Jared felt his nerves stiffening, his muscles growing taut with an undefined fear.

"He is out of my life," she finally said.

"Last week he wasn't."

"Oh, Jared...he was in my office, not in my life," she clarified in a soft, creamy voice. "I left his life three years ago. The only thing he could have done to me last week was to take twenty dollars from me."

"And make you doubt me."

Her arms coiled around his broad shoulders, and he sensed his body beginning to soften. "When I doubted you, Jared, it was *me* doubting you. If I had had the courage to trust you from the start, Curtis couldn't have said anything to change my mind. He only caught me at a very bad time."

"There won't be any more bad times for you if I can help it," Jared promised. "But I'd rather tell him never to catch you again, period. Will you let me do that?"

"I'll do it," Lissa declared. Her eyelids dropped slightly as she tucked her head against his shoulder. "With you beside me. All right?"

"All right," Jared said, sighing, his nerves relaxing as he savored the pressure of her head against him. "Well, we've got one other problem."

"And what might that be?" Lissa drew her head from his shoulder and frowned at him.

"I talked to the construction foreman while they were packing up this evening. Lissa, the ballroom isn't going to be ready until Thanksgiving—and that's just the exterior. The interior still has to be completed. Now how are we going to get married in an unfinished room?"

"I can wait."

"I can't," Jared declared. He had waited long enough. "Would you mind if we had a small civil ceremony for the time being—Paul and Peggy, Nina and Anthony— and then we can have a big celebration when the ballroom is done?"

"Whatever you want," Lissa murmured happily, melting back into Jared's embrace. "I don't even know who we'd invite to a big celebration."

"With all that glass, we can invite the moon and stars," Jared suggested. "A great big room filled with moonshine."

Lissa lifted her face to Jared's. The shimmering moonshine from the window lit her face with a magic glow. He guided her lips to his and drank her in, filling his body and soul with the intoxicating love, with the unshakable faith he had awakened in her. She was his, and he had always been hers. And finally, after far too many years, he knew he was home.

EPILOGUE

"What about all these built-in shelves?" Peggy asked, shifting Suzanne more comfortably across her shoulder and gazing about the bright room. The winter sunlight was surprisingly bright, warming the space through the windows. "It looks more like a library than a nursery."

"It was a library for a while," Lissa explained. "But before that it was a nursery—Jared's nursery. It's so convenient to the master bedroom." She waved toward the open dressing-room hallway connecting the two rooms.

"So what are you going to do with all these shelves?" Peggy persisted.

Lissa shrugged. "Put books on them, I reckon. Who knows? Maybe we'll wind up with a bookworm infant on our hands."

Suzanne grabbed a lock of Peggy's hair and yanked on it, causing Peggy to shriek. "Let's go back downstairs," she begged. "Someone here is getting restless."

They trooped down the stairs together, Lissa leaning against the balustrade for balance. She wasn't that big yet, but since she had been fairly petite to begin with, she felt unwieldy as her hips and legs accommodated her added weight.

They strolled down the hall to the solarium, which, like the nursery, captured the sunlight through its broad Thermopane windows, filling the vast room with natural warmth. Even the thin dusting of snow across the back lawn couldn't erode the room's coziness.

Peggy lowered Suzanne to the carpeted floor, and the pudgy little girl began a lopsided crawl toward the back wall as the two women took seats, Peggy on the plush leather sofa and Lissa facing her on a matching brown chair. "So how were your holidays?" Peggy asked.

Lissa shifted against the upholstery, seeking a more comfortable position. "Exhausting," she revealed. "Two Thanksgivings is one too many. I wish Gramma wasn't so frightened of airplanes—Nina and Anthony wanted her and Aunt Ida to come to Little Compton, but Gramma wouldn't hear of it. So we had one turkey Thursday at Nina's, and another one Friday in O'cha' Crick. It's no wonder my stomach is pooched out to here," she added with a laugh as she patted the round swell that stretched her corduroy jumper below her waist.

The sound of male laughter filtered into the room, followed by the clamor of heavy footsteps climbing the stairs from the game room. Jared and Paul burst into the solarium, Jared moving in broad strides to Lissa and planting a loud kiss on her stomach. "Hello, Ebenezer!" he hollered through her skin.

"Ebenezer?" Peggy gasped.

"Ebenezer if it's a boy, Gladiola if it's a girl," Jared announced. He scanned the room, located an ottoman, and dragged it over to Lissa's chair. Then he eased her legs up onto it.

Peggy glared at Paul. "You see that? You see how he

pampers her? That's what you were supposed to do for me."

Jared laughed. "I'm not doing it for her," he protested. "I'm doing it for me. I'm the one who has to look at her legs. I've got a vested interest in keeping them pretty."

"Does that mean you don't care what my legs look like?" Peggy asked her husband accusingly.

Paul squirmed, then weaseled his way out of the tight spot Peggy and Jared had put him in. "Peggy, love, your legs are so beautiful I knew even pregnancy couldn't ruin them," he offered. Peggy sniffed dubiously, and Jared and Lissa erupted in laughter.

"Peggy," Jared said as his laughter faded, "your husband is a dangerous man around a pool table. Why didn't you warn me that he would clean me out?"

Lissa's smile tensed slightly. "You weren't playing for money, were you?" she asked. Even after all this time, kidding about gambling made her nervous.

"No, we were playing for ego," Jared assured her. "A much more expensive stake. I, for one, would like to drown my sorrows in a beer. Paul, Peggy? Can I get you anything?"

"Just a glass of milk for me," Peggy requested.

"Two milks for the ladies," Jared announced as he and Paul left the ballroom.

Peggy turned to Lissa. "Ebenezer!" she repeated in disbelief. "Is he serious?"

Lissa chuckled. "That's this week. Last week it was Rasputin if it was a boy and Brandywine if it was a girl."

"Suzanne seems awfully mundane in comparison," Peggy said, rising to fetch her daughter, who had thumped her head against the glass wall and emitted a plaintive howl. Peggy scooped up the red-faced baby and carried her back to the sofa. "You're thirsty, too, aren't you," she murmured soothingly, unfastening the buttons of her blouse and offering her breast to Suzanne's round, hungering mouth. "Now tell me the truth, Lissa," she insisted as she settled back into the sofa's cushions. "Have you picked out names?"

"Adela if it's a girl," Lissa soberly informed her. "After my mama. And if it's a boy—Joseph."

Peggy's eyebrows lifted. "Jared would name a son after his father?" At Lissa's confirming nod, Peggy's eyebrows arched higher. "Joseph Isaiah?"

"No, Joseph Jeremiah," Lissa corrected her. "He's got a whole lot of ancestors to honor."

Peggy nodded and tightened her arms around her suckling child. Lissa watched her friend nursing her baby and felt an immeasurable contentment fill her at the tranquil sight. In less than four months, she thought, in three months and twenty-seven days—if Adela or Jay-Jay was kind enough to arrive on time— she, too, would know the unspeakable pleasure and satisfaction of nursing a child. Jared's child.

Last night the baby had begun kicking. Lissa had felt it's gentle stirring before, but last night it had pummeled her so hard that it had awakened Jared. He had flinched, turned toward Lissa in the brass bed, and mumbled, "What do you want?"

"Nothing," she had murmured. "I've got everything I want."

He had folded his arms about her, kissed her and then muttered, "Then keep your damned elbows on your own side of the bed."

"That wasn't me," she had objected. "That was your baby."

"My baby isn't supposed to be waking me up at night until after it's born," he had protested.

"Just getting you into shape," Lissa had teased. "It wants you to be ready."

Jared had shared a quiet, private laugh with Lissa, kissed her again and then nestled himself beneath the starburst quilt as Lissa molded her body to the angles of his.

Now she watched Peggy, who cooed sweet syllables into her daughter's fine blond hair as the baby hovered between eating and sleeping. The serene beauty of the sight transfixed Lissa, and she smiled. Soon, she thought, soon she and Jared would know this, the immeasurably marvelous gift of a child born in love. A Stone, Lissa thought. Noble by birth...no. She shook her head. No, their baby would be noble by love. That was the heritage she and Jared would give it.

PAUL CARRIED IN the tray of drinks, but Jared remained at the doorway gazing into the room, reflecting. The expansive walls of glass gave the ballroom an almost unreal loveliness, allowing the pristine winter vista into the house without its accompanying cold. It was his favorite room in the house—with the possible exception of the bedroom he shared with Lissa.

She was watching Peggy feed her Suzanne, a solemn, intense smile curving her full lips. Taking notes, Jared wondered.

Lissa didn't need to take notes. She would be a wonderful mother. He had a hunch about it.

She looked tired to him. Not surprising, since they

had flown down to Knoxville and then driven to Orchard Creek that past Friday morning, and then returned to Providence yesterday evening. Jared had originally objected to the trip, concerned that Lissa not push herself too hard, but she had insisted on visiting her relatives for Thanksgiving. And Jared was glad they had gone. He liked Lissa's grandmother and aunt. They were so unlike anyone he had ever known before, and he had a bit of difficulty at times cutting through their bizarre mountain accents, but they were such basic, wholesome, unaffected people. And they seemed fond of him. They had laid out a fine feast for Jared and Lissa's second Thanksgiving dinner, and they had done their best to make him feel at home.

And he *had* felt at home, even in their modest cottage in the middle of the Appalachian Mountains. The coal-mining "holler" ought to have been an alien world for Jared, but it wasn't. As long as he was with Lissa, he could feel at home anywhere.

But there would be no more big trips for her until after the baby was born, he decided. He wanted her to get her rest now, while she could. He wanted her to keep up her strength. Last year they had flown out to his house in Colorado for a week after Christmas, and Jared had tried to teach her how to ski. No trips to Colorado this winter, he decided. None for Lissa, and none for himself. He didn't want to leave her alone, even for a week. Even for a weekend. He would miss her too much. Any business he had to conduct he would take care of over the telephone. And Debbie was really doing a splendid job out there without him.

Lissa's pregnancy caused minor adjustments in their lives. The real adjustments would begin once the baby came. With Lissa's guidance and skill, he had converted the third-floor suite of servants' quarters into an in-house office for himself, so that once Lissa was ready to return to Cavender & Morris part-time he would be home to watch the baby. And he had finally persuaded her that they ought to consider hiring a housekeeper to help out. Not a live-in, he had promised Lissa, who had bristled at the thought of servants. She was just an earthy lady from O'cha' Crick, and she didn't want some uniformed maid bowing and scraping and saying, "Yes, madam." Jared didn't want that, either. He had had his fill of that sort of nonsense as a child.

But surely there wasn't anything wrong in having someone help out around the house. It was awfully big, after all, and he had finally convinced Lissa that what free time she would have once the baby was born would be better spent playing with the baby than attending to the house.

A baby. Their baby. Adela, maybe... but probably Jay-Jay. Jared had a hunch about that, too.

Jay-Jay. Joseph Jeremiah. A son. His house had become a home the minute Lissa had set foot in it, but soon it would be even more of a home. Lissa, his beautiful wife, his magic witch who had flown into his life on an invisible besom, had scared away the ghosts of the past to make room for the next generation. Another Stone, another photograph in one gallery, another painting in the other. Lissa's child. And then it would really be home.

His smile expanding, Jared strolled across the room to join their friends. He lifted his mug of beer, touched it to Lissa's glass of milk in a silent toast to their baby, and drank.

Share the joys and sorrows
of real-life love with
Harlequin American Romance!™.

GET THIS BOOK FREE as your introduction to Harlequin American Romance — an exciting series of romance novels written especially for the American woman of today.

Mail to:
Harlequin Reader Service

In the U.S.
2504 West Southern Ave.
Tempe, AZ 85282

In Canada
P.O. Box 2800, Postal Station A
5170 Yonge St., Willowdale, Ont. M2N 6J3

YES! I want to be one of the first to discover **Harlequin American Romance.** Send me FREE and without obligation *Twice in a Lifetime.* If you do not hear from me after I have examined my FREE book, please send me the 4 new **Harlequin American Romances** each month as soon as they come off the presses. I understand that I will be billed only $2.25 for each book (total $9.00). There are no shipping or handling charges. There is no minimum number of books that I have to purchase. In fact, I may cancel this arrangement at any time. *Twice in a Lifetime* is mine to keep as a FREE gift, even if I do not buy any additional books.

154-BPA-NAZJ

Name	(please print)

Address	Apt. no.

City	State/Prov.	Zip/Postal Code

Signature (If under 18, parent or guardian must sign.)

This offer is limited to one order per household and not valid to current Harlequin American Romance subscribers. We reserve the right to exercise discretion in granting membership. If price changes are necessary, you will be notified.

AMR-SUB-1